Her mouth stayed closed and motionless, its shape so perfect, its color so soft and pink. His center of gravity dropped low into his groin, which felt as heavy as base metal.

Kiss her, Jared.

Just once.

Goodbye, maybe.

Goodbye, more than likely.

Don't think about that. Don't think about anything. Just do it. Kiss her. She's waiting for it, isn't she? That's what the frown and the big, troubled eyes and the still, expectant mouth are all about. That's the reason for the little lap of her tongue tip at the seam of her lips. That's the reason for the sharp in-breath.

Isn't it?

No.

It wasn't.

"Small complication in all this, Jared," she said. "It's only fair to tell you. I'm pregnant."

Jared had never been sucker punched before. He'd had no idea that *anything* could flatten a man's lungs so fast.

Dear Reader,

It's hot and sunny in my neck of the woods—in other words, perfect beach reading weather! And we at Silhouette Special Edition are thrilled to start off your month with the long-awaited new book in *New York Times* bestselling author Debbie Macomber's Navy series, *Navy Husband*. It features a single widowed mother; her naval-phobic sister, assigned to care for her niece while her sister is in the service; and a handsome lieutenant commander who won't take no for an answer! In this case, I definitely think you'll find this book worth the wait....

Next, we begin our new inline series, MOST LIKELY TO..., the story of a college reunion and the about-to-be-revealed secret that is going to change everyone's lives. In *The Homecoming Hero Returns* by Joan Elliott Pickart, a young man once poised for athletic stardom who chose marriage and fatherhood instead finds himself face-to-face with the road not taken. In Stella Bagwell's next book in her MEN OF THE WEST series, *Redwing's Lady,* a Native American deputy sheriff and a single mother learn they have more in common than they thought. *The Father Factor* by Lilian Darcy tells the story of the reunion between a hotshot big-city corporate lawyer who's about to discover the truth about his father—and a woman with a secret of her own. If you've ever bought a lottery ticket, wondering, if just once, it could be possible...be sure to grab *Ticket to Love* by Jen Safrey, in which a pizza waitress from Long Island is sure that if *she* isn't the lucky winner, it must be the handsome stranger in town. Last, new-to-Silhouette author Jessica Bird begins THE MOOREHOUSE LEGACY, a miniseries based on three siblings who own an upstate New York inn, with *Beauty and the Black Sheep*. In it, responsible sister Frankie Moorehouse wonders if just this once she could think of herself first as soon as she lays eyes on her temporary new chef.

So keep reading! And think of us as the dog days of August begin to set in....

Toodles,

Gail Chasan
Senior Editor

Please address questions and book requests to:
Silhouette Reader Service
U.S.: 3010 Walden Ave., P.O. Box 1325, Buffalo, NY 14269
Canadian: P.O. Box 609, Fort Erie, Ont. L2A 5X3

LILIAN DARCY

The FATHER FACTOR

SPECIAL EDITION®

Published by Silhouette Books

America's Publisher of Contemporary Romance

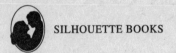 **SILHOUETTE BOOKS**

ISBN 0-373-24696-X

THE FATHER FACTOR

Copyright © 2005 by Melissa Benyon

Visit Silhouette Books at www.eHarlequin.com

Printed in U.S.A.

Books by Lilian Darcy

Silhouette Special Edition

Balancing Act #1552
Their Baby Miracle #1672
The Father Factor #1696

Silhouette Romance

The Baby Bond #1390
Her Sister's Child #1449
Raising Baby Jane #1478
*Cinderella After Midnight #1542
*Saving Cinderella #1555
*Finding Her Prince #1567
Pregnant and Protected #1603
For the Taking #1620
The Boss's Baby Surprise #1729
The Millionaire's Cinderella Wife #1772

*The Cinderella Conspiracy

LILIAN DARCY

has written over fifty books for Silhouette Romance and Harlequin Mills & Boon Medical Romance (Prescription Romance). Her first book for Silhouette appeared on the Waldenbooks Series Romance Bestsellers list, and she's hoping readers go on responding strongly to her work. Happily married with four active children and a very patient cat, she enjoys keeping busy and could probably fill several more lifetimes with the things she likes to do—including cooking, gardening, quilting, drawing and traveling. She currently lives in Australia but travels to the United States as often as possible to visit family. Lilian loves to hear from readers. You can write to her at P.O. Box 381, Hackensack NJ 07602 or e-mail her at lildarcy@austarmetro.com.au.

Chapter One

"Excuse me, I think you've given me a tad too much change." Shallis Duncan held a handful of bills and coins toward the teenager at the checkout, but he continued to look goggle-eyed, openmouthed and blank-faced.

"Huh?" he said.

His glazed focus dropped to her where her cleavage would have been if she'd been wearing a bikini instead of a businesslike dove-gray suit. His mouth fell open a little farther, revealing his disappointment at such a chaste amount of fabric.

"Too much change," Shallis repeated patiently. "See? I gave you five dollars on a two-dollar-and-six-cent item, and you've given me forty-seven dollars and ninety-four cents back." She tried a teasing, big sister kind of smile. "I don't think this is what your boss wants from you."

"Oh. Right," he answered vaguely. "Did you want to see him?"

Okay. Still not getting through.

She gave up.

"Here." She took his hand, turned it palm upward and dumped two twenties and five ones into it. His hand stayed frozen in place as he stared down at it. "Put it back in the till, okay?" she coached him. "And you have a good day, now."

Those last four words seemed to make some kind of low-wattage lightbulb click on in the young man's head. He stopped looking at his hand. "Uh, yeah, have a good—" He frowned. Hadn't someone just said that? "…uh, Miss Ameri—Miss Duncan," he finished vaguely.

On her way out of the drugstore with the tube of lip balm still in one hand and a leather briefcase in the other, Shallis sighed. At some point, surely, this kind of thing had to stop.

But not yet, apparently.

"Well, hey, it's Hyattville's very own home-grown princess!" said the man who'd just emerged from the real estate office she was passing.

"Good morning, Mr. Delahunty," she answered, digging the appropriate smile out of her extensive repertoire the way she might have dug the right lipstick out of a crammed makeup case.

The law office of Abraham Starke beckoned to her, several doors down. It had slatted cedar blinds in the windows, a polished brass knocker and name plate on the door, and a facade of pretty, cream-painted nineteenth-century brick, trimmed in Wedgwood-blue.

If she had pocketed that extra forty-five dollars in the drugstore like a felon, and left the unfortunate youth to explain the discrepancy to his boss, she would have missed crossing paths with Mr. Delahunty. By the time he'd appeared, she would already have gained the comparative safety of a private ap-

pointment with a man who was old enough to be her grandfather and was surely therefore not about to be impressed—
or reduced to a gibbering heap—by former beauty queens.

Should she conclude that sometimes crime did pay?

Mr. Delahunty was her father's assistant manager at the
Douglas County Bank, so she couldn't be rude. In fact, if she
was *ever* rude, to anyone, anywhere in town, at any time, day
or night, the story would probably make the front page of Hyattville's weekly newspaper.

"Hyattville's Very Own Home-Grown Princess says,
'Scram!' to Local Puppy," or something.

It got wearing, after a while. Made some of life's curlier
issues a little harder to resolve. Who she was and what was
really going to make her happy, for example.

Mr. Delahunty was asking questions. How did she enjoy
being back in town? Three months, wasn't it? How did it
compare to L.A.? Didn't she ever hanker for the bright lights
and the celebrity lifestyle she'd left behind?

She couldn't possibly give him a truthful answer. Even if
he had all day, she didn't. Abraham Starke would be expecting her at any moment, and she had to be back in her office
at the Grand Regency Hotel right after lunch, to deal with a
To Do list six feet long.

"Hyattville is a great little town," she told him. "I don't
have any regrets about leaving L.A."

Which was true as far as it went, but it didn't go anywhere
near all the way.

"Well, you have a great day, and I'll tell your dad I ran into
you. You know, if that Miss America had only turned out to
be a prison escapee, or something…"

"I know," Shallis drawled, smiling. "How unfair can you

get, huh? How dare the woman have led such a blameless life!"

"Smart, beautiful and funny, too." Duke Delahunty said to the April sky. His expression began to resemble the expression of the drugstore counter clerk a few minutes ago.

"It was good to see you, Mr. Delahunty," Shallis said quickly.

Then she smiled at him again because, like almost every other citizen of Hyattville, he was genuinely proud of her and genuinely sorry that she'd so narrowly missed winning the Miss America crown. It would be ungracious to get angry about the level of support she'd always had here, when the cleavage gazers were well in the minority.

But the pageant was more than five years ago.

She wondered if Hyattville would ever let her move on.

An old-fashioned brass bell tinkled when Shallis open the front door of Abraham Starke's law office, and his middle-aged receptionist looked up from her computer screen.

"Oh, Miss Duncan!" She beamed. "I'll let Mr. Starke know you've arrived. He's waiting for you."

Instinctively, Shallis looked at her watch.

"Oh, no, you're not late," the receptionist said, fast and breathless. "I'm sorry, I just meant he's expecting you."

She pushed her swivel chair back too fast, stood up and stumbled over one of its wheels. A sharp curse word escaped her lips, and she threw a panicky look back at Shallis, as if a one-time first runner-up in the Miss America pageant had the right of citizen's arrest over any woman who swore in public.

What next? Would Abraham Starke have an attack of hospital-strength heartburn at the sight of her, or something?

He'd been the Duncan family's lawyer since before Shallis was born. Surely he might be one person who wouldn't think of her in a ball gown with a pageant princess's tiara on her head, but would have memories of some less exalted outfit from her past. A diaper and a sunhat, for example. Or a Girl Scout uniform. She'd seriously prefer either of those.

The receptionist rapped at the door of his private office, opened it and poked her head inside. "Miss Duncan is here to see you, Mr. Starke."

"Yes, please show her in," said a voice that didn't sound like it belonged to someone in his eighties.

Two seconds later, Shallis came face-to-face with the man who six years ago had gotten dangerously close to ruining not just her sister Linnie's wedding day but Linnie and Ryan's whole marriage.

Jared Starke.

Not Abraham.

Oh, yeah, this Mr. Starke would have memories from her past, all right.

Her whole body went hot, and then cold. Reaction rushed through her, changed direction, rushed back again. She felt as if she'd been ambushed by ancient feelings she hadn't enjoyed at the time and liked even less now. Surely it all should have gone away, after so long?

She'd felt so fiercely protective of her sister since getting back to Hyattville three months ago, when she'd learned the full story behind the fact that Linnie and Ryan weren't parents yet, after six years as man and wife. She didn't want anything to come along that might impinge on Linnie's happiness any further.

If Jared still had the power to do that…

He was probably the one person in the world who could have made Shallis nostalgic for the princess treatment she regularly received from everybody else in Hyattville—every-

body except her dad. She couldn't stand the princess treatment, but at least she knew how to handle it.

She'd never known how to handle Jared. At best—as on
Linnie's wedding day—she'd only pretended.

He was Abraham Starke's grandson, and she'd had no idea
that he was back in town, let alone that he'd apparently taken
over his grandfather's law firm. He was sinfully good looking, impossible to trust, and she didn't like him one bit.

No, really.

She didn't.

She wouldn't betray Linnie like that, and she wouldn't be
such a fool. She'd developed some pretty powerful instincts
toward self-protection in recent years.

"Shallis," he said, standing at once, and fast, so that he was
on his feet almost before she'd fully entered the room. The
Southern courtesy bred into him since childhood hadn't been
abraded by Chicago's brasher style.

The noon sunshine reflecting into the office through its
east-facing window caught the natural blond highlights in his
hair and made them stand out against the thicker and darker
strands beneath. His tan was no doubt the artificial result of
frequent sessions on a big city tanning bed but it suited him
all the same, even around the outer corners of his eyes, where
a couple of fine, tiny wrinkles had begun to form.

His dark tailored pants and plain white shirt covered a
strong male body that seemed at ease in its own skin, full of
latent power but with nothing left to prove. He must already
have proved himself plenty of times, with plenty of women.
The electric aura of sensual success hovered around him, yet
he acted as if he had no idea it was there.

Yeah, right. Like I'm buying that! Shallis thought. A man
like him would *always* know it was there.

He must be around thirty-three years old by now, or maybe just turned thirty-four, against her own age of going on twenty-eight. He'd been her sister's first serious boyfriend, starting from when Linnie was in senior year of high school and Shallis herself had hit thirteen. Thirteen was an impressionable age, and Shallis had been...

Yup, impressed.

Round-eyed.

Envious of what Linnie had.

In fact she'd had a wild hormonal crush on Jared that had lasted until she was sixteen. For most of those three years he'd hardly seemed aware of her existence, but, *ohhh,* had she ever been aware of his! The kind of aware that resulted in clammy hands and hot cheeks, clumsy outbursts and ill-timed episodes of tongue-tied silence, an obsession with certain hit tracks featured on MTV and the scribbling of secret, tortured and very, very bad poems. The way she'd behaved on the night he'd finally deigned to notice her was not exactly one of her proudest memories.

As if Jared sincerely had no notion that she might have any reason to feel hostile or negative toward him, let alone that her feelings might be a whole lot more complex and jumpy than that, he came around the side of his grandfather's huge oak desk to shake her hand. His smile was as steady as his grip, and contained just the right amount of professional warmth. There was a respect in his golden-brown eyes that you sensed might eventually turn to friendship given the right encouragement and points of connection.

And there was nothing in his attitude or his body language that said, "Another blond bimbo, big yawn...or maybe a one-night stand," which was the way she'd been treated in Los Angeles, and nothing that said, "Oh, wow, I'm in the same room as Hyattville's beautiful prodigal princess," which was the way she got treated here.

Not fair!

He was too good at all of this.

It was exactly the kind of behavior that Shallis wanted from every other citizen in town, but she didn't want it from Jared Starke, not when she knew from Linnie's experience and her own that it had to be part of some game plan of his that could lead to only one outcome—a win for Jared himself.

"Jared," she answered him coolly, because sometimes an ex first runner-up in the Miss America pageant could be good at this, too. And she dropped his grip a little too soon. Deliberately. "I wasn't expecting you to be here."

"I wasn't expecting me to be here, either, until a couple of days ago," he drawled. "Please sit down." He gestured not to one of the two upright chairs that faced the desk, but toward the leather armchairs positioned near the window, on either side of a low coffee table which matched the antique oak of the other furnishings.

Reluctantly, Shallis took a seat. Her lips felt dry, which was why she'd stopped into the drugstore to purchase the lip balm just now. She'd spent most of yesterday out in the open air at Linnie and Ryan's thoroughbred stud farm and she'd gotten burned by the spring sun and wind, as if the weather itself wanted her to regret her recent attempts to wean herself away from full daytime makeup.

And why was she doing that?

The princess thing, again. New theory. Maybe if she looked a little more down-to-earth...

So far, it hadn't worked.

"I arrived back in town Friday," Jared said, "and Grandpa

Abe basically pushed a bunch of keys into my hand, picked up his fishing pole and headed for the mountains." He gave a bland kind of grin and turned his hands palm upward. "I thought I was here for a break, but he had other ideas."

"So this is a temporary setup? Just a few days?"

Shallis let way too much relief show in her voice, and this time it wasn't deliberate. She wished at once that she'd hidden her reaction better. Jared was definitely hiding something.

"That's fine," she went on. "I can arrange another appointment when your grandfather gets back."

Jared looked at her in steady silence for a moment, reading every bit of her discomfort. Hopefully not reading all of the reasons for it. He gave another brief smile.

"Sorry, I guess I'm giving you the wrong impression," he said. "My grandfather and I had a good talk before he left on his fishing trip, and I've agreed to take over his law practice for the next six months while we have a serious look at options for the future. He's overdue to retire, but he wants to take some time to consider things. My dad's death rocked him, six months ago."

"Oh, yes, of course. It would have done. I was sorry to hear about it," Shallis told him.

"It was hard," he agreed. "We didn't see each other all that often after he and Mom got divorced—he moved to Nashville, as you know—but we were still close."

"Of course."

She'd already noted the enlarged, silver-framed photograph on the most prominent shelf of the antique breakfront behind his desk. In the photo Jared, his father and grandfather all grinned toward the camera against a backdrop of the manicured green grass and foliage of Hyattville's members-only golf course.

Jared didn't look much like the two older men. The bone structure in his face was more angular, his jaw more prominent and determined, his build stronger and denser, but the closeness between the three of them was self-evident.

"Anyhow, we're talking a lot more than a few days until my grandfather's return, I suspect," Jared continued. "I've looked at a couple of the relevant files and I'm sure your business can't wait that long."

"My grandmother's estate. No, it can't. My mother is finding it hard."

"I can imagine."

Once more, he seemed to know just how to pitch himself. His sympathy was sincere but not cloying. It had to be a professional skill, studiously worked at, part of the Attorney Ken act. It couldn't be natural, not in a man like him, Shallis told herself. Surely his arrogant behavior at Linnie and Ryan's wedding had given her all the warning signals she needed in that area.

"I've heard a few great stories about your grandmother," he said. "Laughed at most of them. Of course it's hard for your mom."

Shallis stayed cool and wished her throat hadn't gone so tight. She nodded. "They were very close. If I can get the practical, legal stuff taken care of for Mom, some of the decisions she needs to make about Gram's possessions and so forth will be easier."

"Well, you could go to Banks and Moore over in Carrollton, if you want," Jared offered. Was that the glint of a challenge in his eyes? "Or you can deal with me."

"I'm surprised you're here," Shallis said, stalling for time. Then she realized she sounded as slow on the uptake as the drugstore clerk who'd tried to give her too much change.

Jared had just explained why he was here. She added quickly, "I mean, I'm surprised you were available to do what your grandfather wanted. You've been in Chicago for quite a while, now. I would have thought you had commitments there."

"Taking a break," Jared answered, offhand. He was confident that the complexity of his feelings on the issue didn't show.

And he ignored Shallis Duncan's cool tone, because he understood the reasons for it all too well. No doubt about it, he'd behaved very badly in the past. To Melinda Duncan—Linnie—and to Shallis, her baby sister. More than once. He didn't like those memories.

"Thinking about a couple of opportunities," he continued. "I don't want to commit myself to the wrong choice."

He knew that many people in Hyattville wouldn't believe him on this. There was an element in the town that would love to see him crash and burn, and would interpret his return home as a signal that it was about to happen, big-time. He expected rumors about shady dealings, massive debts, financial scandals, or disbarment from the future practice of law.

That was the downside to being a self-proclaimed high flier, in a place like this, and unfortunately his ambition and his arrogance had led him into a few poor choices in the past, which would make the rumors more plausible.

Yep, no doubt about it, at times he'd been a jerk and he made sure he never forgot the fact. Grandpa Abe had put a slew of Jared's old golfing and racquetball trophies on the breakfront shelves, "to put your own stamp on this office, since it's yours, now." Jared had added a trophy of his own— the fake one that a couple of old law school buddies had presented him with a few years ago.

Sore Loser it read, in beautiful copperplate engraving. The

really telling point about the trophy was that when his friends had made the mock presentation, he hadn't been able to laugh. Three years on, the trophy was the first touch of personality he gave to a space any time he shifted offices, and he laughed at himself a lot more often now.

The only thing he could do about his reputation, he knew, was to get his head down, take heart from his own growth and his family's faith in him, and prove everyone else wrong.

No, not everyone.

Just the people who mattered.

The impossibly beautiful Shallis Duncan shouldn't be one of them, and yet without a doubt she was. Six years since he'd last seen her face-to-face, and he still hadn't been able to get her out of his head.

She stood up, and instinctively so did he. "Banks and Moore has a good reputation," she said.

Her golden-blond hair bounced around her face, and her blue eyes looked as big and clear as pools of sea water. Her suit was neat and conservative and plain, but on her curvy, long-legged frame it somehow managed to look as pretty and feminine as a lace negligee.

She appeared to have almost no makeup on at all, apart from a translucent sheen across her lips, but her skin was so clear and fine and her coloring so perfect that Jared preferred her with the natural look, and every molecule of testosterone in his body refused to leave the subject alone.

"Your secretary will be able to arrange to have the files sent over to them, I assume?" Shallis finished.

Jared felt his stomach drop an uncomfortable couple of inches.

Shoot. Drat. Darn.

Or words to that effect.

She'd called his bluff.

Well, no, she didn't look at it like that, of course, and neither should he. She was simply taking the perfectly reasonable way out he'd just offered her—but he might not have offered it if he'd thought she'd catch hold of it so smoothly.

Helplessly he let the rest of their short conversation unravel like a piece of yarn... I mean, sure, if she wanted, yes, she should go over to Carrollton, to Banks and Moore... And it wasn't until she'd closed the outer office door behind her that the real Jared Starke took control of his actions again.

Jared Starke the winner.

Jared Starke the fourth generation lawyer.

Jared Starke who heard the word, "No," the same way a bull saw a red rag.

Jared Starke who could laugh at his Sore Loser trophy now, but who still wasn't going to let what would surely be his last chance to make something work out right with the Duncan family just walk out of his grandfather's law practice on those sexy pale gray heels, while he stood here rooted to the floor, imprisoned by an agonizing rush of physical need as tangible as iron bands.

Chapter Two

"Wait!" said Jared's voice, overtaking Shallis as she went back along the street toward her car, which was still parked in the drugstore's lot.

She stopped and turned reluctantly, watching him catch up to her. His stride lengthened, strong and full of purpose, and then he stopped short, keeping safely out of her body space.

But whose safety was he concerned for, here?

"Do you really have to do this?" he said.

His voice stayed low, in an instinctive bid for privacy that Shallis appreciated. The intimacy that it seemed to weave around them she appreciated a lot less.

"It's a half hour drive to Carrollton," he went on. "Banks and Moore's billing rate is considerably higher than my grandfather's, and they have no familiarity with your family's legal affairs. I'm not sure what's making you so reluctant—"

She threw him a look that said, "Oh, really?" and his face changed.

"Okay. You got me." He spread his hands, then he sighed.

His voice had gone husky, suddenly. Deeper, too. Its masculine notes curled around her legs and misted upward, as sneaky as the smoke from the cigarettes Shallis had tried a few times at fourteen.

"I know exactly what's making you so reluctant, don't I?" he said. "But this is a simple business relationship and I'm a good lawyer. My grandfather wouldn't have handed the practice over to me if I wasn't. I wouldn't be considering partnership offers from three major Chicago law firms if I wasn't."

He stepped a little closer, and Shallis didn't know if it was deliberate or not. She did know that she was far too aware of the movement, and of its results. She could see the tiny chips of gold deep in his brown eyes, now, and a couple of equally tiny freckles just above the corner of his mouth.

She narrowed her eyes and pressed her lips together, but couldn't close off the effect he had on her. The effect he'd *always* had.

"At least let's go through with our appointment this morning," he continued. "We can set things in motion regarding your grandmother's estate. You can talk it over with your mother later. And if either of you still has a problem about my involvement, I'm sure my grandfather will agree to handle the next phase when he gets back from his fishing trip, since your family has been with him for so long."

"When is he getting back?"

Soon. Please let it be soon, so that I don't have to deal with this. Again.

"He wouldn't commit himself, unfortunately. I'd imagine

it's going to be at least a month, judging by the huge pile of gear and supplies in the back of his pickup when he left."

"Why are you so keen about this, Jared?"

He studied her for a moment, and she got the impression he was sorting through his possible answers in search of the one she was most likely to believe. She'd seen a lot of men with that particular look on their face, as they sorted through their possible come-on lines in search of the one that was most likely to get a beauty queen into bed.

"I don't want to be responsible for taking your family's business away from my grandfather," he said eventually.

"It's a bread-and-butter estate settlement, isn't it?" It hurt her to talk about her grandmother's legacy this way, but she could put on a cool front just as successfully as Jared himself. What lay beneath the cool front was surely hotter in her case, however. "Your grandfather must deal with this sort of thing all the time. Losing one client isn't going to bankrupt him."

"Losing the Duncan family is going to send the wrong message around town, and he'll lose other clients as well, as a result. Look, it's up to you." He shrugged. "I just don't think it's necessary, that's all. It seems petty, or something."

"Petty on my part?"

"Petty that either of us should feel that your grandmother's estate has anything to do with a personal and much-regretted mistake I made six years ago. I've moved on. I'm sure you have, too."

Oh, he had a good line in sincerity. The voice really helped, as deep and buttery, now, as a bottomless bucket of popcorn. So did the eyes. And the lashes. And the tiny glint of ironic awareness almost lost behind the lashes.

Shallis almost believed him—enough to consider that, yes,

Banks and Moore would be more expensive and less convenient, and to finally decide to give him the benefit of the
doubt. It was just a straightforward legal matter, after all, and
it wasn't fair to Mom to let it drag out longer than it had to,
or get it tangled in personal feelings.

"All right," she said. Her nerve-endings jumped and
squealed, treacherous things, like giggling teenagers glimps-
ing their latest crush. "We'll do what needs to be done today,
and then I'll find out how my mother wants to proceed."

She would talk to Linnie about it, too, only Jared didn't
need to know that.

"Would you like coffee while we talk?" Jared asked as they
entered the front office once again.

"Yes, please." You could hide a surprising amount behind
a steaming cup, Shallis knew, and she might need to do exactly that.

"Andrea?" he said to the receptionist.

She nodded. "Coming right up." If she was curious about
Shallis's sudden departure and unexpected return, she didn't
let on. "How do you like it, Miss Duncan?"

"Cream and no sugar, thanks."

"And I'm sorry, Mr. Starke, you made your own this morning and I didn't see…"

"Just black."

So he wasn't too exalted to make his own coffee. Or maybe
he was just softening Andrea up with a good first impression
so he could load her down with unreasonable requests later
on.

What, me? Cynical? About Jared Starke? Never! Shallis
thought.

This time, he sat behind his desk while Shallis sat in front
of it, which acted as a useful reminder that their meeting was

purely business. He ran through the steps that had to be taken before the proceeds of the estate could be disbursed, and asked to see some of the papers and documents that Shallis and her mother had found amongst Gram's things so far.

"She wasn't a very organized person," Shallis told him.

"But you forgive that in some people, don't you? From what I've heard, your grandmother was one of them."

"She was wonderful. Generous and fun and creative. Wicked sense of humor. Really surprising take on a whole lot of things. Cared a lot about people. Drove us totally nuts, sometimes, especially my dad, but the whole world always seemed that much fresher and more interesting when she was around. I—I actually can't believe that she's gone."

"No, I bet," Jared said quietly. "And it's only been two weeks, right?"

"Just over." Shallis couldn't have said more than two words, at that moment.

She kind of hid in the coffee for a couple of minutes and Jared didn't rush her, which she had to be grateful for, even though at some level she didn't want him to have the slightest clue about how to behave so well. It would really have helped with this crazy nerve-ending problem if he'd been crude, insensitive, obvious and a flagrant con artist.

Why had she told him so much about Gram in the first place, she wondered. Because he'd paved the way by talking about his father's death, earlier?

"Your mother didn't want to wait a little longer on all this?" he finally asked. "Sorting through a person's whole life can be very draining and difficult."

"I think it's helping Mom, in some ways. And she had a little time to prepare before Gram died. Gram was eighty, and the stroke was a severe one. We knew she wouldn't want to linger for a long time without hope of recovery, and her wish was granted. She died in her sleep ten days after she first collapsed."

"You said she wasn't very organized. Did she at least keep all her papers in one room? Did she have any kind of a filing system?"

"Uh, no." Shallis smiled a little. "There are boxes and stuffed envelopes and loose file folders all over the house."

"Right." He smiled back. "That kind of a filing system. I know it well."

"And then there are all Gram's wonderful knickknacks and souvenirs, precious memories folded away in tissue paper, bits of jewelry, old evening gowns, so much."

"Some hard decisions. You'll need to put aside anything you want valued. There are a couple of local valuers my grandfather recommends."

He reached into a drawer of the desk and took out two business cards. He didn't hand them to her directly, but reached across to put them down just in front of her. There was never any risk that they'd touch, and Shallis wondered if that was his intention.

"Thanks," she said.

She picked up the cards and slipped them into a pocket inside the lid of the open briefcase, which she'd place on the desk to her left. Then she looked back at Jared and found him with his jaw propped on his two thumbs and his elbows on the desk for support.

He looked a little tired. Stressed out, even. She wondered what lay behind his decision to take a break from his jet-propelled ascent up the ladder of success in Chicago, but realized she might never know. She definitely wasn't going to ask any searching questions that might bring the information out.

"Should we make an inventory as we go?" she asked.

"It might be better to sort through everything first."

"There's so much. We're not tackling any of it systematically."

"Room by room?"

"That's what I'm trying to do, but Mom goes off on a tangent, sometimes. We keep getting distracted, and we still have a lot more to go through. I'm taking next week off work, but it's not going to be enough."

Shallis realized that once again she'd begun to unload a level of detail that Jared didn't need. She hadn't expected him to be such a good listener, in his new professional role.

"Anyway…" she added in a more businesslike tone.

"Yes, let's take a look at the papers you've found so far," Jared said. He sat up straight again and started paging through some of the sheets in front of him. "This is the deed to the house."

"That's right, but before you look at that, there's one thing we found that we don't understand and I wanted to ask you about it."

Leaning forward, she slid a sheet of paper out of the file folder that came next in the pile. It was a property tax bill dated just a couple of months earlier, and it had a line of her grandmother's distinctive spiky handwriting scrawled across it in the rich, royal blue ink she always used.

"Paid Feb. 20," it said.

"Look at the address that this tax bill relates to, Jared. Chestnut Street. Gram's never lived in that part of town, and we're sure she doesn't own rental property there or anywhere else. We can't understand why she'd even have this bill in her possession, let alone why she'd have paid it."

"Grandpa Abe lives on Chestnut Street." He looked at the address more closely. "I'm staying there while he's out of

town. Just a half dozen houses down from this place. I'm trying to picture number Fifty-six, but right now I can't."

"It's a very nice street, the whole length of it, with all
those gracious old Victorians."

"It's beautiful," he agreed.

"The grounds of the Grand Regency back onto a part of
it."

"That's where you're working now, right?" He looked up
briefly from the paper he was still studying. Knowing he
would be seeing her today, he must have done some research.
"Their events manager? That's a big job, at a place like the
Grand."

"See these gray hairs?" she joked.

"Oh, yeah, hundreds of them," he drawled in mock agreement.

Their eyes met for a moment and they were ready to share
a laugh, but then memory intervened and both of them looked
quickly away—Jared down at the tax bill, and Shallis toward
the window.

Linnie and Ryan had had their wedding reception at the
Grand Regency Hotel six years ago. Jared had heard about
their impending marriage, flown in from Chicago and gate-
crashed the event, five years after he'd dumped Linnie and
practically shattered her heart—she'd cried for months. He'd
gate-crashed the church ceremony before the reception, also,
hot off the airplane.

In fact, he'd tried to stop the whole wedding, right in front
of the minister at the altar and the entire congregation. "You
can't marry him, Melinda Duncan. I know this is my fault.
I'm an idiot. I always thought I had plenty of time, through
law school and beyond. But you know it, don't you? You've
always known it. You have to marry *me!*"

Wrong, Jared.

Bad call.

You weren't even serious, were you?

You were just testing your power.

Linnie and Ryan were made and meant for each other, but they'd had a whirlwind courtship and they really hadn't known each other all that well, on the day of their wedding. Made and meant for each other didn't always mean that things worked out. Ryan had seen Linnie's flash of doubt.

"You know what we always had together," Jared had claimed, and for a few long, horrible moments, Linnie had remembered all those tears she'd shed for him. She'd bought his whole act.

Jared had grinned at Ryan, already acting as if he'd won. "Sorry, buddy, but this woman belongs to me."

Only then had Linnie been able to speak. "No, Jared, you're wrong. I don't."

You could have cut the air with a knife, even after Linnie and Ryan had gone through with the ceremony as planned. It took the whole of the wedding reception and some important talks with other family members for the two of them to sort out what they really felt and what they really wanted. A couple of times, Shallis had seriously feared they were headed for an instant annulment or divorce.

She would never forget it, and she would never forget the way Jared had purely wanted to win, the way he'd selfishly wanted to prove he still had power over Linnie's heart. Shallis had spent nearly an hour with him at the reception, decoying him safely away from Linnie—flirting outrageously, in fact— so she knew how he'd really felt. He hadn't cared about her sister, and he hadn't even pretended to care about Ryan's feelings.

Winning was all.

Shifting the power balance in his favor.

Showing the whole town who was in control.

And even though he'd lost the game that day and Ryan had won, Jared had finally left the big hotel with the cocky attitude of a cheating gambler who *knows* his luck's going to come around again one day, because he has the aces up his sleeve to prove it.

A part of her wished the subject of the Grand Regency had never come up, but another part of her was very glad that it had. She didn't want to lose sight of the kind of man Jared Starke really was, beneath the smooth and adept professional facade, beyond the unwanted havoc he wrought with her woman's needs.

What the heck was wrong with her?

"Back to this mystery property tax bill," she said, making each word clipped and cool. "Will you follow it up for us? My mother is a little concerned that Gram could have been conned into parting with her money to cover some false tax claim."

"If you find anything else of a similar nature, bring it in right away, won't you? You're right, there are people who'll take advantage of an elderly woman living alone, and someone comes up with a new scam every week."

"I can't imagine Gram falling for something like that." Shallis clicked her tongue and sighed between tight teeth. Jared's gaze seemed to follow the sound of her escaping breath, and her lips felt dry again. She gathered her train of thought and kept speaking. "She still seemed so sharp in her mind, right up until the day of the stroke, and she was very vocal on the subject of men who preyed on naive women. But we're definitely confused so, yes, anything else we find I'll bring right over."

She stood up and looked deliberately at her watch. It was after noon. "I'm sorry, I need to get back."

"I'm about to order in a sandwich lunch." Jared stood, also. He narrowed his eyes for a moment, then looked down at his thumbnail and pushed the cuticle back with his middle finger. His head came back up, his regard steady again. "Andrea can pick up something for you, too, if you want. It'll only take twenty minutes."

"I'm fine, thanks."

"You're sure? There are a couple more things we could get through while we eat."

He came around the desk and put a hand under her elbow. Suddenly their eyes were fixed on each other, locked together, giving off naked heat, drowning. A blast of awareness hit her—the same physical and emotional ambush Shallis had felt when she'd first found him here instead of his grandfather. Jared looked at her as if the chemistry of her physical response to him was written on her skin, as if it had made her whole body turn blue.

She froze, unable to pull away as she needed to, unable to stop looking at him or hide her reaction. It scared her to feel like this, when she so seriously didn't want to, when she had so many reasons not to.

Whatever had happened to the strength of the human will?

"What do you want from me, Jared?" It came out on a whisper.

There was a tiny beat of silence before he spoke. "I'm just trying to do my job."

"No. I don't think you are." She snatched her arm out of his grip, about thirty seconds too late. "I think there's something more."

And it wasn't the princess thing.

"Do you?" His lids flickered, and a shuttered look came onto his face.

He was lying, evading the truth in some vital area, only she didn't know what. The whole way he held himself right now, so stiff and wary and closed, reluctant and almost angry, in such contrast to the bland professional bearing he'd seemed to have in the beginning.

Everything had changed with her mention of the Grand Regency Hotel. The air itself seemed electric, crackling with complex tensions she couldn't read.

"If you want me to tell you that I forgive you, and that Linnie and Ryan forgive you, and it's all water under the bridge and we know you've changed, that's not going to happen," she told him. "If that's what this is about, then you can have it straight, without the sandwich lunch."

"Why, thank you, ma'am," he drawled.

She ignored him. "I don't believe you have changed. If you could behave that badly six years ago, on Linnie's wedding day, you could behave that badly still. I love my sister, and she's hurting right now, over Gram's death and—and—other stuff. If she has anything whatsoever to do with why you're back in town for the next six—"

"She doesn't," he cut in, hard and fast. "Okay? Let's get that on the table right now. She doesn't have anything to do with my being here."

"No? Good." If she believed him. What had she seen in his eyes? "Because some mistakes you just have to live with. *You* have to live with this one, Jared. Linnie doesn't, Ryan doesn't and I don't."

"I guess not."

"We're done here."

"Sure…"

"Thanks for your time."

He put on a crooked, cynical smile. "Thanks for the insights."

"You're more than welcome, if they've gotten through."

"Oh, they have." He glanced behind him toward the shelf where various polished trophies gleamed, as if reminding himself that he was still a winner. "I'll keep you and your mother posted on how I'm doing with the estate."

"Sure. And I can leave any messages or papers with your secretary."

"Right. No personal contact necessary."

But Shallis didn't reward this barbed observation with a reply. She simply snapped her briefcase shut, picked it up and left.

Jared watched her go—the graceful walk, the squared yet feminine shoulders, the pretty, bouncing hair.

"You are such a damned idiot, Jared Starke," he muttered to himself seconds after the door shut behind her.

It didn't slam, because Jared couldn't imagine that Shallis Duncan, ex Miss Tennessee, would ever slam a door.

She was far too perfect for that.

As perfect as a splinter stuck under his thumb. As perfect as a melody in his head that wouldn't go away. As perfect as some twisted form of hell, in which a man didn't see a certain woman for six years and when he did, he discovered that he still hadn't gotten over a gut-level response to her that he'd never wanted, that maddened him and embarrassed him and confused him to the point where he could barely walk straight.

He ought to feel proud of his performance this morning. Professional and courteous and pleasant. Bland as vanilla pudding. For most of their meeting, he was positive she'd had no idea. Even when his guard had slipped a little and she'd seen something, she'd gotten it wrong. She still thought he was on some twisted quest to change the balance of power between himself and Linnie.

Thank heaven, he wasn't. One thing to be grateful for, at least.

He'd behaved despicably toward Melinda Duncan Courcy in the past—twice—his arrogant ultimatum on her wedding day wasn't the first time—but he was in no doubt as to how he felt about her now.

There remained a brotherly sort of affection which she'd probably never know about and wouldn't value if she did. There was also a recognition that her wedding day had started a chain reaction of questions inside him that he was still trying to deal with.

But nothing more.

Nothing like what Shallis feared.

It was Shallis herself who twisted him up inside, and he was as appalled about it as she would be, too, if she knew.

Apparently she didn't know, and he would make sure he kept it this way until he could somehow delete the unwanted attraction from his emotional hard drive like deleting a piece of e-mail spam.

"Yeah, and how're you going to do that, tough guy, if you have to have a half dozen meetings with her over her grandmother's estate," he muttered again.

He should have let her go to Banks and Moore.

It was the same problem he'd always had. Against all good judgment, against everything the rational side of his brain understood, and even with the odds stacked monumentally against him, his instinct was always to try to win.

Frowning, he stepped over to the breakfront and moved the

Sore Loser trophy to a more prominent position on the shelf, right next to his favorite golfing photo of Grandpa Abe, himself and Dad.

Chapter Three

"Linnie, oh, no, what is it?" Shallis gasped out as soon as she saw her sister. "What's happened?"

It was five-thirty in the evening, and Linnie had just opened the front door of her modest ranch house for Shallis, her pretty gray eyes reddened and swollen, and tears streaming down her cheeks. Her shoulders shook with suppressed sobbing.

"Oh, it's just the usual," she said, trying to smile. "Not pregnant. Again. Come in." Her voice cracked into a high-pitched squeak as she struggled for normality. She looked down at the decorative wicker basket in Shallis's hands. "Oh. Nice. You've brought fruit."

"Left from a conference at the hotel on the weekend."

"You're good. It looks l-lovely, with the r-ribbons and all." Her shoulders shook some more. "Ryan's not in from the barn yet, thank goodness."

The house was plain and small, but it was situated on a beautiful piece of land, part of the infrastructure of the horse-breeding business Ryan had been building for several years. He'd recently renovated a couple of old cabins on the property, also, and they would be open for paying guests this summer, with optional breakfast and dinner included in the package.

Ryan worked very hard, as did Linnie, and Shallis wasn't surprised to hear that he wasn't yet back at the house. She'd been counting on his absence because she wanted a sister-to-sister talk, but she didn't understand why Linnie would be feeling the same.

Linnie stepped to the side and Shallis crossed the threshold. "You don't want to see Ryan?" she asked carefully.

"I don't want him to see me. Like this." Linnie flapped her hands at her blotchy face and attempted another smile. It looked heartbreaking. She kicked the door closed behind her.

"Oh, Linnie." Shallis put down the fruit basket and hugged her sister, burning with love and empathy that just had no place to go, no way to translate into the right words.

"I'm sorry," Linnie whispered in her ear, her voice tight and harsh with a continuing effort not to cry. "It's so stupid. It usually only lasts around twenty minutes, so I'll be okay again soon."

"Twenty minutes? What does, Lin?"

"The sobbing." Her body shuddered suddenly, and went still. "There. See? It just stops. And then I sometimes laugh at myself a little bit, because it shouldn't feel so…so…*tragic*, you know? Ryan and I love each other, we love the farm and the horses, I love my teaching job, we have great families, plans to extend the house, we have so much going for us. And still I'm sobbing like a maniac every month just because I don't have a baby. What more do I want out of life? The moon and stars on a big silver plate?"

She threw the words over her shoulder at Shallis on their way down the short corridor toward the kitchen. Her golden-brown hair looked limp and tired, and so did her green-toned skirt and top.

"Of course you want a baby," Shallis said, following her with the fruit basket. "Of course it's hard. You had an appointment with the specialist last week. Weren't there some test results coming in?"

"His nurse called today, just after I got in from school. Which is why I guess I was already a little upset, even before…you know. Nothing conclusive, she said."

"But that's good news, isn't it?" Shallis felt so far out of her depth.

She'd been on the pill for six months. A doctor had prescribed it in Los Angeles when the stress she'd been under there had led to painful and wildly irregular cycles. She had no idea how it must feel to be so desperate to conceive.

"Oh, sure," Linnie answered. "I mean, it's better than, 'Guess what, you don't have any ovaries,' or something. But it leaves us still in the dark, nowhere to go. Technically there seems to be no reason why, in more than three years, I haven't conceived. And if there's no reason, then there's no action you can take to correct it, you know?"

"I get it. Oh, Linnie…"

"Hey, want a big, stiff drink? Please say yes, because I'm having one."

"What're you having?"

"Bourbon and Coke, nice and strong. Two weeks every cycle I don't touch a drop of alcohol. You know. Just in case I'm— Then on this day each month, I pretend to myself that getting a little tipsy is just what I've been looking forward to. Woo-hoo!"

She sounded so cynical and self-mocking, so *not* like the sunny, caring, capable Linnie that Shallis knew Ryan had fallen in love with. It scared her a little. Until three months ago, she'd been caught up in her life in Los Angeles, and she'd had no idea.

She'd known Linnie had some kind of fertility problem, of course, but she'd never suspected her sister felt that badly about it. Linnie was only thirty-two. She had time, didn't she? And modern reproductive medicine could do so much.

In her e-mails and phone calls, Linnie just hadn't let on the full truth, and neither had anyone else. Protecting Shallis's important career, as usual. The PR career she hadn't even liked, in the end, which was one of the reasons she'd come home.

"Does—could—does the specialist think that tying yourself in knots about it might be making it worse?" she asked carefully.

"That's the myth, isn't it? Just relax, and you'll conceive. If I had a dollar for everyone who's told us to take a cruise or a trip to Paris and just do what comes naturally… I'm telling you, Shallis, it doesn't come naturally, any more. It's like an Olympic event, with training and warm-ups and electronic timing. Ryan is getting—" She stopped suddenly. "So, want that drink?"

With scary efficiency, she reached into the fridge, the freezer, and a couple of cabinets just above her head. Slosh went the bourbon, fizz went the Coke, crack went the ice cubes. She pushed one brimming glass in Shallis's direction and took a huge gulp from the other. Then she stopped with the glass and her hand in midair.

"Don't worry," she said. "It's one day a month that I do this, and it's one drink. But boy, do I need the effect!"

Shallis nodded slowly and took a much more cautious sip of her own. She'd had a stomach upset over the weekend and was still eating and drinking carefully. "You were, um, saying something about Ryan."

"Oh. Yeah. But I rethought."

"Rethink again. I'm your sister. And I care about you. So much, Linnie." Oh-oh. Foggy voice alert. They'd both cried enough in the past couple of weeks, about Gram's death. She swallowed.

"Oh, it's just… He hates this," Linnie said. "In a different way than I do, but he hates it just as much. He hates that I'm a mess. He hates the Olympic event mechanical sex. We've had a couple of—" she stopped again.

"Arguments," Shallis suggested.

"Fights."

"Fights?"

"Yelling. Ryan never yells. It reminds me of his dad." Who was a difficult man, Shallis knew. "I don't like it."

"No, of course you don't."

"And I don't think he does, either. He's always hated the thought of getting like his father." She took another gulp of her drink, let it roll around her mouth for a moment, then swallowed and squared her shoulders. "Okay, can we close this subject for the moment?"

"Well, if you want, but—"

"What I want is to hear about your appointment with Mr. Starke today."

She only said Mr. Starke, ran Shallis's thoughts. If she'd said Abraham, I would have been obligated to say, no, it was Jared. This way, I can let her think it was his grandfather, if I want.

Yeah.

Right.

That level of honesty between sisters? After Linnie had just more or less admitted to a serious fear that her marriage was in trouble, on top of everything else? When Shallis had come out here pretty much on purpose to tell her about seeing Jared?

No.

"Well, I convinced Mom not to come, in the end," Shallis began. "She really didn't need to. And that was good, as it turned out, because it wasn't Mr. Starke, senior, it was his grandson, who's taking over the practice for a while. Jared."

"Jared," Melinda echoed blankly. *"Jared?"*

"Yes." Your old boyfriend, Linnie, whom I would have stolen from you at sixteen, if I'd had the power. The one who dumped you, then tried to get you back at the altar, when you were marrying the man who was perfect for you.

"But he lives in Chicago," Linnie said. "City of big shoulders and hogs' breakfasts, or whatever that poet said."

"Carl Sandburg. But I don't think the hogs' breakfasts bit is quite right." Although Jared's shoulders were certainly big enough... "He's taking some kind of break." Shallis took a breath. "And he was pretty helpful, actually. Professional. Sensitive. He said we could take our business over to Banks and Moore in Carrollton if we wanted, or let him get things rolling and then hand over to his grandfather as soon as he gets back."

"Where has he gone?"

"Smoky Mountains. Fishing trip. Lo-o-ong fishing trip, Jared thinks. I went with the second alternative, but I have to ask how *you* feel about it, Linnie. You're the one whose life he tried so hard to mess up. I wouldn't blame you if you didn't want anyone in the Duncan family to have anything to do with him."

"He's probably not someone I'd enjoy having around,

true," Linnie agreed slowly. "In any personal sense, that is. You know, for fun family barbecues, and stuff. But the way I'm feeling right now, it would seem so petty and unimportant to sack the family law firm just because its temporary new partner spoiled a few of my wedding pictures six years ago."

"He did a heck of a lot more than that, Linnie!" Shallis put down her drink, most of it untouched.

"You know what I mean. Jared didn't change the bottom line. Ryan and I had a beautiful wedding, and we—" *huge* foggy voice alert "—love each other." The words were barely even a whisper.

"He tried to tell you that you didn't love Ryan at all!" Shallis's indignation rose. "He hung around at the reception like a bad odor, with a nasty smile on his face."

And I flirted with him to keep him away from you, and part of the time I *enjoyed* it.

"You sound as if you mind about it more than I do."

"I'm just worried about you, Lin."

"Thanks. But worry about the important stuff, okay? Our marriage, and our fertility, not Jared Starke. Keep him to deal with Gram's estate, because it has to be more convenient that way. I expect he's changed a lot now. Grown up. We all have." Her face said very clearly that Grown-up Land wasn't always a fun place to be. "You said he acted like a professional this morning?"

"Yes, he did." And so did I, thank heaven.

"So give him the benefit of the doubt."

This is not what I wanted you to say, Linnie. You were supposed to give me the perfect way out...

Shallis hadn't realized until just now that this was what she'd been hoping for. So who was the person she really didn't trust?

Herself?

Was that possible?

Ohhh, yeah!

"Did you get a chance to ask him about that strange property tax bill?" Linnie was saying.

"Yes, and he's going to look into it."

"Was he concerned?"

"He thought it seemed a little odd. But don't start worrying about that…"

"…on top of everything else. No, I won't. I think I hear Ryan. Are you staying to eat?"

"Can't. I have a function at the hotel tonight. I'll say a quick hi to your hubby, then I'll head back to town."

"So you only came out here to break it to me about Jared in person?" Linnie took another mouthful of her drink. She gave a wan smile which suggested it was sweetly funny of Shallis to think the issue important enough to warrant the price of the gas, and the wear and tear on the car.

Illogically this only made Shallis feel even more fiercely protective about her sister, and even more determined not to risk hurting her in any way. She said her hello to Ryan, and under the cover of a sisterly hug managed to whisper in his ear, "Look after her. She's hurting today."

"I know," he answered, gruff and male and helpless. He'd never been big on fluent speeches, but his heart was in the right place. "I can tell just from her face."

Shallis was back in town at ten after six.

This was the house on Chestnut Street. Number Fifty-six.

Shallis slowed the car and pulled close to the curb. She must have passed this place dozens if not hundreds of times in her life, but she'd never really looked at it before. The street contained a mix of Victorian architectural styles, and there'd been a mix of changes made to the original dwellings over the years, also. No two houses were alike.

Some of the best places in the street had been gorgeously restored for use as suites of doctors' and dentists' offices, elegant dwellings or the kind of bed-and-breakfast inns that featured in glossy travel magazines, but Number Fifty-six hadn't. Made of a rust-colored brick, it seemed a little tired.

The guttering needed some attention, and so did the floorboards of the wraparound porch. The garden looked as if it received regular care, however. The lawn had been recently mown, and the shrubbery in front of the porch was free of weeds. But the bushes themselves were gnarled and old.

Was anyone living here?

From the street, Shallis couldn't tell. She parked the car, then sat in it for a moment, debating her options. Several people at the Grand Regency would commence predictable panic attacks if she wasn't back by six forty-five, but the hotel was only three minutes drive from here, right around the block, and everything had been under control when she left. She had a little time.

She climbed out and went to the small metal mailbox. Tentatively lifting the back flap, she saw two or three days' worth of junk mail inside. Maybe whoever lived here was away. If the place was unoccupied, someone was definitely collecting the mail. The flap of the mailbox squeaked as she lowered it shut.

She walked up the slate path toward the front door, aware of the ambient sounds of the town around her. High overhead, a jet plane faintly roared, while closer at hand a car or two swished by, a dog barked and muffled radio music played. No sounds came from the house itself.

Stepping onto the porch, she felt like a trespasser. She

rang an old-fashioned electric bell which seemed to peal inside the house like a fire station alarm, and she knew she probably wouldn't have pressed that little black bakelite button if she'd really thought that anyone was home. After a two-minute wait and another press of the bell, she hadn't sensed any sound or movement inside.

Time to leave.

Except that she couldn't seem to do so just yet. She really wanted to know if the house was empty and unlived in, or just temporarily unattended. Its secrets seemed to whisper at her in the breeze that stirred the trees. The front windows were curtained, but she cupped a hand against her cheek and forehead and peered through the glass anyhow, in case there was a gap.

Yes. A couple of inches. It was dark inside the house, however, and she couldn't see. Just a few dim shapes, edges and angles. Furniture? She thought so, but wasn't sure.

She decided to make a quick trip around to the back of the place. Successful ex-beauty queens tended to be thorough. If there was anything to be learned here, she would learn it now and not need to make a second visit.

The back porch, like the one at the front, was wide and substantial and in need of repair, and a couple of the windows that looked onto it had raised blinds and no drapes. She saw a dining table through an open doorway and a primitive-looking kitchen with this year's calendar on the opposite wall, still showing the February page.

Behind her, she heard footsteps and a voice. "Shallis, hi…"

Whirling around, she found Jared half way up the back porch steps. She took a too-hasty step and her dove-gray spiked heel rammed through a splintery crack between the old floorboards. She tripped, ending up on both hands and one painful knee, with the other foot bare and its shoe still jammed in the crack, some inches behind her.

"Shoot, this porch needs some work!" Jared dropped beside her and touched her shoulder. He didn't let the contact linger, but his voice was resonant with concern. "You okay?"

"I'm fine."

"Sure? Your foot—"

"Apart from the crowd of splinters having a family reunion in my knee."

Shallis steeled herself for Jared to make the kind of comment that usually came next. Something along the lines of how lucky it was she hadn't tripped like this on pageant night in front of the whole of America. She geared up to laugh and politely pretend she hadn't heard variations on the same joke a hundred times here in Hyattville, on every occasion when she did anything even the slightest bit graceless or messy or natural.

But all Jared said was, "Let me have a look, okay? Got tweezers?"

"I possess tweezers, yes." *Go away. Stop looking at my knee like that.* "But I don't carry them around with me."

This was another assumption she had to contend with on a regular basis—that she carried an elephant-size makeup and grooming kit in her purse everywhere she went, and did she happen to keep aloe vera tissues/a corkscrew/spare panty hose/a socket wrench set in it, by any chance?

"Mono-brow doesn't grow back that fast, I guess," Jared murmured, with such a straight face that it took her several seconds to react with a very unprincesslike snort of laughter. "You don't look comfortable," he added.

"I'm not."

Still thrown off balance by a kind of humor she wasn't used to, except maybe from Dad, Shallis rotated to a sitting position, and mentally added twenty minutes to her schedule so she could go home and change. The splintery wood had pulled several threads in the fabric of her skirt, and the gray of the porch dust wasn't an exact match for the gray of the silk.

Since it was an expensive designer suit, she cared about the pulled threads a lot more than she cared about the splinters in her knee. Skin healed. Silk didn't.

"Let me take a look," Jared repeated. "Can I remind you that helplessness is considered an attractive quality in a Southern woman?"

"I can do it, thanks. I was an L.A. woman for five years. I don't do helpless anymore."

Especially not with you.

"People always wuss out on their own splinters. Splinters need tough love." She felt the warmth of his breath on her knee, but he didn't touch her. "None of these are stuck all the way under the skin, from what I can see. I can get them."

"You don't have tweezers."

"We've already discussed this." He looked up from his inspection. "Neither do you."

"I have nails."

And a gorgeous French manicure that would probably get as ruined as her skirt if she used her nails to get the splinters out. She'd counted five of them. Too bad. She wasn't letting Jared's fingers anywhere near her knee.

He'd gotten the message now, apparently.

Gritting her teeth, she scraped at her skin, pincered her nails and got four of the splinters out while Jared took out a pocket knife—not the kind equipped with tweezers, unfortunately—and used its strongest blade to lever the gap in the floorboards wide enough to pull her jammed shoe heel free.

"It doesn't look too good," he said, examining the piece of expensive Italian footwear. "The leather is all scraped."

She glanced up from her inspection of a section of newly chipped nail polish. "It looks better than my knee."

"How're you doing, there? I haven't heard any ouches."

"I'm keeping them to myself. The last splinter wouldn't come."

"Okay, my turn."

"I'll get it out at home."

"No, let me have a try." He put the shoe down beside her, rested a hand on her knee before she could make another protest, and told her in a cheerful tone, "This is probably going to hurt."

"Did you ever consider going into medicine?"

"For a couple of months when I was eighteen, but I dropped the idea pretty fast and took on the traditional Starke family career. Why?"

"Good decision. Because your bedside manner is way off. Ouch," she added.

"Yeah, can't help it," was all he said, still cheerful.

How do I loathe thee? Let me count the ways…

He pinched up her skin, scraped, pinched again. Shallis sat back on her hands and closed her eyes. She could hear his breath whistling softly between his teeth and over his firm lower lip. She could imagine the golden glint of concentration in his eyes. His hand was warm—ouch, again!—and confident. His knee pressed into her outer thigh, chafing her skin softly with the fabric of his summer-weight suit.

Focusing on the splinter, he probably wasn't aware of the contact, but Shallis was. She felt like a traitor to Linnie and Ryan, but even more of a traitor to herself for the powerful and familiar tingle of physical response that built inside her.

He'd dropped the lawyer facade, and he was such a sexy man. A thousand women must have thought so. Chemistry on two legs. A dangerous assailant on at least four of her senses.

But he was the wrong man.

He always had been.

She'd met enough men with the same win-at-all-costs mentality in Los Angeles. And thanks to Linnie's history with Jared she'd always recognized pretty fast what they were really like underneath the charming, sexy veneer, and that they hadn't really wanted *her,* they'd wanted…

Well, take your pick.

Arm candy.

Another notch on their belt.

A passport to the next level of success.

She'd met losers, too, and they could be even worse.

Surely there had to be some kind of middle ground. A man of her own generation who had the same basic qualities as her dad. A man who knew what he wanted but had limits on what he'd do to get it. A man she could be attracted to for his strength and even, yes, his arrogance, but who knew how to laugh at himself, too. A man who hadn't already proved himself to be a total jerk in the way he'd behaved to Linnie six years ago.

If she was crazy enough to give in to her chemical attraction to Jared Starke she could never say she hadn't been warned.

She *had* been warned, so why didn't this act as the perfect antidote to the delectable poison that was running through her veins?

She had little tingles chasing each other all the way up her legs and, darn it, a red-blooded woman needed a few tingles in her life. There had to be a couple of decent single men in this world who knew how to deliver them. If only she could get this man out of her system first.

"Got it," Jared said, and his touch evaporated from her knee before she could open her eyes.

She wanted the contact back, and hated herself.

"Thanks," she muttered, and sat forward again, to inspect what he'd done. There were a couple of pinprick sized droplets of blood forming. Jared produced a clean tissue, pressed it into her hand and stood up, watching her dab the blood away.

"That's your car out front, I take it," he said.

"That's right."

"Nice."

"It gets me from A to B." The European-styled sports car was a part of her pageant winnings, five years old now but still widely admired. In the past, she'd had numerous dates with men who were more interested in the car than they were in her. "I had a few minutes, and I was curious about the house, so I stopped by," she added.

"Same here. I walked down from Grandpa Abe's place, in time to see you disappearing round the back."

"It's furnished, but do you get the same impression as me that no one's living here? Not quite sure why the sense is so strong."

"I know. Just a feeling, but you're right, it's definitely there." He went and peered in the windows, just as she had. His body language was intent and focused. "Something about the stillness," he murmured.

What was it? It wasn't the words. It was the delivery.

"And the calendar in the kitchen, still on the February page," she added. "Do you know any of the neighbors?"

"I don't, but my grandfather must. I had a closer look at your grandmother's files this afternoon, after you'd gone, but couldn't find anything. I've tried calling him, but he only has a cell phone up at his cabin, and he has it switched off. So it doesn't scare off the fish, I imagine."

Shallis laughed. She kept doing that. He kept saying things that weren't exactly hilarious, but somehow surprised her enough to tickle her funny bone, purely because they weren't the same lame beauty queen jokes she'd heard dozens of times before. He was refreshingly different from most men in ways that didn't really count, and exactly the same as the worst of the species in other much more dangerous ways that counted for everything.

"It's twenty till seven," he said. "I'll try calling him again soon."

"Oh, it's that late?" She'd been here almost half an hour. Drive home to her garden apartment, freshen up, change. If anything was going wrong at the hotel... And speaking of cell phones, she'd left hers in her briefcase in the car, so if there had been a catering catastrophe, or something, she'd been out of contact. "I need to get home."

He nodded. "It's getting late. And there's something about this place. It could get spooky after dark. Porch rocker starting to creak when there's nobody there. Whispering voices echoing down the stairs."

"Stop!" She went to slip her foot back in the damaged shoe. "You're too good at creating atmosphere, Jared Starke."

Various kinds of atmosphere, none of which she wanted.

"Don't put on the shoe," he said. He had that husky note in his voice again, that she'd heard earlier today. "Take off the other one and go barefoot. The path around the side of the house is pretty uneven, too, and I think you might have weakened the heel. Can't guarantee I'll be able to save you, next time."

"You didn't save me this time," she pointed out tartly, bending a little and lifting her foot to scoop the second shoe off. The soft leather slid across the sensitive skin of her instep and heel. "You didn't even have tweezers."

"True." He watched her movement, his focus casual yet intent, as if her action with the shoe was significant.

Or sexy.

Her body warmed, as if beneath a row of hot stage lights.

"We'll be in touch, then, as soon as either of us finds out more about this place," he finished.

"Yes." She walked ahead of him, since she knew he was hanging back so she could do so—her knight in shining armor, ready to be there for her if she stumbled.

No.

Not quite.

Ready to ogle the shimmy in her walk, more likely. Shallis hadn't taken that kind of thing as a compliment since she was seventeen. And she couldn't *believe* that she was even the slightest bit tempted to respond to it now.

The slate path felt cool under her feet, however, and she started thinking about the house again. It could be one of the grandest places on the street if it had the right treatment. It was three stories high, with a big round turret on one corner and a steeply sloping roof, made of slate that matched the path. Looking up, she saw that some of the slates were a slightly different color than the majority, as if the roof had been repaired with new stone, not too long ago.

Slate was expensive. A lot of people didn't try to repair it anymore, just got rid of it altogether and put on a tar or wood shingle roof instead. Someone had cared about this place.

Her grandmother? Gram would have used slate. She

wouldn't have wanted this grand old lady to wear cheap tar when she was accustomed to being coiffed in elegant stone.

"If Gram owns this house, though, why on earth don't we know about it?"

Turning to ask the question out loud, Shallis almost came to collision point with Jared. He'd about caught up to her, now, ready to head up the street toward his grandfather's house. They both stopped, managed not to touch, and blurted awkward apologies.

"Can't answer your question," Jared said.

They were standing too close, he realized.

Again.

He stepped back, hoping it didn't look too obvious that he was attempting to get himself safely clear of her space. With any other woman for whom he felt this powerful level of attraction, he would have used the opposite strategy—stepping closer, turning on the charm like turning on garden lanterns on a summer evening.

His history with Shallis and her sister was like the repelling force of two magnets pointing at each other the wrong way, and his questions about his own future and priorities only strengthened that force.

He wasn't back in Hyattville to get involved in some disastrous, short-lived relationship with a blast from the past that would leave a sour taste in everybody's mouth. He was here for some space, in order to work out, once and for all, who he wanted to be.

"No, I didn't expect you to answer it," Shallis said, cutting in on his thoughts. "If you'll excuse me, Jared, I have a function at the hotel tonight and I really need to go home and change. But… uh… thanks for your help with the splinter and the shoe."

"You're welcome. Talk to you soon."

He gave a short, careful nod, not too friendly, not too sharp—he hated controlling his every word and gesture this way—and set off along the sidewalk toward his grandfather's house.

About thirty seconds later, he heard the smooth purr of her expensive car drift past him. They waved to each other again—casual hands, polite smiles—and he wondered what it was going to take for this to get easy.

Go back and erase the past, maybe?

Six years back, to Linnie and Ryan's wedding, and then another five to the night of Shallis's sixteenth birthday party, when he'd almost kissed her. That little word "almost" was the only thing that gave him any hope and any self-respect, when he looked back on his behavior that night.

He'd wanted to, and Shallis at that point in her life would have practically fainted with ecstasy in his arms. Yeah, her crush had been as obvious to him as the sweet champagne on her breath, and as innocent and doomed as a baby doe caught in the headlights of an oncoming car.

She wouldn't have turned him down, even though she wouldn't have had a clue what was really happening. She'd have gone as far as he wanted, believed everything he said. The sweet-natured seventeen-year-old boy who'd been agonizingly and just as innocently in love with Shallis that year wouldn't have had a chance.

And Linnie, who'd considered herself just about engaged to Jared at the time, would never have known… unless Shallis herself had told her. Jared would have gone on his merry way, feeling like a winner after an easy victory, as usual.

Two sisters wrapped around his little finger, when he didn't have serious plans for either of them.

But he hadn't done it. He'd run his fingers softly through Shallis's golden hair. His mouth had come within an inch of hers. She'd sighed up at him, her eyes huge and awed and gorgeous, as she waited.

She was young enough to trust him, to have faith in her own feelings, and to believe that Linnie would forgive her such a betrayal, because this was love, and love conquered all.

He didn't understand how he'd been able to read her layered feelings so clearly, but somehow he had.

Finally he'd muttered, "I can't do this," and he'd torn himself away, left with an enduring sense of protectiveness toward Shallis Duncan that he didn't understand, either.

It was one of the few moments in his life that had had the power to convince him, over the past six years, that he had any sense of honor in him at all.

Chapter Four

"Here's another thing that doesn't make sense," Sunny Duncan said to her daughter.

"Show me, Mom." Shallis hid a yawn behind her hand as she spoke.

Last night's function at the Grand Regency had run until after midnight, and she hadn't gotten enough sleep. To be honest, though, her serial yawns weren't happening just because her job had kept her up late.

Instead, blame Jared.

No, blame herself for the fact that he'd stuck around in her head all night, along with memories of those tingles running up her legs when he'd worked on her knee. She was shocked at how powerful the memories were. Fingers were just fingers. A knee was just a knee. This shouldn't happen.

With a quiet day at the hotel today, she'd taken the morning off work, but she'd known her mother was going over to

Gram's to sort through more of her things so she'd set her alarm for seven anyhow, and they'd both arrived at Gram's house at eight.

Now it was just after ten, and the two of them had worked for two hours without a break. Even with the windows open, the place felt dusty and musty because of the things they'd unearthed, and Shallis craved coffee and some kind of carb-loaded, totally unacceptable snack.

"It's a bill for roof shingles," her mother said, holding out a creased invoice. "From a slate company."

"Fifty-six Chestnut has a slate roof," Shallis said.

She shivered suddenly. What was that old saying? *Someone is walking over my grave.*

"So you've been past the house?"

"Yesterday evening. I didn't tell you—" And I know why I didn't tell you. Because I ran into Jared there, and I had his fingers on my knee all night. "—but I got out of the car to take a look at the place, and saw that the roof had been repaired with new slate. I actually thought—"

She stopped, because it sounded too strange, and her mother finished the sentence for her, looking a little spooked, also.

"—that your grandmother would choose slate if it was her place, even though it costs a bundle. I know. Of course she would."

"But it can't be her place."

"Exactly. This is her place. My Lord, I grew up here, and I visited her here practically every day. I love this house, but good gosh, Shallie, it's nowhere near as big and nice as the places on Chestnut Street. It doesn't make sense that she'd own a house there that she never told us about, and never lived in, and never sold."

"It doesn't, does it?" Shallis frowned.

"Was anyone home?"

"I think it's unoccupied. Although from what I could see it hadn't been that way for long. Since February, maybe."

"We need to take this invoice over to Mr. Starke's office right away." Sunny caught sight of her daughter's expression. "Yes, and talk to his grandson. You managed it yesterday without hitting the man. I can probably do the same."

There was the definite suggestion that this would be an act of heroic restraint on Sunny's part.

Shallis hesitated for a moment, then asked, "Have you talked to Linnie since the weekend?"

Sunny sighed. "Oh, trust me, honey, I know her cycle as well as she does. I called her last night and I could tell just by the sound of her voice that she's not pregnant again this month."

"Nobody told me how bad it's been hitting her."

"Did you really need to hear it, out in L.A., with so much else to think about?"

"Yes, I did! I didn't need to be shut out. She's my sister. How can you stay close if you don't know what's going on? And nobody considered that. Not Ryan or you or dad. Nobody told me it was threatening her marriage."

"Threatening her marriage? No!" Mom looked shocked. "Her and Ryan? No! It's not doing that."

"She seemed pretty upset about it last night, Mom. She stopped trying to pretend with me—the way you've all been pretending to me for *months!*"

"What? The same way *you* didn't admit to us how miserable you'd gotten in L.A?"

Two points to Mom, to level the score.

"Okay… The thing is," Shallis said, "is whether Linnie's

going to get even more upset about what's happening with her and Ryan if she has to deal with Jared being back in town as well. She says she's not."

"But you don't think we should believe her."

"I'm not sure that we should risk having her find out the hard way that she was wrong," Shallis said slowly. "And I want to know how you feel, yourself, about Jared being involved in dealing with Gram's estate. We could go to another lawyer. He offered me that option himself, and I said I'd discuss it with you. If you want to bail out, now's the time. If you think there's any risk to Linnie at all…"

"I never trusted Jared when he and Linnie were going out. I wasn't sorry when he dumped her, in my heart of hearts, even though she felt for a long time as if he'd broken hers."

"Why didn't you trust him, Mom?"

"Because he's the type who does break hearts."

"So it's a lifelong habit?"

Did she really need to know Mom's opinion?

"A habit or a hobby. It can be, honey, in my experience, unless a man is given a good reason to change. But I don't think he could break Linnie's heart anymore. She has her priorities in place, even if they're painful ones right now. Let's take this invoice over to Jared, and keep it businesslike."

Another Duncan family member who didn't seem to understand that Shallis wanted an easy way out, the way they'd never realized how miserable she was in L.A. while she was attempting to build a career in PR. Apparently thanks to her pageant years, she was simply too good an actress.

"How about we call first?" she suggested. "In case he's—"

Left the country. Wouldn't that be nice?

"—on another appointment." Mom nodded. "Yes, let's do that."

She was already reaching for her neat little cell phone. She spoke to Andrea, then waited while the receptionist put her through to Jared's office. And then…

Uh-oh.

The Voice.

The one that could probably shatter a champagne glass at twenty paces.

The one that said, loud and clear, I don't like or trust you but you'll never be able to pin me down on that in a hundred years because I'm *wa-a-ay* too well mannered and well raised.

Shallis was all too familiar with The Voice. It was high and cooing and polite, dripping with honey yet still somehow sharp as a razor and cold as Arctic ice. She'd heard it many times during her pageant years, when Mom spoke to another pageant mother whose daughter was, say, bitching about the other girls behind their backs, or wearing a gown that Mom considered inappropriate for her age. "Your daughter could pass for twenty instead of twelve in that outfit, couldn't she, bless her heart!"

Shallis only focused on her mother's tone, at first, but then the tone changed—got warmer by about five degrees, kept the honey but lost some of the razorlike edge—and she started to listen more carefully.

"Oh, you have?" Mom was saying. "And you want us to come in? Right away? Yes, because we're very anxious to hear. We'll be right down."

She flipped the phone shut a few seconds later and looked at her daughter with raised brows.

"He's found out something," Shallis said.

"And he doesn't want to discuss it over the phone. Doctors are like that, too." Mom sounded edgy. "They want to see that you're sitting down. What in the blue blazes could Gram have had going on in her life that we would need to hear about sitting down?"

Mom was already on her way to the bathroom with her lipstick in her hand. She tended to wear makeup the way medieval knights wore suits of armor. Shallis felt an instinctive urge to follow her and do some facial repair work of her own, but she resisted and simply retrieved her lip balm from her purse instead.

"You're not going to change and do your face?" her mother asked. She looked shocked.

Shallis looked down at her jeans and top, and brushed away a few token specks of dust. "Nope," she answered.

Put on full cosmetic battle dress for Jared Starke?

She wouldn't stoop to such desperate measures.

Mysteries weren't supposed to be this easy to solve. As soon as he'd gotten home from his exploratory visit to Fifty-six Chestnut Street last night, Jared had called his grandfather and found his cell phone switched on at last.

"Darn it, I meant to tell you about that place before I left. Too much else on my mind."

"Like trout fishing flies, I'm guessing," Jared drawled. He understood his grandfather pretty well. "So you know about it?"

"Of course I know about it. Find something in this town that I don't know about and you can sell me the Empire State Building while you're at it." He clicked his tongue. "I wanted Caroline McLenaghan to do something about the place, but she didn't feel ready, and then she had her stroke. I was her lawyer for fifty years. More to the point, I was Flip Templeton's lawyer, too."

Jared sighed. "Tell me the whole story, Grandpa Abe. I have a feeling none of this is going to make any sense until you do. Beginning, middle and end, please, in that order, and don't make any assumptions about what I already know."

So now Jared knew, and Sunny and Shallis Duncan were on their way to his office at this very moment to find out. He'd spent half the morning wondering when and how to give them the story. Mrs. Duncan's phone call a few minutes ago had made the decision for him.

He didn't know how they would take it. It wasn't so much the fact that Caroline McLenaghan had secretly owned a very substantial Victorian dwelling for the past thirty years and more, it was the reason why she'd owned it that might knock the whole Duncan family for a loop.

This was what small town legal work was all about, he'd begun to discover, after just a day and a half on the job. Friends and enemies, rumors and facts, individuals and families, secrets that echoed down the generations.

Jared hadn't known it would be so interesting...or such a responsibility. By his own admission, Grandpa Abe would have more stories locked away in file drawers and safes and his own memory than anybody but old Dr. Taylor, who'd finally retired at eight-five, just last year. As manager of the Douglas County Bank, Bob Duncan must know a good few town secrets, also, but his mother-in-law Caroline McLenaghan had always banked with Tennessee State and Main, so Bob hadn't known this one.

The phone on Jared's desk rang, and he heard Andrea's voice. "Mrs. Duncan and her daughter have arrived, Mr. Starke."

"Yep, bring them on in, Andrea."

"Coffee?"

"If they want it." He suspected this was going to take a while. He might have to shuffle them out, shell-shocked, to clear some space for his next appointment at eleven-fifteen.

Actually, they already looked shell-shocked, as soon as they walked through the door. Sunny Duncan, who didn't have the word casual in her vocabulary, wore a bright, swirly skirt, a white blouse, watermelon-pink shoes, full makeup and pearls, but her daughter had dressed down today. Apparently they'd spent the morning at Caroline McLenaghan's house, going through more of her things, and Shallis had expected to get dusty.

Her blue jeans fit her like surgical gloves, stretching over her perfect peachy backside and down her long, long legs. Her top was just as snug—one of those long-sleeved, round-necked things…blue, with a misty sort of pattern…that shouldn't have looked all that sexy because there was very little skin on show, but in fact looked as sexy as hell.

It had to be the close fit, Jared decided, the way it clung to the exact shape of her shoulders and her waist and her…mmm, yes, those. Round and full without being too heavy, high and soft inside what had to be a lace bra because he could see the texture of it showing slightly through the stretch fabric of the top.

How much of a sleaze was he, to be thinking of something like that now? Shallis would walk right out of here if she knew…wouldn't she?

"Please sit," he invited both women, tuning his voice to the right professional pitch. "Andrea's bringing coffee, and then we'll start."

Shallis was nervous. She didn't stand with her usual poise, but hugged her forearms across each other, gripping a hand around each elbow. She looked relieved at the offer of a chair.

"Obviously this isn't something simple like a real estate investment we weren't aware of," she said.

"I'll start at the beginning," he promised, as Andrea brought in three bone china cups on a tray, along with a plate of cookies. He waited the appropriate interval until the receptionist had left again before he continued. "Your father Henry died in 1957, didn't he, Mrs. Duncan?"

"Yes, when I was only seven years old."

"Two years later, your mother met Felix Templeton. Flip, everyone called him."

"I remember Flip," Sunny Duncan said. "And I remember his wife Martha."

"Yes, he was married. My grandfather says he would have left his wife but your mother didn't want that."

Shallis was listening intently to his words, Jared noted, as he reached the difficult part. Her eyes looked even bigger and bluer and more beautiful than usual, beckoning to his hot, prickling body like a sparkling swimming pool on a scorching summer day. He tried to keep his focus on her mother instead.

"The Templetons had no children and Martha was a difficult character," he went on. "Selfish and not emotionally strong, according to Grandpa Abe. Mrs. McLenaghan didn't think Martha would be able to function on her own if her marriage broke up."

"So you're saying—?" Sunny Duncan frowned. "You can't be saying—"

"Flip and your mother were lovers, yes. For a long time. Their relationship lasted eleven years, until Mr. Templeton's death. He left her the Chestnut Street house in his will, as well as a cash sum to be used for its upkeep and—"

"None of it went to his wife?" Shallis asked.

"No, because his two unmarried sisters were living in the house, and according to my grandfather Mrs. Templeton had always been quite vocal about wanting to turn them out on their own in order to sell. Flip trusted your mother not to do that, Mrs. Duncan, and she didn't let him down."

"Well, of course not," Shallis said. "But—"

"In fact, as well as giving them companionship over the years, she supported the Templeton sisters financially to a generous extent, above and beyond the money Flip left her, through payment of various property tax, yard maintenance and repair bills for almost thirty-five years. Shallis, that's why the lawn still looked freshly mown yesterday."

"Right." Her voice was tight. "Thirty-five years. My whole life and more."

"Until the last surviving sister, Ivy, died in February this year," Jared explained. "The other sister, Rose, was mentally handicapped so Ivy had never worked and had cared for Rose devotedly, until she died several years ago. Apparently at the time of Mrs. McLenaghan's own death, she hadn't yet made up her mind what she was going to do with the house. She knew she couldn't put it on the market without you asking questions she didn't want to answer, after so long."

"All these years!" Sunny Duncan spoke at last. She seemed, yes, shell-shocked, just as Jared had expected. "I know she and the Templeton sisters were friends, but I never knew why, nor that Gram was doing anything to support them." Her words came out with a strangled effort, and even her careful makeup couldn't disguise her loss of color.

But Shallis had a soft smile on her face. "You know, that's so like Gram," she said. Her eyes had filled with tears. "I mean, it's incredible. It's unbelievable. But it's so like her. In so many ways."

"How can you say that, honey?" Sunny turned to her, even more shocked now. "An affair with a married man? For *eleven years?* A whole other life that she didn't tell us about? She didn't tell me, her own daughter."

"You know she always made her own rules, Mom. She had her own sense of honor. It might have been different from some people's version, but it was every bit as strong, and—and—*upright,* really. It doesn't sound as if Martha Templeton was a particularly considerate person, if she was prepared to throw her own husband's sisters onto the street. Gram never would have done that, and we have the proof of it."

"Well, that's true," Sunny conceded.

"And I wonder if her secrecy had more to do with wanting to keep her generosity from being known. Maybe she wasn't ashamed of the affair itself at all. Oh, and I bet the affair was wild and romantic and full of Gram's surprises. Flip Templeton must have been swept off his feet. He knew he'd found someone special, someone he could trust, and Gram stayed true to his trust for thirty-five years."

"Where did my daughter get to be such a romantic, I wonder," Sunny drawled.

Shallis smiled again. At her mother, not at Jared. "Maybe from Gram."

Sunny hardly seemed to hear. She slumped in her seat. "I still can't get my head around this. It means I own the house now, is that right, Jared? That's what you're saying? Martha went back to her people in Ohio after Flip died, I seem to remember. And I think she died not long after. Just a few years."

"Yes, that's what my grandfather said," Jared answered. "And yes, Fifty-six Chestnut Street is a part of your inheritance."

"Why didn't Flip leave it direct to Ivy and Rose, and the money, too?"

"He did leave them some money directly, but according to my grandfather, he felt they were too trusting and too vulnerable. He thought they'd risk losing the house and the money if it was in their name, either through bad management or someone cheating them."

"So we have a second house. And my mother had a whole other life that she never shared. I'm just—" She shook her head, looking like a rag doll with half its stuffing gone.

"Shall I take you home, Mom?" Shallis said. She reached out and touched her mother's arm.

"I'm going to take a moment in the powder room. No, honey, I'm fine on my own," she added, as Shallis started to get up.

When she'd gone, Shallis sat in silence until she apparently felt that Jared would want her to speak. Clearly she still didn't know what to say, and was almost as thoroughly knocked for a loop as her mother.

She had her hands clasped around her knee so tight her knuckles were white, and her face had set with a distant, troubled expression. A whole lot of things she thought she knew about her family had just gotten turned in a radical new direction. And family was important in a place like Hyattville. As a fourth generation Starke lawyer, Jared knew this very well.

"This is…uh…" Shallis finally began, when the silence had thickened to breaking point—Jared's fault more than hers. He should have jumped in sooner, taken the responsibility of speech.

"Would you like the keys?" he asked, thinking it might be easier to get down to a practical level. Easier for him, as well as for her.

"The keys?"

"To Fifty-six Chestnut."

"Oh, you have them?"

"My grandfather did. He told me which safe they were in, on the phone last night, and there's no reason why you shouldn't take them."

Jared had taken them out of the safe first thing this morning, and put them in his top desk drawer. Aware of Shallis watching him, he opened it, picked them up and gave them to her. Her fingers felt almost as cold as the metal, and her hand dropped as soon as she'd closed the keys in her fist, as if they weighed too much.

Emotional weight, he guessed.

The heaviest kind.

As heavy as the weight of all the other Hyattville family secrets contained in his grandfather's files. Why did people do it to themselves? And to each other? He didn't believe in evasions and hiding and lies. The truth always came out in the end, and like a jar of badly preserved fruit it had rarely fared well in long storage.

Chapter Five

"Shallis, before you go, could we run through next month's calendar? I need to check a couple of things."

"Sure, Mr. Lonsdale." Shallis halted obediently in her tracks, on the way out to the staff parking lot behind the rear door of the Grand Regency Hotel.

The hotel manager often needed to check a couple of things. He was as fussy as an old hen or an overprotective father. Even though he'd hired her himself to perform a fairly demanding and responsible set of duties, he frequently treated her more like a ten-year-old who'd shown up with her mom for Take Your Daughter To Work Day.

Another variation on the princess thing.

Another decent, well-meaning man whom she didn't want to offend.

Sigh.

This evening, Shallis was particularly anxious to get away.

Those cold metal keys in her purse had been on her mind all day, from the moment Jared had given them to her, and she wondered if she'd been wrong not to tell Mom that she had them in her possession. But Mom had been so knocked for a loop, she just hadn't dared.

Shallis had taken her to Dad's managerial office at the Douglas County Bank to put her into his concerned hands, as soon as Mom had recovered enough of her customary poise in the powder room. The poise had evaporated again as soon as Mom had seen him.

"You just will not believe this, Bob. I still cannot believe it myself. I am so tied up in knots I don't know what to do."

They'd probably talked about it for most of the afternoon. Shallis had tried calling them, both at the bank and at home, but had only gotten the answering machine and the information from a junior at the bank that Mr. Duncan had left for the day. They hadn't called back. Maybe they'd gone to Linnie and Ryan's, or to friends, unable to keep the news about Gram and the house on Chestnut Street to themselves.

"Now, we have the Parmenter-Robinson wedding on the fourth," Mr. Lonsdale said. "And we need to take particular care with the flowers…"

Half an hour later, Shallis finally managed to leave. She was hungry and tired and had been too churned up to eat lunch, but she also felt too annoyed with her boss to let him ruin her planned visit to Chestnut Street.

Those keys were practically singing in her purse, and she wanted to be able to tell Mom more about the place next time they talked—and that would be soon, she had no doubt.

The front door lock of Fifty-six Chestnut Street was ratly and loose, and the key turned in it easily. Just inside, an old light switch pull-cord dangled, but when she yanked at it nothing happened. The power had probably been disconnected, or switched off in the basement.

No problem. It wasn't dark yet.

She opened drapes in the dining room and the parlor. You had to call it a parlor. The old-fashioned word fit. The place smelled musty-sweet, redolent of some genteel, lavender-laden perfume—fifty years of it seeped into the heavy furniture. Even the crowded ornaments seemed to give off the same flavor, set out in their glass-fronted cabinets, on round rosewood tables and above the open fireplace.

In her lightweight pink suit, Shallis shivered.

If the man who kept the lawn in shape had entered the house since February, or if Gram herself had visited here before she died, it didn't show. Dust had begun to felt itself on the flat surfaces, but in the fading light you didn't immediately see it unless you looked. She had the impression that an elderly, stiffly moving figure might appear at the top of the stairs or in the kitchen doorway at any moment, to ask her if she took lemon in her tea.

It wasn't spooky. Not exactly. Not when there was a new-looking drip coffee machine sitting on the kitchen bench, and plastic utensils hanging on a hooked rack above the stove, and that calendar from the local hardware store on the wall, showing a picture of three cute ginger kittens.

But it was…unsettling.

She went upstairs, heels tapping on the hardwood as she tried not to think about personalities and secrets and old emotions that must have been as powerful as the lavender scent. She schooled herself to think about possibilities, instead.

Really, with the clutter stripped away and the place renovated and revamped, it would be fabulous. The rooms were spacious, the ceilings were high, the hardwood floors and skirtings and stair rails were of a solid quality and craftsmanship you just couldn't find anymore.

Did Chestnut Street need any more Southern Living type bed-and-breakfast establishments?

For the buyer to decide, she realized.

And yet she somehow didn't like the idea of selling the house right away—letting go of a part of Gram's life they'd never known she even had, letting the place go to strangers.

Shallis opened the drapes in one of the back bedrooms on the second level, and saw the far corner of the Grand Regency's extensive grounds coming right up to the house's back fence. The hotel needed to expand its conference facilities. Could this house possibly work for something like that?

The idea seized her imagination and eased her sense of anticipated loss.

There were two sets of stairs, one of which must have been for servants to use in the early days of the house's life. It would be easy to achieve a good flow of traffic between the levels. Add a couple of bathrooms and an elevator. Use the third level for office space. Hire out the facility to smaller conferences and conventions. Women's groups would love it, in particular, with its gracious Victorian atmosphere.

Some strategically placed antiques would help. A piano. A marble washstand. Paintings of still life. She found one in the main bedroom—a pretty little thing, showing a standard bowl of summer fruit, but it didn't look like the work of an amateur.

Or a gifted one, maybe. Someone who'd once lived here? Someone who'd owned that pretty blue and white bowl, and picked those realistic, glowing peaches from one of the gnarled, ancient trees that still grew in the yard? Someone who'd had joys and sorrows and secrets like those of Ivy and Rose and Gram...

Looking at the painting in silence—wishing she could see it better, because the light wasn't good in here, even with the drapes opened up—Shallis heard something creak.

Twice.

And twice was enough.

The shadows and the scents and their effect on her imagination were more than enough.

She hadn't realized how dark it was getting outside. No wonder she couldn't see the painting. Right now, she couldn't see anything, because the details of the house which had fascinated her so much a few minutes ago were now just a blur as she raced down the stairs with her heart thumping, her breath coming in shallow pants, shoes threatening to fly off and spots strobing before her eyes. The seventh step down from the top creaked like a screeching child and the hairs at the back of her neck stood up.

In the front hall, the rattly old door handle wouldn't turn beneath her grip and she panicked completely. Whirled around ready to head for the back door. Saw another shadow.

Moving.

Was it moving?

Or was it just her dizzy vision?

The empty stomach and her bad night didn't help. She made another dizzying one-eighty-degree whirl. She rattled at the front door handle again, and this time the catch let go and she yanked the heavy old door open and fled out into the dusk, gasping.

Gasping, and right into Jared Starke's waiting arms. They felt warm and strong and real, and way more familiar and right than they should. He smelled instantly of something she'd always wanted but couldn't name, some unique combination of fragrant shower products, beer, smoke, clean laundry, male skin and just a hint of sweat.

The bones in her legs dissolved, she grazed her almost trembling chin on the shoulder of his gray T-shirt and her heart jumped against his chest like an animal trying to escape a cage.

"What's chasing you?" he said, and let her go at once.

Shallis weakly wished he hadn't. His solid, nonghostly male bulk had begun to ground her again at once, and now the grounding effect had gone away. But at least she could put a hand up to her pounding heart and press on it until it settled down. "Just my imagination," she said.

"I thought it might have been a ghost." He glanced up at the still, silent windows of the darkened house.

The movement stretched his neck a little, emphasizing the uncompromising push of his jaw. His breathing was faster and heavier than usual, and Shallis guessed he must have been running. He had a small towel draped around his neck, so he was on his warm-down phase now. He must have grabbed the towel from his front porch, or somewhere, and then walked back along Chestnut Street at a tapered down pace so his muscles didn't stiffen. He would have seen her car parked in front of the house.

"It *was* a ghost," Shallis said. "Ghosts, plural. But I don't think they were really there. I did the scaring all by myself."

"Powerful woman." He grinned at her like an old friend, his chest still pumping in and out as his breathing began to slow.

"Powerful atmosphere inside that house."

"You should go back inside." His gaze flicked to her tight shoulders, her hand on her heart, and her panting mouth. He stopped longest at her mouth—or was that her overactive imagination, too?—but then he looked away again, and lifted the end of the draped blue towel to wipe his face.

"No, thanks!" she told him.

"I'm serious. Like getting back on a horse after a fall." He stepped a little closer, touched her arm, then let the contact drop at once. "You should go in there again right now and look in every room so you can see that nothing's there, cure yourself of your own imagination."

"You'll offer to escort me, of course," she drawled. "Maybe check on some of the really spooky rooms all by yourself?"

"Definitely." He grinned again, and someone started flipping pancakes in her stomach. "But first I'll check the fuse box and see if we can switch the power on." He flourished a small flashlight she hadn't seen in his hand until now.

"It hasn't been disconnected?"

"Grandpa Abe doesn't think so. When I saw your car on the way back from my run, and saw the house was dark I thought I should come help you out."

"The ghosts were half a minute ahead of you."

"My timing was still pretty good, don't you think?"

Yeah, timing was one of the things he'd always had down exactly right.

Zing!

Their eyes met just as he clicked the flashlight on. He had it still pointing at the ground so it didn't blind them. It didn't even create much additional light in the place that counted— the two feet of air space between them. But the light was good enough to see, and more than good enough to feel.

Except that it didn't even count as feeling. It was more like *knowing*.

Somehow, Shallis just knew.

That the connection between herself and Jared wasn't only skin deep.

That all his bland professionalism yesterday and this morning had been designed to mask exactly the same awareness that she felt herself—they were in the same boat, here.

That he was going to matter in her life, in some elemental way.

That his smile was the most important thing she'd ever seen.

That he recognized it all just as clearly as she did.

And she didn't like any of this recognition one tiny bit. It unsettled her and horrified her and filled her with a profound distrust of her own judgment. It was worse than the ghosts in the old house who weren't really there. As with the ghosts, she didn't believe in the feeling but couldn't banish its effect.

"Come on," Jared said. He didn't try to touch her, and his smile was *almost* not really there, also. He had a watchful look in his eye, now.

What was he thinking? What had he seen?

"I'm not going down in that basement with you," she told him. "Not in a million years."

"I won't ask you what you're so scared of."

"No. Good. Don't." Because I think the thing that scares me most is you. "I'll wait here by the door, and I'm not moving until lights come on."

"By magic?"

"By you pulling switches." She kept her hand on the door handle, with the door still hanging safely open, and he laughed at her as he left her alone.

She heard his progress all the way through to the back of the house and down the stairs that led from the kitchen, but then the sound of his footsteps died away and the spooky feeling came back.

It really was nothing.

She knew that.

Unfortunately, knowing and feeling—especially in the dark on an empty stomach—were two different things.

Like *recognizing* and *believing*.

Those were two different things, also.

She heard another of those creaking sounds and held on to the door more tightly.

And then she heard footsteps.

His.

Coming back up the stairs.

The squawky, almost musical sound of a pull-cord came to her ears, and she saw light glowing from the direction of the kitchen. Another pull-cord. More light from the dining room. She found the pull-cord she'd first tried herself nearly an hour ago. It was hanging right near her shoulder, and this time it worked. Light shone through the dusty glass teardrops of the chandeliers and chased the ghosts away for good.

They'd never been there in the first place.

"Give me a tour," Jared said, "and tell me what you were thinking about the place before the denizens of the night came out of their lairs."

"Stop it, Jared. I've just gotten them all chased away. Don't make them come back." He laughed and she glared at him, adding, "In fact, give me that flashlight. I need a weapon, and I don't trust you."

…Although it occurred to her with a flash of insight that this was the kind of thing you only said to someone you did trust, because if you really didn't trust a person, you kept that information to yourself.

How could she possibly trust Jared Starke?

She didn't!

She held out her hand, and he laid the flashlight's plastic barrel in her palm with an extravagant gesture of Victorian courtesy. His expression teased her a little, and the plastic felt warm from his grip. His breathing had gone back to normal now.

"Thank you," she drawled.

"You're welcome."

The atmosphere in the house seemed so totally transformed this time that it was like a different place, or a hiccup in time. The dust showed up more under the lights, but the rooms felt airier, more welcoming, less still. Was it just because Jared was here with her?

He picked up a video movie sitting beside the television in a small sitting room adjoining the main parlor, and they both laughed because it was an unlikely choice for two elderly ladies—an action film with a hunky Hollywood star baring some impressive muscles on the cover.

"Are we talking about a rich fantasy life, I wonder?" he said.

A few minutes later, he found a crystal decanter and lifted the stopper so they could both smell what was inside. Sweet sherry.

"That's more in character."

"I wish Gram hadn't kept Ivy and Rose such a secret," Shallis said, as they wandered into the kitchen. Just behind her, Jared was still picking up occasional objects and putting them down, like a crime scene investigator looking for clues. "I feel as if we've all missed out on a set of relationships that might have enriched our lives, as well as theirs. Mom's pretty upset. She prided herself on being close to Gram, friends more than mother and daughter, and now she's doubting all of that."

"Family pressure is a strange thing," he answered. "And it doesn't only go from the old onto the young. Sometimes it's the other way around."

"Do you think so?"

"I think people can often care more about what their children think than what their parents think."

"I guess that's true. And don't forget what their friends think, their work colleagues, their neighbors…"

"The whole town, in a place like Hyattville."

"Tell me about it!" She led the way up the stairs, noticed the creak on the seventh step down from the top and couldn't understand why it had bothered her so much when she was here on her own.

"So tell me why you came back to the goldfish bowl, Shallis," Jared said just behind her.

She reached the top of the stairs and half turned. "Too many sharks in the ocean?"

"You were afraid of getting eaten."

She thought for a moment as they walked into the turret-shaped master bedroom, which apparently the sisters had used for craft-related hobbies, not for sleeping in. Their own rooms had been the modest-size ones farther along the corridor.

"No, I think I was more afraid of growing six rows of sharp teeth and gray skin," she answered Jared eventually. "I saw it happening to a few people. I heard the double-speak they used to convince themselves it wasn't. My dad used to come down pretty hard on me if I ever behaved like the bitchy beauty queen stereotype. He's a down-to-earth kind of man, a really good balance to my mom, great at giving people the right space, and he uses humor like a guided missile system. His attitude stuck. I really didn't want that sharky gray skin."

"And how's the goldfish bowl treating you so far, by contrast?"

"The water's too warm, and the other fish are too tame. I might have to punch a hole in the glass with my little orange fin and—" She stopped and shook her head. "Nope. Sorry. The metaphor is breaking down at this point."

"We can forget the metaphor."

"Yeah, let's, because it's going to give me a headache in a minute." She took a breath. "I'm glad I came back. I'm still getting used to some of the frustrations. No place is perfect, but—getting back to the metaphor—I think I've got a good shot at arranging my goldfish bowl the way I want it. And this navel-gazing must be boring you stupid."

"Nah. Not yet. There'll be a ten-second warning buzzer when it starts to."

"Oh, good! I'll listen out for it."

"What's all the gear in this room? For sewing?"

"Quilting, crochet, tapestry, pressing flowers."

"They kept themselves busy. I wonder what they did with it all."

"Sold it at church bazaars for charity, gave it to friends. I'm guessing, here, but it would fit. And I'm glad they had an outlet, something satisfying and creative."

Jared wandered back out of the big bedroom and into the adjacent smaller one, where Ivy must have slept. She had probably made the pretty blue and yellow Ohio Star quilt on the bed, as well as the framed tapestry showing a vase of roses and the lacy crocheted doilies on the dresser, where her silver-backed brush and comb set still sat.

"How long would Gram have left the house empty and unexplained like this, I wonder?" Shallis murmured. "Oh, now look." She interrupted herself. "There's a connecting door between this bedroom and the turret room. Open that up, and you'd have a nice-size meeting room with adjoining space that could be used as a kitchen or an office. I'm seeing possibilities here."

"It might work. The street doesn't need another dolled up Bed and Breakfast. Did you open this window?"

"Yes, I opened a few. The room smells quite fresh, doesn't it? Imagine how pretty it would look in early spring with that cherry tree in flower just outside. We should close it now, though." She stepped toward it, but Jared got there first and dragged the wooden sash down. It stuck a little, and he reached up and pounded on the top with the flat of his strong hand.

"That gray skin problem you mentioned, it's not unheard of in the Chicago legal professional, either, by the way," he said, while he still had his back to her.

"So you fit right in." Was she teasing him, she wondered inwardly, or delivering a barb?

Seeking out information, more like, she quickly decided. She wanted to know how he'd react to what could have been read as an accusation.

"Yep." He turned, and he was grinning. "Ran with the pack. Sharpest teeth in the water. Capable of smelling a molecule of blood in the middle of a four-foot high pile of legal deposition papers."

"Okay, so you didn't fit right in," she suggested, with a definite edge. "You were a cute, colorful little Disney fish, and that's why you've swum back home, too."

They went into the next bedroom along, where the green-clothed ends of the cherry tree branches still fingered the window. Shallis had left this one open, too, even though the screen was missing. She went over to it and leaned on the sill, breathing in the cool evening air. The crickets had started singing outside. Jared came up beside her, despite the fact that there wasn't strictly room for two.

"People thought I already had gray skin when I left here,"

he answered. "People don't forget your past in a small town. There's a group of guys that still don't talk to me because they think I cheated my way into the quarterback position on the high school football team when I was fifteen."

"And did you?"

"Yes. I did."

"Oh," she murmured politely.

"You probably want the story now."

"Only if you want to tell it. Did Linnie know?"

"Not from me. She probably heard. And she probably gave me the benefit of the doubt. One of the few people who did."

"Wrongly so."

"Yep. Not that I would have had the, oh, guts or integrity to tell her that at the time. The coach had scheduled an extra pre-season friendly game, because he couldn't make up his mind between me and a guy called Pete Stafford."

"The name sounds familiar."

"He's taken over his dad's hardware store in the strip mall off of Route 41. You might have gone past it."

"But not into it, right, because beauty queens think a screwdriver is just a cocktail?"

"Sorry." He spread his hands, then added innocently, "So what's a Phillips head?"

"Screwdriver with a cross-shaped tip. Get on with the story before I find one and eliminate two rows of those sharky teeth. I have a father with a twenty-by-fifteen foot toolshed and a brother-in-law on a farm."

He shook his head, laughing, then picked up his story again. "Not much more to tell. I said I'd give Pete the message about the extra game, and I…just…never did."

"So of course he didn't show up. Meanwhile, you played the best you ever had in your life."

"Yeah, I did."

"Are you still proud of it?"

"I was never proud of it. I did what I thought had to be done."

"You could have just stuck with the playing your best part. Might have worked on its own."

"Yeah. I could have. But I didn't. Wanted to stack the cards a little more in my favor. Which is why Pete hasn't spoken to me since."

"At least you're honest about it. Now. Eighteen years later."

"Right." He went still, his upper arm just an inch from hers. "Well, huh," he said.

"Well, huh, what, Jared?"

"I'm thinking…"

"I'm sorry to see that it's such hard work for you," she murmured.

He gave a snort of laughter, and she grinned, pleased with herself in an over-the-top way which didn't really fit with the reaction she'd gotten from him. Why did it feel so good when they made each other laugh?

"…thinking about why I came back."

"Let me know when you get a result."

"Might. Getting some kind of answer, here. Might be too personal."

"More personal than admitting you cheated your friend?"

"I'll get back to you on it, okay?"

"Okay." She stepped back and he reached up for the window. This one came down smoothly. "I think I left one more open downstairs, which we should close and then…well, I'm fine now. No more spooks. I'm back on the horse after the fall, so we can go."

"Sure."

"Thanks for coming in, Jared."

He didn't answer directly, but said instead, after a moment, "Do you want to stop by my grandfather's house for dinner? Nothing fancy. We can talk about the house, if you like. About your grandmother, and what's happened. Or not. Whatever you want. It's getting late, and I know you haven't found this an easy day."

He looked at her, with his hand on the rounded top of the newel post at the head of the stairs. She looked back at him.

Zing!

Say no, Shallis.

Sneeze in his face.

Put up some defenses, before it's too late.

"Before I consider the offer, how much do you bill for after hours?" she asked, slathering the sarcasm on thick.

Regretting the line two seconds after it fell out of her mouth, she waited for him to treat it as a joke. She'd left herself wide open to several familiar lines, delivered with a super-size order of sleaze on the side.

Don't worry, sweetheart, my after hours service is free.

I'm happy to take another form of payment, if you're running low on cash.

Why don't we see how many hours it takes, first?

But Jared didn't use the opportunity. Didn't even blink. "Same as my daytime rate, as it happens," he said. Neither of them had yet started down the stairs. They were both…frozen? Waiting for the other to make the first move?

"Are you joking?"

"Yes. Of course. As if I'd offer dinner and then charge for it! Skin's not that gray. Say no, if you want. It was just a thought. You look tired, and you still don't have much color in your face. Low blood sugar can hit and a person doesn't realize it's happening, especially after a scare."

He said it as if he cared. He said it as if it was the most natural thing in the world that he cared. And he said it as if they both knew he cared and were totally okay with that.

He was wrong.

He had to be wrong.

What argument had he used, just a short while ago, to get her back inside this house?

So you can see that nothing's there.

It was a good theory, and it had worked with the house.

Could it work with all this other stuff that she didn't want? This stuff about liking to make him laugh? About their shared understanding of shark ponds and goldfish bowls, pointy teeth and gray skin?

"Dinner would be nice," she answered, and caught his complicated look of surprise and sparked satisfaction at once.

At heart, he'd expected her to say no, and he had no idea why she'd taken the opposite route.

She knew, though.

Or she told herself she did.

Just like with the ghosts in Ivy and Rose's house, however, Shallis planned to spend the evening with Jared Starke purely in order to prove to herself that nothing was there.

Chapter Six

This was definitely Abraham Starke's house, Shallis thought as she stepped past Jared and into the wide front hall. Jared hadn't yet had a chance to put his own stamp on it, of course. The sky was almost completely dark outside by this time, but a small chandelier and two wall lamps lit the interior with Jared's flick of a switch. The golden light banished the night.

An old wooden coat rack of Grandpa Abe's looked as if it might collapse beneath the weight of at least a dozen jackets, windbreakers, overcoats and hats. The red carpet runner on the stairs was threadbare in parts, but the oil painting of a nineteenth century landscape mounted on the wall had the kind of heavy gold frame that made you look more closely and realize that this was a fine quality picture.

It was worth money, no doubt, only it belonged so completely where it was that no one with any heart would think of selling it. Everything in this house belonged, including

Jared. He moved through it with the ease of someone who'd known a place since the dawn of his earliest memories, who took its best features for granted and didn't even see its comfortable flaws.

"Let's go on through to the kitchen and I can pour you something to drink," he said. "I bet those ghosts got you dry in the mouth."

"As dust," Shallis agreed.

"Me, too, although maybe in my case it wasn't the ghosts." He slid the towel smoothly to and fro across the back of his neck a couple of times.

"How far did you run?"

"My usual five or so miles, give or take. I tried a new route tonight. Some uphill stretches. Legs were feeling it some." He paused for a moment and bent down to rub one muscular calf, then the other. "Feels so good, though. Your whole body feels like stretched elastic, and your skin sings. It's the best kind of fatigue. Do you ever run?"

"I power walk." And sometimes she danced—variations on the old jazz routines she'd performed in pageants, only now she did them for her own private pleasure. She didn't often admit to it.

"Treadmill?"

"No, why stick myself in the stale air of a gym, in a place like Hyattville? I prefer pavement or grass. The grounds of the hotel, usually, before work."

"So you'd know."

"How great it feels? Yes."

Passing the opened double doors that led to a spacious front parlor, Shallis saw that it was filled with antiques—the kind that acquired this status simply by sitting in the same place for eighty years or more, until they turned old. Set in the bay window opposite the double doors there was a beautiful grand piano which probably hadn't been played since Jared's grandmother had died. It was covered in ornaments saved from gathering dust, no doubt, by a weekly professional cleaner who clearly did her job well.

Even with an active old man's comfortable clutter, the house was way too large for one person. Had Jared ever lived here with his parents as a child? If so, the arrangement hadn't lasted. When he'd been going out with Linnie in their teens he'd lived in a Sixties-era ranch house on a nice street just a couple of blocks from her parents' place.

That place had been sold, Shallis thought, when his parents divorced and his father moved to Nashville. She knew his mother was still in the Hyattville area, but wasn't sure exactly where.

"Okay, so, to drink," Jared said. He still had the towel draped around his neck, but he looked cool and relaxed now, his limbs loose after his run, the way he'd described. Shallis felt unsettled about being in his private space, restless as a cat, and ready to second-guess any wisdom in coming here. "Coke? Juice? Iced water to start and then something stronger?"

"I'll take the iced water to start." She wasn't going to think about anything stronger just yet.

While he poured water into two glasses from a plastic jug in the refrigerator and added a couple of ice cubes from the freezer, he suggested, "And to eat we could do takeout pizza, or steak and salad…"

"Steak and salad sounds good."

"If you don't mind, I'm going to take a shower first." He handed her one cold glass and took several big gulps from the other before setting it on the white ceramic sink.

"Of course I don't mind if you take a shower," she answered automatically, her mind still on the steak, and the second-guessing. "Is there anything I can do to help?"

His eyebrows lifted and the corner of his mouth quirked. "Hmm, let me think about that for a second," he murmured. His gaze locked onto hers. She realized what she'd said. Or how a man could interpret what she'd said, if he was so inclined…and in her experience a man usually was.

Wanna help me undress? Soap my back? Lick me clean? With the steak. Help with the steak. That's what I meant. Get it thawing in the microwave. Make salad. Is what I meant. Not help with the shower.

She didn't stoop to gabbling any of this, just silently anticipated the inevitable smug, stale, suggestive line. Would have drummed her fingers on the big old-fashioned kitchen table in an exaggerated "I'm waiting" rhythm, only the table wasn't in reach.

He stayed silent for a pregnant moment, keeping her captured with that wicked glint in his eye and that smile hovering around his mouth. She couldn't be angry with him. He was good at that. She wondered if any woman had been able to stay angry with him for long, once he'd made up his mind that he didn't want her to be.

"Get it over with, Jared," she finally said on a sigh. "Tell me the help a grown woman can give a grown man in the shower."

"Nah." He shook his head, then grinned. Lord, those eyes! "Think I'll leave that to our separate imaginations."

"I guess I set myself up for it," she admitted, disarmed by the way he'd handled it.

"You surely did," he told her solemnly. "And you have to know, for a moment there I wanted to." He opened a hand, palm up. "But it would have been too easy."

"So you'll wait until I deliver some more challenging material?"

"Something like that."

"You don't like things that are too easy, I'm theorizing."

"Nope. Never have. Sometimes that's not good, by the way. Some challenges, a man should learn to resist."

"Okay, I'll remember that about you," she said slowly. He was watching her mouth, and she didn't care.

"But if you actually meant you wanted to help with dinner…can't imagine why you'd expect me to interpret your words that way…you could search out some steak in the freezer. I know there are a few packages of it, but they tend to get buried beneath Grandpa Abe's caches of fish. Which—here's a hint—you can tell from the steak, even inside the plastic wrap, because of the scales."

"Right."

"Back soon." He clicked his tongue and disappeared, unwinding the towel from his neck as he went in an unconscious and strangely graceful masculine neck strip tease.

Can I change my mind about helping you in the shower? said a treacherous part of her. Can I soap your neck? Yum. Please? Some men's necks are so nice. Women's magazines should feature them in centerfold…

"Find the steak, Shallis," she coached herself under her breath, through gritted teeth. While it was circling in the lit up microwave interior a few minutes later, she prowled.

Jared kept his living space pretty neat. She could tell it was him, not the cleaner, because his morning coffee cup and juice glass and plate were sitting upside-down and clean in the draining basket on the sink, where a professional cleaner would have gone one step further and put them away. She tested the three pots of African violets on the window sill and found their soil damp but not sodden.

Well, that could have been the cleaner.

And this plastic container of mixed salad greens in the refrigerator could have been his grandfather's purchase, but she didn't think so.

Interpreting the refrigerator's cool interior like a desk-based intelligence agent interpreting spy satellite pictures, she discovered a man who'd acquired Chicago's big city gourmet food preferences and an ability to take care of his nutritional needs, if not to actually cook much.

He must have been to the enormous new supermarket near the Interstate exit since getting back here last week. As well as the salad, there were containers of fresh pasta with sauces to match, smoked salmon, chili-marinated olives, salsa verde and European cheese, honey yogurt, fresh strawberries and four different kinds of beer.

There were probably other things, too, only she stopped looking because it really did start to feel like spying, which implied…

Yeah, that she was interested.

Women who weren't interested didn't look in men's refrigerators and interpret their contents.

She wasn't allowed to be interested because of Linnie—no, not just because of Linnie, it was more complicated than that—so she'd better stop.

She started reading the sporting magazine on the kitchen table instead, making both her and the steak in the microwave look perfectly innocent when Jared came back into the room.

He looked innocent, too.

Clean and innocent.

Gorgeous and innocent.

Nothing nearly so obvious as a half unbuttoned shirt or a tight, muscle-hugging tee, just a loose navy cotton knit sweater pushed up to the elbows and a pair of faded jeans. The jeans did a certain amount of muscle-hugging, but not too much. His freshly washed hair was damp at the ends, and he moved with an aura of satisfaction at his well-earned cleanness and fatigue.

He didn't seem anything like the smooth, polite and some-times bland professional who'd greeted her in his office twice over the past couple of days. He was like an Olympic athlete an hour after a big race, magnetically physical, mag-netically a winner.

Shallis's aching, heart-fluttering, mystifying desire came right back into the kitchen with him, on big, powerful wings, smelling of clean skin and sunlight, taunting her and beguil-ing her at the same time. Her mind buzzed, so confused she couldn't have walked a straight line.

She shouldn't be here.

She couldn't imagine how she'd leave.

She'd forgotten all the reasons why this was impossible and wrong, but couldn't understand how anything could feel so right.

The microwave beeped and shut off, catching Jared's at-tention.

"You found the steak? Great. Thanks." He took it out, slid a heavy cast iron grill plate onto the stove top and lit the gas beneath.

Shallis took a breath and went with her impulse. "And you managed to lather that tough stretch between your shoulder blades without me, I'm guessing."

His tone fell into a seductive lilt, but he didn't turn toward her from the stove. "I'm impressively flexible with most parts of my body, I've been told..." Before she could frown or laugh or walk off in a huff, he added with complete truth, "Hey, you lobbed it up and this time I went for it."

"Uh, yeah, okay, I did, didn't I?"

Only now did he turn, still standing several safe paces from her across the big kitchen. "Why did you lob it up, can I ask?" His focus on her was serious and total, fraying her certainties still further, making it impossible for her to break the eye contact. He leaned one splayed hand on the counter top, making his strong shoulder lift.

"You can ask, but...I—I don't know the answer, Jared."

"Think about it, because I want something better than that."

"Oh."

"You're a very socially adept, poised, grown-up woman, quick on the uptake, practiced with people, and you're beautiful."

Did she roll her eyes?

He added quickly, "That's not a come-on. Or even a compliment. That's just a fact. You know it, because your mom's been telling you so your whole life, along with plenty of other people. So if you're telling me you don't understand your own behavior and your own reactions tonight, then something's going on here."

"Jared—"

"I don't know how to pitch this, so I'm going to pitch it straight. No lines. No games. Nothing underhand or unfair. I asked you to come eat here tonight because I could feel the vibe between us—or *thought* I could feel it—and only *thinking* I could feel it is pretty unusual for me, because normally I'm one hundred percent sure. Tell me why you came, Shallis, if it wasn't for the same reason. And tell me what you're planning to do about it."

"Do about it…" she echoed.

"You could step across this kitchen right now, reach your hands up to my face and—"

He stopped, while her imagination careened onward like a runaway horse. She could practically feel the texture of his skin beneath her hands. She could smell the shampoo in his freshly washed hair.

"You know I wouldn't turn you down," he went on, after a few seconds. "I did turn you down once, almost twelve years ago, even though I came *so close*…and then the way you flirted with me at Linnie's wedding was as aggressive and over the top as a lioness protecting her cubs. It wasn't sexy, so we were both pretty safe, but—"

"I was a lioness that night for a good reason, Jared."

"I'm not denying that. Yet even then there were a couple of times—"

Okay. He was right. There *were* a couple of times—times when if she hadn't flirted to a frantic degree she would have swooned against him and begged to join with him in a bridal waltz, her old teenage crush swamping her at its most physical, incomprehensible level. She didn't want to admit to those times yet.

"Let's just make it dinner," she cut in. Was tempted to pick up the sports magazine and fan her cheeks, because she knew they were bright pink. "I'm not saying—" She tried again. "I need time to work out what I'm saying. I'm not saying I don't appreciate that you didn't just take it for granted I'd…"

Too many negatives in that sentence. If she couldn't follow it herself, how could she expect him to?

She tried yet again. "I just want to make this dinner, okay?"

And waited.

"Okay," he answered, after a pause of about six heartbeats. "Just dinner. For tonight, anyhow."

Finally she managed to look away. Down. The old inspecting-the-fingernails trick that her mother would have slapped her knuckles for. Pageant girls never had a problem looking anyone in the eye. According to Mom, pageant girls had Star Moments, Room Radiance and above all control.

"I'll toss in some pasta on the side," Jared said after a moment. "I can put on some music and we can hang out here while it all cooks. Are you cold? You are. This kitchen chills down fast when the heating's turned off and the nights are cool."

He slid an ancient radiant heater out from under the table and switched it on. Like some of the furnishings in the front parlor, it could almost count as an antique, with its little arrangement of artificial logs and fake fireplace molding, surrounding a heated coil of glowing wire.

Shallis laughed at it. "Do you have a plastic cat we can set in front of this? A dog with a mechanical wagging tail, maybe?"

"I'll check the attic on the weekend."

The metal of the heater ticked as the contraption warmed up, and the tension in the kitchen seemed to cool in balance. At least she was breathing again, now. Enjoying herself, even. Tingling with an energy she'd never felt quite in this way before. Whatever was happening between them, it sure set her adrenaline flowing.

"Grab whatever salad fixings you like," Jared said, flipping through a CD rack on the heavy and ornately carved sideboard just through the kitchen's far door. He put on a greatest hits collection by Sheryl Crowe, and her smoky, cynical lyrics and hip-swaying rhythms seemed to fit.

Shallis went to work in the refrigerator, and if Jared noticed that she was already strangely familiar with its contents, he didn't comment. When their meal was ready, he looked at the clock on the microwave, then tossed a too-casual glance through into the dining room and said in a careful voice, "You know, there's something not right about steak and salad for two at a French-polished rosewood table that comfortably seats twelve every Christmas. Wanna do this in front of TV?"

"Sounds good. Do you happen to have a copy of that action movie we saw at Ivy and Rose's place?"

"Uh, no, 'fraid not."

"Pity. I wanted to check out the attractions." Except that as she said it, she suddenly thought about the time on the microwave clock, too, and remembered that this was her favorite TV night of the week. The action movie lost its appeal.

"We only have about two movies," Jared said, "And one of them's Mary Poppins. However Grandpa Abe has this strange taste for recording British cooking shows and historical dramas from PBS."

He turned off the music, picked up their two steaming plates and carried them through to the less formal sitting area at the back of the house, while Shallis remembered she hadn't set the recording timer on her DVD, back in her little garden apartment five minutes drive from here.

"He has stacks of 'em," Jared went on, coming back for the antique radiant heater. "We could do Regency ladies and nine-teenth-century men's whiskers, or strings of royal wives and gouty royal lovemaking, or this scary pair of women with long red fingernails who go around on a motorcycle cooking for British cricket teams and raising everyone's cholesterol by about six hundred percent."

"I'm sensing you want to steer me away from the cooking and the history. There's a game on, right?"

More than one game, possibly. The sporting one on TV,

and a sneakier one in which they were both going to try to win their own viewing preference without making the other person look like a pushover, or realize what was going on.

Thinking out her strategy, Shallis laid napkins, silverware and beer-mugs on the coffee table, while Jared slid a low wicker-and-chintz couch closer to it.

"There's always a game on," he said. "This one, I'd like to watch, yes, but I did get a lesson on the weird way my grandfather has his DVD hooked up, so I can record it if you want." He just couldn't manage to keep the little boy reluctance out of his voice. Man, he wanted to watch that game, but he was wa-a-ay too polite to say so. He just wanted her to buy the little boy act and cave.

"Well, it's no fun watching sport when it's taped," Shallis conceded. "Because by then you've lost the chance to influence the result."

"You believe you can do that?" He grinned and frowned at the same time, a little alarmed at the idea, and Shallis hid her smile behind a gulp of beer.

"Oh, I *know* I can do that!" she said. "The second I start rooting for any one team, I'm sorry but their chances are shot."

"You're scaring me. I seriously do want the—"

She put down the beer and put her hands up to her ears. "Don't tell me which team you want to win. Just don't."

"You could root for the other one, couldn't you?"

"It doesn't work like that. You can't play tricks with these psychic phenomena. I might honestly try to want the other team to win, but if underneath we both knew all along that I was doing it so your team could win, I'm afraid the effect would be—"

"Okay, we're recording the game, and we're watching…"

Shallis named her current favorite crime show. The one

whose characters and interactions developed to a new, enticing level with every storyline. The one she hadn't missed an episode of yet. The one she recorded every week but much preferred to see when it was actually screening. Jared hopped channels until he found it, set the DVD player to record the game, then shot her a suspicious glance before she could wipe the satisfied smile from her face.

"You were playing me just now, weren't you, with that stuff about influencing the result? Taking shameless advantage of my weakness for the—"

"I'm telling you, don't spill the name of the team! They're doomed if you do."

"Playing me," he repeated in disgust. "Like a fish on a line."

She didn't try to hide her smile, this time. "You'll never know. The way I'll never know if you were playing me with that stuff about the cholesterol levels on British cooking shows."

"Truce. I'm calling a truce."

"Only because you already lost. Seriously, Jared, we can watch the game if you want."

"We are not watching the game. You can win on being tricky, but I'm damned if I'll let you win on being generous as well."

He was laughing at himself—at both of them, actually—and Shallis liked that. She liked the meal, too. Juicy steak, crisp salad, cheesy pasta, yeasty beer. She liked the way they only talked during commercial breaks, and the way the coil of wire on the old heater glowed as it warmed the room. It really did need a cat stretched out in front of it. A real one, purring.

She kicked off her shoes and poked them under the coffee

table with her bare toes. Jared followed the movement with his eyes but said only, "Your fingernails have a French manicure but your toenail polish is red. I noticed that yesterday when I was getting out your splinter, but I was too polite to comment."

"Today you're not?"

"After that charade over our TV viewing options, the gloves are off. You're getting it straight now. The red clashes with your shoes, your suit and your fingers."

"I know. Don't tell Mom. I've been having a pedicure crisis for the past six months. Summer's nearly here—all those open-toed shoes—and I'm still in denial."

The moment her show finished, she grabbed the remote and switched direct to the game, then told Jared, "You sit. Don't take your eyes off the screen and don't tell me your team."

"Don't tell me you're serious about that."

"I seriously don't have a great track record. My dad used to ban me from the TV when there was important sport showing. He swore I was a jinx. I'll make coffee, and clear up a little."

"There's ice cream in the freezer, too, if you want. Swiss chocolate almond, I think. And cherry. Microwave hot fudge sauce in the pantry."

Perfect.

Completely perfect.

They sat and drank coffee and let Swiss chocolate almond and hot fudge melt on their tongues. Jared's team won the game. He didn't tell her this until it was over, although his reactions and his body language hadn't been hard to read. "I can break it to you now. I was rooting for the White Sox."

Shallis let out an exaggerated squeak. "No! You shouldn't have said that!"

"What, you're going to go your whole life not knowing my teams?"

"I could live in such ignorance without despairing about it, I think."

"You know what? We have *nothing* in common!"

But they both knew that wasn't true.

"I should go, Jared," she said, after a dangerous beat of silence. The radiant heater gave a couple of its periodic clicks. "It's getting late."

He didn't argue. They both stood up and he came out with some polite, well-practiced lines about the evening. How much fun they'd had. How soon they should do it again.

She responded in the appropriate way.

He asked if she was sure she didn't want more ice cream or coffee.

She said yes, she was sure, but thanks.

He said he still didn't seriously believe she would have jinxed the game.

She told him to talk to her dad about it sometime.

She put on her shoes.

Without hiding the direction of his gaze, he watched the bits of past-their-use-by-date red nail polish disappear beneath the pink leather.

"The clashing nail polish is our little secret, okay?" she said, feeling hot.

"Okay."

She waited for him to renege on the "just dinner" deal, waited for her chance to turn him down for the second time, because she desperately needed to prove to herself that she still could.

He didn't renege, he just said something else about it being a nice night, or whatever, that she didn't even listen to.

He walked her to the door.

They said good-night.

Or, at least, he did. She said something like, "Um, yeah, thanks."

She stepped out into the night.

He stayed at the open door as courtesy required.

She managed, "Good night," after all.

He said it again, back to her.

Game over.

Her heels clacked on the porch.

Jared watched Shallis step out onto the porch and begin to cross the wide expanse of boards, her hips swinging just the right amount beneath the pale pink fabric of her suit. She wasn't wearing any hose. Her legs looked perfect, tanned and silky and soft and smooth. He ached at the thought of those unrepentant, red-daubed toes running slowly all the way up his—

Okay.

What was happening now?

She'd turned, as if she'd read his thoughts. Swung around on her heels, with her shoulders very square. She was coming back.

She didn't say a word.

Just kissed him.

Loosened her tight fists, held his face between her hands and imprinted a soft, fast kiss on his mouth, then took her lips away, swung around again and hurried toward the brick steps, heels clacking, as if she needed to get safely out of his aura *fast*.

Until she'd reached the bottom step, he was frozen, too surprised to take action, brain totally off line, while his whole body buzzed and stood to attention.

Hell, was he just going to let her go?

Even if it wasn't an open invitation, he had to reply, kiss her back so she'd know he only hadn't done so just now because she hadn't given him a chance.

He tried to speak, to call her back, but his throat seemed to have rusted shut and he couldn't get out a sound. He raced down the steps and she heard him coming, stopped and half-pivoted in his direction just as his voice finally returned. Sort of.

"Hey." Sounded strange. Creaky. Intense. He touched her shoulder. "Don't I get a turn?"

She smiled, looking almost shy, as if that hadn't really been her, just now, smooching him like that out of the blue, without a word, when they'd both agreed earlier that it wasn't going to happen. "If you want."

"Oh, I want. I want."

He did it the same way she had, no leading up to it, just a direct hit. A plain, short, ordinary kiss firm and square on her mouth. Then they both stood back a small half-pace with their arms loosely around each other and waited for the earthquake to hit.

It did.

"Oh, dear lord…" she said, with breath more than voice.

He pulled on her hips and she sank against him, cupped her hand and touched his face. Her eyes were huge. They fell to his mouth and studied its shape with an intensity that was as powerful and intimate as touch. His legs felt like tree trunks, with roots pushing deep into the soil.

Shaky tree trunks, now that he thought about it.

He tightened his arms around her because if he hadn't they might both have sunk to the ground.

This *so* wasn't the way he usually did this!

He usually had the whole thing sewn up from the moment a woman walked into his space. It played out like a piece of theater, from the Act One dinner at a fancy restaurant to the Act Two pretense of her coming in "for coffee" to the Act Three bedroom scene. The woman never kicked off her shoes and ate ice-cream. He never suggested TV. He never said goodnight without a kiss.

No, correction, he never said good-night at all, because the woman was always still there in the morning, at which point he usually impressed her—so that the decision whether to see her again would be his, and his alone—by slipping out of bed just as she began to stir and racing down to the nearest bakery for croissants and lattes or bagels and cappuccinos, which they ate in bed.

Tonight, he'd seriously thought that Shallis needed more time, and he'd intended to give her that. To give himself more time, also.

But now they were standing here, drowning in each other's eyes. He wanted to take her to bed *so bad* and he didn't have a clue where to start, because he didn't want it to be like all those other times. He didn't want this to be theatrical and perfect, with all the control in his own hands, he wanted it to be real.

Lost in thought, he lifted his hand and touched a fingertip to her lips, tracing their soft, pouting shape. Her mouth fell open on a tiny hiss of breath, and then her tongue lapped at his finger and her teeth nipped it, each movement slow and thoughtful just as his had been. She took the finger into her mouth and sucked, and fire jetted to his groin.

"I can taste fudge and ice cream," she murmured, when she'd let his finger go.

"If you want more, I have nine more fingers…"

And there's my whole body, the second you tell me you want it. Please tell me you want it.

She brushed the ball of her thumb against his mouth, frowning as if she hadn't decided what to do next, as if she needed to know the exact shape of his lips before she kissed him again.

His patience vanished, and he got right to the point. "Are you coming back in?"

She took a shaky breath. "Yes."

"Good."

He grabbed her hand and pulled her up the path, stopped on the steps and kissed her, kissed her again when they'd reached the front door and stepped inside. None of it was especially elegant, all of it was impatient, eager as a puppy, erupting from deep in his heart.

"This is crazy," he said, laughing and shaking his head.

"Crazy is good."

"It *is* crazy, though, isn't it? As of yesterday, I hadn't seen you in six years. Now I'm going to make love to you—that's what I'm going to do, right?—and I'm dizzy about it. I don't know where this is coming from."

"Do we have to know, Jared? I was thinking about that before, when you first touched my lips. I was trying to, oh, work something out, put this in some kind of box, but…let's not. Let's just…"

She didn't finish the sentence.

He kicked the door shut and wound his arms around her, as tight as wrapping paper. She felt like a gift to him. Precious. Perfectly packaged. Exactly what he wanted. A total surprise. Her body was willowy and soft and strong, all at the same time. She smelled of ice cream and a light fragrance like spring flowers, the sweet-scented ones his mother raved about—freesias and daphne and gardenia.

She kissed him while he was still thinking helplessly about the way she smelled, and she whispered against his mouth, "I'm making all the moves here, Jared."

"No, you're not, you're just getting to them first. I'd be making 'em if you gave me half a chance."

"Okay." She closed her eyes and whispered, "So here's your half a chance."

He took it. Slowly. Savoring every second. The soft mouth and softer sounds she made. The press of her breasts. The sinuous rock of her hips as they swayed together. The way she touched him, with her hands light on his body, *everywhere*, driving him wild with wanting more.

He throbbed for her, ached for her. Pressing against the swollen mound between her thighs, he knew from the way she gasped just how much she throbbed and ached for him. Yet weirdly he didn't feel impatient, because he didn't want this part to end. He wasn't operating on a program, which meant he could live intensely inside this moment in a way he couldn't ever remember doing before.

Cupping her breast through the lightweight fabric of her jacket, he wasn't thinking about the next maneuver or about how to push her reaction to breaking point and getting his own reward. All he cared about was the delicious sensation of warmth and weight, the perfect curve, the hard nub he could feel thrusting against his palm even through her bra.

Their kiss went deeper and deeper, until he could hardly tell where his mouth finished and hers began. He barely needed to breathe or see or hear. He only needed to taste and feel. Her hair slipped in a bouncing, silken curtain against his face. Her hands flattened against his back and slid down to the waistband of his jeans.

It must have been, oh, half an hour, forty minutes even,

before she captured his jaw softly between her palms then brushed his eyes open with her thumbs. "Hello, in there?" she whispered.

"Hi…" That creaky, rusty voice again.

He blinked.

She frowned and tucked in the corner of her mouth.

Uh-oh, he thought. If she tells me some kind of thanks-for-a-nice-evening-I'm-going-home-now thing at this point, I'll *die*. I will.

But no, apparently she wasn't saying that.

"So I'm making this next move, too, Jared?" Her smile was tentative and mischievous at the same time. "I'm having to beg for it?"

The blood rushed to his head and once more he forgot to breathe. All that came out when he tried to speak was one tiny, strangled, nonsensical sound.

Shallis sighed.

"Okay, then I guess I'll beg," she said. "Please, please, Jared, can we go upstairs?"

Chapter Seven

The flare of light in Jared's eyes told Shallis that she'd said the right thing.

Not that she had been in a great deal of doubt. When a man clearly enjoyed kissing a woman that much, he didn't usually want to say goodnight and goodbye at the end of it. He wanted the next step. Only in this case he'd taken a heck of a long time getting to it, and in the end she'd gotten confused.

Was he waiting for a timer to go off? Did he think she needed longer? Couldn't he feel the heat she was giving off? Would he feel that he was pressuring her if she didn't say it herself?

So finally she did say it, all pride gone.

Which wasn't such a bad thing, as it turned out.

"Come on, then." He took her hand and led the way.

Three steps up, her sharp heels snagged on the worn carpet runner so she kicked off her shoes and they bumped back down to the bottom. He let her ahead of him and ran his hands up her legs when she got high enough on the stairs, making her whole body erupt in a fresh volcano of tingling need.

At the top of the stairs they kissed again, teetering on the edge. He unfastened the buttons at the front of her suit jacket and discovered that all she had on beneath it was a bra—red, in an accidental match with her shop-worn pedicure.

"You couldn't have done this on purpose," he said, "But I'm going to wonder whenever I see you from now on whether your underwear clashes with your clothing or tones in with your toes. It's going to half kill me every time, because I'm going to know you could be wearing *anything*."

He slid the jacket off her shoulders and it fell to the ground. She shimmied her skirt off to keep the jacket company, and said, "See? The rest of my underwear matches, too."

"Oh, it does? There's not enough of it for me to tell. Three pieces of ribbon and half a handkerchief."

"Red, though."

"Red." He fingered the satiny elastic of her thong, making it slip across her skin and pull deliciously tight against her flesh. "I like red."

"What color is your underwear?" she asked.

"Black."

"I like black. Let's see." She reached for the front of his jeans, but he'd gotten there first, so her hands closed over his knuckles as he worked the snap fastening and the zipper. She didn't take her hands away, just let her fingers brush the satisfying weight and hardness of his arousal through the dark stretch cotton fabric.

Breath hissed in through his clenched teeth. He left the opened jeans in place and pulled her hips against his body, sliding his hands around to cup her cheeks, silky and naked.

Heat pulsed inside her. This wasn't close enough. It was *almost* as close as a man and a woman could be, but still it wasn't close enough.

She dragged his sweater upward and he folded his arms above his head so she could pull it free. It landed on top of her discarded suit, leaving his torso bare.

No, not totally bare.

More accustomed visually to the waxed chests of L.A. actors and models, she hadn't expected this patch of impressive masculine hair. Oh, but it felt good against her fingers. Different. Strong. Male. Silky and rough at the same time. Prickly and springy. Darker than the hair on his head. Real.

Mmm.

"If we don't get as far as the bed soon, I'm not going to be able to walk," Jared said.

"Walking is overrated." She kissed him and pushed him ahead of her, making him walk backward. "This way?"

"To my room, yes." An opened door loomed behind him.

She pushed him as far as the bed. He grinned at her and she grinned back. "You're going to tip back any second, Jared, and I'm coming right after you, so hold out your arms."

He caught her and she arched her body over his, fitting oh-so-snug against him from stomach to ankles. He flicked her bra straps down then pulled her close enough to kiss her breasts, easing the lacy fabric from her darkened, aching nipples with his mouth.

"We could do this for quite a while, unless you're in a hurry," he murmured.

"I think…I'm in a…hurry," she gasped.

"Too bad. Because I'm not. I'm going to make you wait."

With one movement, he rolled her sideways toward the two fat pillows at the top of the bed. One breast rested against her upper arm. He brushed his fingers lightly over it, and over its twin, thought about suckling her—yes, she could tell, she could see it in his face and the little flick of his tongue between his teeth. She could read the image so vividly that her nipples felt wet as if he really had. Then he pivoted to his feet and dragged down jeans and briefs together.

Sliding back onto the bed, he stroked her hip and thigh, easing her open. He cupped his hand over the tiny patch of red fabric above her inner thighs and her body pulsed again. "You can't make me wait, Jared. You— Oh!"

This kind of waiting, she could handle. For hours. No hurry at all. Why anyone would ever want this slow, fluid, intimate caress to end, she couldn't imagine.

Oh.

Unless it was to have this next sensation take its place.

He slid the patch of fabric aside, so slowly that she felt every fiber brush against her damp curls. He bent closer. He used his mouth. Her body threatened to splinter and buckle and explode but he held her in place, kept that little piece of red pushed out of the way so that its elastic was a taut seam of friction against her swollen flesh.

Then, when she was actively fighting him, gripping his head with her hands, not even sure if she was pulling him closer or pushing him away because the sensations he'd made in her were just too powerful to bear, he whipped his body upward and slid into her, filling her completely, pushing against her core, making her pulse and ache and tighten around him, close, close, close.

She held him, almost sobbing, and his rhythm built and intensified. He kissed her neck, whispered words in her ear that she didn't need to understand, bucked and thrust and groaned, drowning her own mounting sounds of astonished pleasure.

It was minutes more before they came to earth, breathless and still locked together, gripping each other and not ready to let go. He lay against her chest and she stroked his hair, wondering for quite a long time if she would ever bother to speak again. Words seemed irrelevant. Pressing skin to skin in the darkness like this seemed to communicate so much more.

For a long time, they didn't move. They might even have slept. Shallis didn't know who stirred first, only that the moment one of them did, her senses crashed to life again. His fingers slipped across her skin, and he made a lazy, sleepy sound of appreciation. Her hips rocked slowly as she eased herself closer against him. He appreciated that, too.

He began to caress her, in no hurry. She opened her eyes and found him watching her, his lids heavy and his pupils huge and dark. She ran her finger down the strong, straight line of his nose, and he pushed her hand away and kissed her, sweet and soft at first, then with a depth and intensity that she gave back to him in full measure. She could easily have cried.

He moved his mouth down her body, lavishing her breasts with heat, pulling on her nipples until she gasped. Suddenly neither of them could wait. She touched him, guiding him to her, letting him know exactly what she wanted. He was hard as a man could be, and she'd never felt so ready for the tight fill, the aching contrast of his hot pressure and her own fluid softness.

They both shuddered as he slipped into her. His hands tightened on her back, his fingers digging into her skin. She cupped his backside, holding him even closer against her, loving this sense of possession, loving the way he moved back and forth, loving everything. His male weight and strength. The way he smelled. The dizzying loss of control that hit them both at the same time and swept them forward over the edge of release for the second time.

Through all of it, through all their cries of ecstasy, they hadn't said a coherent word.

Jared was the one to break the silence.

With a short, sharp curse.

"I didn't use any protection," he said. "I didn't ask. I didn't even… I told you I was going to make you wait and that was one of the things you were meant to wait for, but then both times when it came to the point I didn't even—"

"Hey, stop. It's okay." She told him about her doctor's prescription of a contraceptive pill in L.A. six months ago, and he whooshed out a sigh of relief.

Not going to get her pregnant.

Whew.

Her heart lurched with a suddenness that made her queasy and she thought about Linnie and Ryan going through the exact opposite experience. Tears instead of relief. Not pregnant, when they wanted a baby so much. Planned, dutiful sex-by-the-calendar instead of a tide of desire that neither one of them could control because neither one of them wanted to.

When she'd turned around on the front porch to come back and kiss Jared, two hours ago, any thought of her sister had been far from her mind, and now that seemed wrong.

If Linnie knew I was here with Jared, what would she really feel? Shallis wondered. I asked her how she felt about us working with him over Gram's estate and she said she was okay with that. Mom is sure that Linnie has her priorities in place, too, but…

Sleeping with the man was just that teensiest bit more personal, after all. Shallis hadn't gotten Linnie's okay for something as drastic as that.

"Breathe, Shallis," Jared said softly, while her mind still churned.

"I'm sorry?"

"You stopped. I could feel it. What's up?"

"Uh, just thinking it's probably best if I'm not still here for breakfast in the morning. It must already be late. Very late. I have a big day tomorrow, and—"

Right now, she didn't have the slightest idea about her day. Her work diary was on her desk in her office at the hotel, and her mind had gone blank regarding its contents. Maybe she had a tiny day. Maybe major regrets about sleeping with Jared would turn out to be the only big agenda item on it.

"Sure," he said, after a little too much silence.

"I mean, it's fine, Jared."

"Are you sure?" He spoke with care, sounding too polite. It was the Attorney Ken persona again, as if he could easily have let down his guard and shown a very different attitude. Anger. Dismissal. Hurt. "This wasn't in the original program. We had other stuff planned, but we never got to it. We never talked about it. How you're feeling about your grandmother, for one thing."

"Oh, you mean how I feel about her whole clandestine life revolving around a big old house on Chestnut Street?"

"Yeah, that." He went silent for a couple of seconds. "Hey. You're saying this is clandestine? That's a pretty negative word."

"It's causing me some trouble," she admitted.

"Suddenly it's trouble, what we just did?" He rolled to the side and sat up on one elbow. His eyes looked much darker in the dim light coming from the hallway than they looked in bright daylight. His emotion was much closer to the surface, genuine and impossible to hide. He did sound angry. "Is that why breakfast isn't on the agenda?"

"No! Yes… This was—oh, Lord, you *know* this was good."

"Yeah? Yeah…it was." His voice had dropped.

"But I didn't plan it. You know that, too. You know that the way I came back to kiss you was—" Oh, what? She couldn't find the right words.

"A pure impulse?" he suggested.

"Yes. Very much."

"And now you're having regrets about acting on it. A little too late, can I suggest?"

"No," she answered. "Not regrets. Just questions. Which I'd like to answer for myself, in my own space, I think."

"This is about Linnie," he guessed.

"Yes." In part, anyhow.

"You told me she's moved on. I told you I was glad about that, and I meant it."

"She has moved on, but this is real life, Jared. Her happily ever after has turned out more complicated than she or Ryan were expecting."

"Their marriage is in trouble?"

"I'm not going to say that. But they have things to deal with, right now. It wouldn't be right for me to tell you the details."

He shrugged. "That's okay. Men don't tend to push for details, we're happy with the bottom line. So tell me straight what that is, and I'll let the subject go."

"Space. That's the bottom line. Time."

To work out what had made Jared so impossible to say goodnight to, earlier. To find out just how fragile Linnie's marriage and happiness really were. To get a little of Shallis's own cynicism about this guy back in place and use it as a lens for examining everything that had happened tonight.

Twice.

Was he playing games? Was his winner's instinct stronger

than ever, but cleverly masked by a more subtle veneer than he'd had in place six years ago? How far did he understand that treating her like a regular human being, the way her father did, instead of a bimbo-slash-princess had been the perfect way to break her defenses down?

Bottom line—what did he want, what would he do to get it, and how much was she prepared to give?

"Could be that I need time, too, when I think about it," he said.

"So there's no conflict of interest."

"Seems that way."

"Then why are you looking at me like that?"

"Looking forward to watching you get dressed."

She laughed as she went into the hallway to retrieve her clothing, because she believed him. Some men would go to great lengths to watch pageant girls get dressed. They weren't usually as open about it as Jared, however, and didn't usually have such a lazy, easy glint in their eyes.

"You're really good at getting people...women...not to be angry with you, Jared," she told him when she came back.

"People." He stressed the first word she'd chosen. "Not just women. I like people. And people like to be liked. You can get a long way in life on making people feel that you like them."

"Even when you really don't?" She slid her arms into her jacket.

"Well, some people would use that strategy. I don't think it's necessary. I like a lot of women...people."

"People? Really? Not just women?" She stepped into her skirt and shimmied it up over her hips, covering the little red thong that was still—more or less—in place. "No gender bias?"

"None at all."

"Somehow this time I'm not buying it." And you sure do like to win, don't you, Jared Starke? Even when it's just hitting clever lines back and forth like hitting tennis balls over a net.

Shallis didn't say the words out loud, but she stored the idea away in her mind as something she should never let herself forget. There were a few things about tonight that fell into that category.

Unforgettable.

"And you're dressed," Jared said. "And I got to watch. And you didn't even notice."

"If my shoes weren't still at the bottom of the stairs, I'd throw them at you."

He sat up, grinning. His eyes arrowed to her fingers buttoning her jacket across her breasts, then came back to her face. The grin got wickeder. "And I'd pick them up, stretch your legs across my lap, slip your feet into them, and kiss your ankles until you writhed."

Their eyes met.

Oh.

Her ankles.

His mouth.

His mouth travelling slowly, slowly, up from her ankles, all the way up her legs.

"Don't go get your shoes just yet," he said.

"No?"

"We don't really need them for the ankle kissing thing."

"No, I guess we don't…"

It was another hour and a half before she left.

"Honey, I'm sure if you could just relax and forget the whole thing, then it will happen on its own." Sunny Duncan put her gin and tonic water down in front of her at Linnie's kitchen table. "You've gotten yourself so twisted up over it. Nature's very wise that way, don't you think? She's not going to let you get pregnant until you learn to go a little easier on yourself."

"Mom…" Shallis began. She was on her way to the other table in the small L-shaped living and dining area to lay out the silverware for the evening meal, but didn't want to duck out of the conversation now, when Mom was saying all the wrong things.

She knew her sister didn't want to hear any of this. She knew Linnie had heard it way too often already. Mom and Linnie had never learned to find an easy relationship with each other. Linnie still believed that she wasn't the daughter her mother had wanted, and there was a tinge of truth to the idea.

Shallis had always been the one to go along so successfully with all of Mom's beauty queen ambitions. From her earliest years, Linnie had been the number one Daddy's girl, and when Mom pushed her too hard or talked at her too much, she closed up—with the occasional explosion thrown in for good measure—just like their father did.

Dad and Ryan were out with the horses right this minute, while the three women stood in the kitchen, enveloped in the heavenly odors that seeped from cooking pots and casserole dishes. Linnie was trying out some new recipes, building her repertoire for when the first set of paying guests were due to occupy the two vacation cabins in a few weeks' time. She was a wonderful cook. Ryan appreciated the fact immensely, and Dad appreciated Ryan just as much.

He was the ideal son-in-law for Dad, steady and strong, and with a career that allowed a respectable bank manager his part-time share in a whole lot of outdoorsy, he-man, horse-related activity that he'd always dreamed about but never had time for. As far as Dad was concerned, he was a four-year-old boy again, and Ryan Courcy had the best sandbox in town.

Tonight, however, Shallis wished that Dad didn't always have to streak for the barns and corrals the moment he stepped from the car at Linnie and Ryan's. Mom wouldn't be speaking her mind quite so painfully if he was around. He'd always been the one to keep her feet on the ground and her focus on what was right and sensible and best.

"Don't try to shush me, Shallie," Sunny Duncan said. "It needs to be said."

"It *has* been said." She put the silverware down on the countertop, on a pile of paper napkins.

"It needs to be said until Linnie can let herself listen. I'm not being harsh."

"No?"

"Of course I'm not! My Lord!"

She stood up, scraping chair legs on the floor, and gave her elder daughter a hard squeeze, but Linnie stayed stiff and stubborn in her arms. Shallis sensed a storm about to break. Tears or yelling, she didn't know which.

"I feel as bad as she does about what's happening," Mom went on, "but I've always said that she's been working too hard, and a half dozen specialists messing around with laparoscopies and blood tests and sperm counts isn't going to throw up any clearer answer than that."

"So instead you're making it sound like it's Linnie's fault?"

"Her fault? No!"

"Mom, I have to say, it sounds that way."

"Well, you're wrong! I'm just saying—"

"Stop it, both of you!" Linnie cut in. Her face looked hot

and red and angry. "Will you just please stop it? Mom, you're hammering at me to relax? You know what that's like? It's like someone saying, 'Whatever you do, don't think about the blue elephant,' and then you can't get blue elephants out of your head. People can't relax through force of will. Lord, if they could, I've got the strongest will in the world! And Shallis, I appreciate your support, I really do, but you don't have to treat me like I'm made of spun glass."

"Linnie, I didn't mean—"

"I do not want to have this conversation!" Linnie yelled. She threw up her hands. "I have had it four hundred times! Why does everyone in Hyattville think it's their business to tell me to relax? Would it hurt to have a little more respect for Ryan's and my privacy?"

"Now you're saying I've told the whole town?" Mom's voice rose with indignation.

Linnie slumped into a kitchen chair. "Okay, no, I'm not saying that. I've told people, too. It just gets around, doesn't it? I'm not all that great at secrets."

"Not like your grandmother," Mom said, her tone suddenly taking on a new edge.

And me, Shallis thought, stabbed with guilt and memory as sharp as one of Linnie's professional quality cooking knives. She'd slept with Jared Starke last night. They'd made love three glorious times, and she didn't have the remotest intention of spilling that juicy little secret to anyone.

"Mom, you're still upset about Gram and that whole thing with Flip Templeton and the house?" Linnie asked.

"Oh, 'still!' We've known about it for, what, thirty-six hours?" Mom said. "Less! Linnie, is something burning?"

"No," she answered calmly, "and you're not getting off that lightly after putting me through your 'Just relax' speech yet again." She got up, went to the stove, lifted a pot, stirred something. "Dinner is fine."

Shallis was tempted to ask what they were having, because it smelled so good. She'd been starving all day, despite eating a decent if health-conscious breakfast and lunch. All her senses were zinging, hungry, demanding their share, and every time she thought about last night and Jared, her stomach went through a gymnastic Gold Medal floor routine, flip, flip, flip, drop.

Linnie turned from the stove back to Mom, watching her closely as she asked, "Can someone tell me why we're treating Gram's secret life as bad news? It's not, is it? Really? We've found out that she was happily involved with a good man for eleven years, when we'd thought she hadn't had a man to love her since Grandpa died, so long ago."

"Yes, but—" Mom began.

"We've found out that she made a major contribution to the happiness of two vulnerable people. And the frosting on the cake—she's left you a second very marketable residence, Mom. The world cruise with Dad is in your lap, if you want it. I'm sure Gram's up on a cloud somewhere—" she blinked back a few tears, but she was smiling "—and she's chanting at you, 'Get the travel brochures, get the travel brochures.' What's not to like about any of that?"

There was a short, strained silence.

"Oh, you wouldn't get it, Linnie." Mom's voice was hard. She had sat down again and was staring at her fingernails— a pastime which Shallis knew she was deeply opposed to on several levels. At the same time she was…surely not…yes, really…making a series of sharp little blinks to keep the tears out of her own eyes.

Steam billowed out of one of Linnie's cooking pots, making the metal lid jump noisily up and down. Linnie shut off the gas. The kitchen went quiet.

"Okay. What wouldn't I get, Mom?" Linnie said, her voice way too calm.

"That I thought your grandmother and I were as close as a mother and daughter could be, and it hurts real bad to find out that wasn't true, because if it *was* true, she would have told me about Flip and Rose and Ivy and the house years ago. It really hurts!"

"So why wouldn't I get that?" Linnie's voice was stony now, also.

"Because you and I—I've tried. We love each other. I know we do. I know you love me. But you push me away. I'm *not* going to go to my grave, twenty years from now, and leave *you* feeling like you've lost your best friend as well as your mom, the way I've felt since Gram died—or the way I felt until yesterday, anyhow," she corrected, her lips thin and tight. "I know it's not going to be that way for you, when I go. And that hurts, too."

In front of the stove, Linnie closed her eyes. "Oh, Mom…"

"You're not going to disagree, are you?"

"I guess not." She thought for a moment. "No…I guess not. We're not best friends. But I don't mean to push you away. I really don't."

"You do it, though. All the time. Your father can do no wrong in your eyes, but me, every little mistake, every time I say something the wrong way, it's as if that gets added to the jail time I'm serving for pushing you too hard in the pageants. I'm on a life sentence, now."

"The jail time? Good grief, Mom—!" Linnie crossed the room, knelt down in front of their mother, took her hands and began to squeeze and stroke them, lost for words, appalled.

As appalled as Shallis.

"Only I'm not locked *in*," Mom said. Her eyes, still a glorious blue, glittered and swam. "I'm locked *out*. Of your heart." Her voice cracked. "And now I feel like I was locked out of Gram's heart, too, without even knowing it. And I keep thinking, what did I ever do that was so wrong? Yes, I spoke my mind, I pushed. Gram. And you. But I always did it out of love, and that doesn't seem to have counted…for squat…with either of you."

Shallis had never heard her mother cry like this. Linnie surely hadn't, either. They exchanged a helpless glance. Neither of them knew what to do. Shallis understood that this wasn't the moment to get in the way of what was happening, since so much of it was between Linnie and Mom.

Linnie started making little sounds, tutting and shushing as she might have done to a tearful child. She was going to make such a great mom, if she ever got the chance. Awkwardly she reached for Mom's shoulders and hugged her, and Mom hugged her back, still shaking with sobs. It was several minutes before she managed to speak. Shallis finally came over and joined her sister, hugging their mother, too, tight in the throat and crying just as hard.

"I'm sorry, I'm so sorry," Mom whispered. "To be laying this on you. I didn't mean it to come out. You know, Gram's gone, we're all grieving, and I can't ever say it to her now, and that makes it worse."

"Oh, Mom, no," Linnie said. "It had to come out. We're all in a mess, right now, aren't we? We don't know what we're doing or saying or feeling. Because of Gram. Because of everything. And I don't think we should expect to solve any of it in a hurry. I'm not punishing you for the beauty queen thing. I'm really not. Not anymore. I know I used to in my teens.

Teenagers do that! But you know I love you. We just have to try harder to reach each other."

"You know I'd cut off my arm if that would help you get pregnant."

"I know you would."

"And, Linnie, I have to say, I'd be telling you to take a vacation even if you weren't trying for a baby. You and Ryan have worked too hard since the day you got back from your honeymoon and you need to make some time for yourselves. Yell at me for saying it, but that's the real threat to your marriage, not the fact that you're still not pregnant. For heaven's sake, schedule in a break, the moment school lets out, before you start on the summer visitors. Go to the Caribbean and lie on a beach, even if it's only for three days."

"Maybe that's what we all need," Shallis said. "To go easy on ourselves for a bit. Before we conclude that we're completely dysfunctional, hey? Save the postage on our letters to Dear Abby? We've all had a lot to deal with, lately."

And how crazy was I to add a sizzling fling with Jared Starke into the mix?

What am I going to do about that?

Mom went into brisk and efficient mode, suddenly. "Goodness' sakes, I must look a mess. If you're going to call those boys in to eat, favor to me, Linnie, don't do it until I've gotten myself fixed up, okay? Your dad will want to know who's been upsetting who, and does he really need to?"

"Since we've all been upsetting each other, maybe not," Shallis said. "Not tonight, anyhow. Put us out of our misery, Linnie, tell us what we're eating."

"Oh, good stuff, I hope." She put on a bright face that fooled no one. "Curried squash and apple soup, blue cheese tarts, beef carbonnade with steamed vegetables, and berry summer pudding with vanilla crème fraîche."

"I'm going to cry again. It sounds too good to be true. Sell the horses and just open a restaurant, Linnie."

The oven door squeaked. "Forget that idea, I've just scorched the edges of the tarts…"

They all laughed and let the emotion go, for the time being. They'd taken some little baby steps into areas Shallis hadn't even known existed, bubbling away under the surface of family relationships that she'd thought were strong and secure.

They *were* strong, too. But they would need some extra tending—nourishment and time and love—the way the garden at Fifty-six Chestnut Street could do with fertilizing and planting and new flower beds, even though its grass was still mown and its shrubs still pruned.

And if I'd known about all these undercurrents this time yesterday, would I have let Jared get added to the mix, she wondered. Laying the silverware on Linnie's little dining table, she didn't have an answer to that question.

Chapter Eight

Jared hadn't heard from Shallis all day.

To be honest, he wasn't surprised. He remembered what she'd said as they were touring Fifty-six Chestnut Street, about her father knowing how to give people the right space. He'd gotten the impression that she needed space right now—space to step back and look at what had happened between them last night, not just in bed but in the hours before that. He'd been stepping back and looking at several related issues for the past twenty hours.

He was way more surprised when the phone rang at nine forty-five in the evening and he heard her voice at the other end of the line:

"Jared?"

"Yup, it's me. What's up, Shallis?"

Of course you can come over!

Now? No problem.

Whipped cream and gold underwear? Great. Ready and waiting.

Not that last night was just about the best night of my life, or anything.

"Unh…" She made a helpless sound.

He jumped in with both feet, feeling as needy as a nerdy teen but—he hoped—not letting it show in a voice he deliberately dropped to a gravelly drawl. "Look, about last night, neither of us has anything to apologize for, so if that's what you're thinking, please don't. And it doesn't have to interfere with our professional dealings. Your call, on all of it."

"Right. Yes. Okay." Another silence, during which he could almost hear the buzz of her thoughts. "I was actually calling about Gram."

"Sorry, my mistake."

Jared reminded himself belatedly that he'd actually done the phone-conversation-after-spending-a-first-night-together thing before. Maybe not after a first night as spectacular as his and Shallis's, but still, he'd always been pretty good at those conversations, and there was no reason why he shouldn't be just as good now. Solid ground coalesced beneath his feet again.

"It being a quarter till ten, and all," he said, "and less than twenty-four hours since we, uh, spent some pretty nice time together, I wondered if your agenda was more personal."

Silence.

"I should have waited until the morning," she said.

"Absolutely not, if it's important."

"Uh…okay."

"Listen, if you want to talk in person, I can jump in the car. You're only five minutes away."

"No, it's fine. I've just had dinner with my parents and Lin-

nie and Ryan. We all got pretty upset. That is, Mom and Linnie and me. Mom, especially, is really hurting because she
doesn't understand why Gram never told her about Flip and
the house. She always thought they were closer than that."

"I could tell it hit her pretty hard, yesterday."

"Jared, I can see her questioning all sorts of stuff about
their relationship, and Linnie and I would both like to find
some way to reassure her. If there's any chance we can find
out more about why Gram felt that secrecy was so important,
I think it would really help. I wondered if your grandfather
might know, or at least be able to tell us where to look."

"You're talking about letters, papers…"

"Anything, yes. Any clues."

"I heard from him tonight. He's coming back to town on
the weekend to meet up with an old friend. Do you want me
to arrange an appointment?"

"Please, if you could."

"At the office?"

"That's probably best, yes."

"I'll talk to him, come up with some possible times and
get back to you about what suits you."

"Thanks. That would be great."

Another silence, big and juicy.

With Shallis's voice unconsciously a little breathless and
hesitant in his ear, Jared's memories of her presence in his
house were even more vivid than they'd already been the
whole evening.

What did he want?

More nights like last night, obviously.

But was it as simple as that?

Ten years ago, he'd been at law school, where certain stu-
dents thought it was fine to give themselves an edge by cut-

ting chunks of required reading out of library law books so that no one else got a chance to look at the material. Jared had never done such a thing. He hadn't struggled with the moral ramifications on that issue. No ifs or buts, it was a scummy thing to do—especially when the subject of the class was Professional Ethics.

But ethics in the real world of corporate law had proved more difficult. Where did your loyalty lie? Where did professional and personal boundaries fall? How far did you go to get information? Who were you prepared to hurt by holding information back?

He'd sheared close to the ethical edge at times over the past few years... No, if he was really honest, he'd gone over it. He'd slept with an attractive partnership-track attorney in a rival practice largely because of information she could give him. He'd told a close friend about a company that was in trouble, while keeping the same information from a colleague he didn't care for. The guy had lost a lot of money when the company went under. He'd gotten praise and approval from the senior partner in his Chicago practice for conduct he'd secretly despised in himself.

Technically Shallis wasn't a client of the Starke law practice. Her grandmother had been, and her parents now were, since Mrs. McLenaghan's inheritance had gone exclusively to Sunny, her only child. A week ago, Sunny and Bob Duncan would have been in his grandfather's hands, not his. He could hide behind fine distinctions such as these, or he could look at the underlying issue.

For some reason, a couple of well-worn phrases from his father came into his head. "You make your own destiny," Dad used to say. "Never forget that, Jared. It doesn't matter what raw material you're given to work with, it's what you do with it that counts. You start with a clean slate, and if you mess it up, you're the only one who can wipe it off and start again."

Yada, yada, yada.

How many times had he heard it? Dad had a minor obsession with destiny and slates and raw material, and an apparent belief that he had to deliver the message over and over in order for it to get through.

Had it gotten through? Jared wondered now.

Sleeping with Shallis Duncan was dangerous. But then, any relationship was dangerous. There was always the capacity for hurt and miscommunication, betrayal and loss. If human beings hadn't been prepared to risk all of that, down the ages, the species would have died out long ago.

There were particular risks where Shallis was concerned, however. Jared didn't think his instinct to win had dropped away in the slightest, but he suspected the prize had changed, over the past couple of years. The prize, this time, would be his certain knowledge that he hadn't behaved like scum.

He knew what he wanted from Shallis right now. More time together. More nights, in particular. But he couldn't guarantee anything else. He might be back in Chicago six months from now. Did that mean he should never have slept with her? How could you work out what you wanted without trying it first?

Letting her make the moves seemed like the only decent strategy right now, so he put an end to the lengthening silence by saying, "I'm glad you called. You know you can call any time, about anything. For now, I'll let you wind down, and I'll be in touch tomorrow about the meeting on the weekend."

"I've arranged to take a second week off work," Shallis said. The private office at the Starke law practice was crowded this morning, with Abraham, Jared, Sunny, Bob, Linnie and Shallis all in attendance. Ryan had offered to accompany his wife but as always there was a mile-long list of chores to do around the property, so Linnie had said no.

It was a warm spring day, and Jared hadn't turned on the air-conditioning for the sake of one short meeting. He'd opened a window, but the room was still stuffy.

Was this why Shallis felt so tight in the chest and so hot everywhere else?

No. Of course not. She knew exactly why she was hot.

"My boss isn't too happy," she continued, looking at her mother, not at Jared, "because we're getting up to wedding season, but—"

"Oh, nonsense," Mom said. "You can wrap that man around your little finger with one smile, Shallie."

"Yes, but my little finger doesn't like having him there."

"He fusses like an old hen. Your assistant is competent, isn't she?"

"Very, and I've hired an agency temp to come in. It's fine." She turned to Jared's grandfather, who had taken the big chair behind the desk automatically, just as if Jared hadn't spent the past week sitting in it. "Mr. Starke, if you can give us any hints about what we're looking for, because I do want to make the best use of this time. Do you have any ideas?"

Abe gave a fleeting frown in Shallis's direction and addressed her mother instead. "Your mother was a very sharp-minded and levelheaded woman, Mrs. Duncan," he began.

"You wouldn't say that if you could see the mess her papers are in!"

"I didn't say she was tidy, but where it counted she was levelheaded."

"She was, Sunny," Dad said. "I'm wondering if we're all

making too much of this. It's been a shock, but she was old and she was your mother. Maybe she felt uncomfortable and just…never got around to talking about it."

"If she chose to keep something secret for so long, maybe we should all respect that," Abraham said.

Shallis knew that Jared's white-haired grandfather was over eighty years old—older than Gram herself—but he still gave off a strong air of competence and almost patriarchal authority. She fought her instinct to defer to his age and experience. This was too important. "Even beyond the grave?" she said.

"Sometimes beyond the grave is the best place for certain things," Abraham Starke intoned.

Shallis felt as if she'd been put in *her* place, and as if that place was a miniature wooden toddler's chair, painted buttercup yellow, with a heart-shaped cutout in the back. Speak when spoken to, Little Missy. Stay out of grown-ups' affairs.

Jared shifted in the secretary's swivel chair he'd brought in from the outer office. "Grandpa Abe, I think the family has some valid concerns. The secrecy does seem out of proportion to the facts we have. You don't know any more about this than you've already told us, apparently—" he waited a moment, but his grandfather didn't correct the assumption "—but do you have any suggestions about what they might look out for?"

"I don't know what Caroline McLenaghan kept or didn't keep," the old lawyer said, sounding a little fretful, now. "And I don't know what Rose and Ivy kept, either. I do know they were a whole lot neater than your mother was, Mrs. Duncan! You're going through everything anyhow. You might find something. If you do, bring it to me and I'll tell you what I can make of it. Interpret it. Follow up on it. Long lives can get complicated, however. I'm not taking responsibility for any unpleasant discoveries."

He stopped and shot a narrow-eyed look at his client.

"I'm sorry, Sunny." He seemed much humbler now. "That sounded too harsh. You know how fond I was of Caroline, and how much I respected her. I can't believe she's gone, when she was three years younger than I am. Felt like her big brother sometimes. Makes a man feel his age. You have no idea."

He stood slowly and awkwardly. Shallis tried to imagine Jared so stiff and portly, fifty years from now, but she couldn't superimpose his strong body and much squarer facial features over Abraham Starke's silhouette. She also had the odd feeling that Grandfather Abe was emphasizing his frailty rather than hiding it, right now.

For a man who took pride in being able to vacation on his own in a mountain fishing cabin and pull prize trout from a stream for hours every day, this looked an awful lot like fobbing them off.

"As you say, Mr. Starke," she told him, gentle but firm, "we're going through everything anyhow. Anything we don't understand, we'll put aside in the hope of some clear answers. Thanks for agreeing to meet with us in the middle of a weekend."

"Oh, you're welcome, Shallis," the old man said. "You're more than welcome."

Outside, Linnie said, "I'm glad Ryan didn't come. We didn't learn much."

We learned that there's something still to find out, Shallis thought, but she didn't say it out loud, in case she was wrong.

She'd also learned that she couldn't sit in the same room as Jared without getting hot all over, but she wasn't saying that out loud, either.

* * *

Back at the Starke residence on Chestnut Street ten minutes later, Jared asked, "Mom's coming over for lunch?"

"Thought it would be nice for the three of us to get together before my golf game with Ed this afternoon. When she offered to cater, I didn't say no." Grandpa Abe chuckled. "I've always liked your mother's cooking more than any fancy restaurant. Told her some baked trout in lemon and cream sauce might be nice. Few toasted almonds on top. Salad on the side. Gave her a couple of fish from my freezer to get her started."

"Then that's what she'll bring," Jared predicted.

His mother had always tried hard to please her father-in-law, and Abraham had rewarded her with a sincere affection that hadn't faded after Jared's parents' amicable divorce, nor after Dad's death last year.

Jared didn't fully understand the bond between them, but he liked it. It was one of the fixed points in his universe, and he'd come to value those more, over the past few years. He couldn't imagine what it would be like for either himself or Mom when his grandfather had gone. "So how many holes of golf have you scheduled, Grandpa Abe?" he asked.

"Eighteen, of course."

"Taking a golf-buggy?"

"Ed likes to walk."

"Ed's twelve years younger than you are."

"But we have plenty in common, despite the age difference, because I like to walk, too."

Stubborn. You couldn't even hint to the man that he might be in danger of overdoing it. Eighteen holes of golf around a very roomy course, after all that fishing up at the cabin? Grandpa would only argue that the fishing had made him fitter.

Mom arrived on the dot of twelve-thirty, with the trout still piping hot in a foil-covered dish, and the salad in a wooden bowl. "And you bought some fresh bread, Abe, I hope?"

"Did you ask me to, Judy?"

"Yes, I did!"

"So the bread's on the table." He spread his hands and gave her a look of reproach.

She clicked her tongue. "As if you've never forgotten an errand I've asked you to run for me."

"Not when it involves food, I haven't, honey." His eyes twinkled. "We're eating on the deck. Your son doesn't get enough fresh air now I've been locking him in my law practice all week."

"It's still more than he was getting in Chicago, I'd bet on that!"

"Most people in Chicago settle for air conditioning," Jared came in.

"I wouldn't *sell* you air-conditioning."

They ate in the spring sunshine and talked about safe, comfortable things. Mom's garden. Her job as a veterinary nurse. The weather. Grandpa Abe's friend Ed's visit. Jared found it difficult to concentrate and to express the right interest. Must be all that unaccustomed fresh air and sunshine.

Or not.

Shallis was still on his mind.

Filling it.

Memories of Tuesday night.

Calculations as to how to have Tuesday night happen again, while still making her feel as if she was calling the shots.

He'd wanted to leave the next move to her, but so far, four

whole days later, she hadn't made it. He felt impatient, and he felt bad about being impatient. She had a lot on her plate right now. She wouldn't appreciate any extra pressure. He'd resolved to let her dictate the pace but, man, did that feel out of character!

"This stuff with Mrs. McLenaghan's estate is strange, isn't it?" he said, putting down his silverware after a last scrape of the china dish. "Has Grandpa told you about that, Mom?"

"He mentioned that Shallis Duncan has been doing a lot of the work, which sounds a bit too much like real work for a former beauty queen. I thought she had some big-time, glittery PR career in L.A."

"She came back a few months ago. Wasn't happy there. And she isn't like that," Jared heard himself say. "She's pretty down to earth."

"Well, good for her!" his mother drawled, smiling at him. "I haven't seen her since the whole town watched her on TV five years ago, losing out to that other girl, who couldn't hold a candle to her, in my opinion—"

"In the whole of Hyattville's opinion, I'm guessing."

"—but I have to say, if I was as beautiful as she is, I can't imagine being down to earth about anything. I would just adore being a prima donna and an absolute bitch."

"No, you wouldn't, Judy," Grandpa Abe groused.

"She gets a little tired of those kinds of assumptions about her, too, is my impression," Jared said.

"Is she still just as beautiful, then?"

"Uh, yeah. She's—" Don't make me start thinking about it. "I mean, she hasn't let herself go."

"I guess she's only, what, twenty-six or twenty-seven? I'm surprised Hyattville offers enough opportunities for her."

"We're not talking about Shallis, we're talking about her

grandmother's estate," Jared said, because he really, seriously, did not want to talk about Shallis Duncan with his mother. "Caroline McLenaghan owned Fifty-six Chestnut Street, eight houses down from here, that's what I wanted to tell you about, and none of the Duncan family or the other McLenaghan relatives knew it for thirty-five years."

"The Templeton sisters' house," his mother answered.

"So you did know?"

She looked at her father-in-law, then back at Jared. "I'm sure I don't know all of it."

"Have you been breaking attorney-client privilege, Grandpa?"

"You start to forget," he said a little fretfully. "What's professional and what's private. Your mother's been living in this town her whole life. She first went out with your father when she was eighteen."

"Mrs. McLenaghan must have inherited the house not long before you and Dad got married, Mom."

"Around then," Grandpa Abe answered on her behalf. "Hard to keep track of exact dates. I don't know why Sunny's getting so het up over it, why she's treating it like a slap in the face. It's not."

"People shouldn't try to keep secrets when they're bound to come out some day," Jared said. "I don't see the point. Mrs. Duncan thought she had a good relationship with her mother, and now she may be left to question that perception for the rest of her life."

"I'm sure that wasn't Caroline's intention."

"I'm sure, too. That's why I don't see the point. Who's being protected? No one that I can see. Instead people are getting hurt."

"No, I think you're right, Jared," his mother agreed, with another glance at Grandpa Abe.

"Maybe so, maybe so. If you'd been privy to some of the things I have in my career, however… Should have opened some wine to go with this," Grandpa Abe muttered vaguely, interrupting his own trailed off sentence. "Something fresh and dry. A California chablis, or a Chardonnay. I can get one now, if anyone wants. Nothing's chilled, but we can add some ice."

"Not for me, thanks, Abe," Mom said. "I'd want to sleep all afternoon, even after just a half a glass."

"Nor me," Jared said. Didn't need anything to blunt his willpower today, thanks. He'd be unable to resist showing up at Shallis's door. "I'm going for a run, soon."

"Coffee instead, then. Judy?"

"Yes, please."

Jared didn't wait for coffee. He needed that run.

Judy Starke waited until her son had changed into his running shorts and T-shirt, slapped a baseball cap on his head and pounded off down the sidewalk, in the direction of Fifty-six Chestnut Street.

"Abe…" she began.

"Don't say it, Judy," he growled.

"You're so sure you know what I'm going to say?"

"And I'm right, aren't I?" the old man grumbled.

"You heard what he said about secrets. How he doesn't see the point, especially when the truth has to come out some day."

"There's a point to this one. And why does the truth ever have to come out?"

"Because it should. And because it just will."

"My son married you, Judy."

"I'm aware of that." She smiled slightly, to soften the sardonic comment. "You've held it over me for years. And you've been able to hold it over me because I've appreciated so much about your attitude, Abe, and about Ray's. There aren't a lot of men who'd view things the way you have, especially after the divorce."

"I've seen too much bitterness. I didn't want to create any more. I didn't want to feel bitter, or to encourage it in my son. You were young, and you made a mistake. Rose and Ivy Templeton would have made a worse one, if Caroline McLenaghan and I hadn't been there to save them from it."

"Oh, let's not go over it all again."

"No, let's not."

"You know I'm not going to say anything to Jared without your agreement, Abe, but you also know I'm never going to stop asking you for it."

"When I'm gone, do whatever you think right." He made a theatrical gesture that Judy didn't buy for a second. "I'll have no say over it, then, beyond the grave."

"That's what you want? To wait until you're gone? That sounds very out of character to me, I have to say."

Abe gave a tired shrug. "Thought that'd make you feel better about it."

"No! Good lord! Sometimes I don't understand you at all!"

He smiled at this. "I can take it. Nothing's worked out too bad. Have a feeling Jared's going to take over the practice permanently. Not pushing him too hard on it."

"No, please don't."

"Has to be his decision. Chicago wouldn't be such a bad result, either. He'll learn a few things while he's here, and they'll help him in that shark-pond up north. I'm proud of him, Judy, and I'm taking a lot of credit for what he's become."

She laughed, shaking her head in disbelief at the same time. "Yes! You would! I'll take a little credit myself, if you don't mind, on my own behalf and Ray's."

"Be my guest. Ray was a good father to the boy. I'm getting ready for my golf game." He took a token dish or two back to the kitchen, while Judy puttered around clearing up the remainder of their lunch, still shaking her head about a whole lot of things.

Chapter Nine

Shallis's boss was late, which meant that there was some crisis, real or highly exaggerated, at the hotel. He should have been here ten minutes ago, for his tour of the house. It was three-forty in the afternoon, on the middle Friday of Shallis's two-week break from her job at the hotel, a time of day when there wasn't anything in the least mysterious or spooky about Fifty-six Chestnut Street.

No, seriously.

Shallis had opened all the drapes, blinds and windows so that cheerful sunshine slanted into the house and gleamed on pieces of gorgeous china. Wallpaper dating back seventy years revealed the subtleties in its pattern under the fresh light. Music played on the radio/CD player that Shallis carted around with her from room to room, for company.

The player had belonged to the Templeton sisters, and Shallis alternated between her own favorite rock and coun-

try music stations, and dips into their extensive CD collection—compilations of hit love songs from the fifties and six-
ties, old-time country music, a little smoky jazz and *lo-o-ots*
of Elvis.

The sisters had had a strong appreciation for music, Shallis guessed. They were slowly becoming real to her. Their
tastes, their foibles, their limitations, their joys. Much more
real than ghosts.

When the doorbell pealed across Mary Wells singing the
chorus of "My Guy", Shallis expected to find Alan Lonsdale,
fussy and apologetic, but instead it was Linnie, on her way
home from school. "Mom said you were here, all on your
own. Let me help for a couple of hours."

"For heaven's sake, Linnie, you're going to sandwich it between seven hours of grade school kids, ninety minutes of
gourmet cooking and three hours of horses?"

"Only one hour of horses. I want to."

"Have you booked that Caribbean vacation yet?"

Linnie gave a triumphant I've-got-you-now grin at this.
"Yes! We leave the day school lets out, just a week from now.
We found a short-notice package deal on the Internet. Five
whole days. And it's already making a difference to how I
feel. So you have no leg to stand on, you or Mom."

"You should have made it fifteen days, but okay, five still
deserves a hug." Shallis reached out and took her big sister in
her arms, registering weight loss and stress just in the way Linnie felt. She shouldn't be this fragile and bony and stiff. Stepping back from the hug, she added a long morning at a good
hair salon to her mental list of things Linnie needed. "Who's
taking care of your place?"

"One guess, Shallie."

"Dad. And he's in heaven, right?"

"Almost as much as we are. We've been talking about it and our tongues are hanging out. We do need a break. So you'll let me help?"

"I guess it's not that brutal. I itemized the furnishings earlier in the week. Now I'm just taking inventory of half a homewares store's worth of very nice glass and china, and going through papers and letters for a change of pace. Ivy sure did like to write to her local elected representatives, and she kept every reply she got."

"Where are you finding it all?"

"Up in the attic, mainly, and the spare bedrooms—four of 'em—this is a big house—but I'm bringing each box downstairs because it's…well…"

"Less spooky down here?"

"Why is everyone so determined to draw my attention to the possible spookiness of this place?"

"Maybe because they can see the terror in your face, barely held in check."

"Curse of a vivid imagination. I keep feeling that there's *something* here. Not ghosts. Surprises? Secrets?"

"Now you're spooking *me!*"

"Sorry… Here, take a fresh box and start reading."

"How're you sorting it?"

"Jared gave me a kind of archival crib sheet." Shallis held out a couple of pages of basic guidelines that Jared had printed off the Internet for her, and listened to the echo of his name in her head. Had she said it the way all the women in town who *weren't* sleeping with him would say it? Like, naturally? As if it wasn't significant in any way?

"Take a look, Linnie." She pointed at the array of papers in four piles on the floor. "This pile's trash, this one's historical value, this one's important documents, this one's personal keepsakes."

"You have nothing in that last pile. And not a whole heck of a lot under 'historical value,' either."

"Take a look at what's in the trash pile, and you'll see why. But there's boxes more. I don't think I've hit paydirt, yet, but I'm living in hope."

No such luck. Linnie was the one to find something interesting, with the very first box she opened. It wasn't fair. "After I've been doing this all day," Shallis complained. "Not to mention hours and hours last week doing the same thing at Gram's. Is that typical, or what?"

"Totally typical. And there's still more at Gram's right?"

"Mom's throwing up her hands, even with Dad helping her this week."

"I think this is Gram's handwriting, isn't it?" Linnie held out a little packet of letters, tied with a rubber band so stiffened with age that it broke as soon as Shallis touched it. "If this is the first interesting thing we've found, then you look at them, Shallie."

"We'll divide the packet in half and both look." She tossed the brittle bit of broken rubber into the trash pile and slid her thumb into the middle of the bundle, dividing it in two.

There weren't more than ten or twelve letters in total, still folded inside their envelopes, each of which had a neat slit right across the top. Gram had only ever written to the sisters when she was out of town for an extended period, and in her later years she'd cut down on travel. She'd used the fountain pen and royal-blue ink that Linnie and Shallis both remembered, and her spiky handwriting wasn't easy to read. Descriptions of Niagara Falls and Ireland, news of friends whose names weren't familiar. Both of them skipped bits.

"Here's something," Linnie said after several minutes. "I'll read it out." She frowned at the letter in her hand. "'I'm concerned about this Mr. Grausam you've mentioned so much in your last two letters, Ivy. It certainly sounds as if he's had more than his share of misfortune, and I'm glad he's doing such a thorough job with the garden and being so good to you, but if he asks to borrow any more money, please talk it over with Mr. Starke before you say yes.'"

"Mr. Starke. That's our Mr. Starke." Jared's grandfather.

"It must be. Okay, she goes on, 'You must remember that not every man is what he seems, and that to him you and Rose must seem, as well as sweet and wonderful women, a little friendless and unprotected. We know that's not so, of course, you have friends who care about you very much, but please be careful, and do write again soon, because I get anxious when I don't hear from you.'"

"What's the date on that one?" Shallis asked.

"August 6, 1970. Remind me, Shallie, isn't that the year Flip Templeton died?"

"Yes, back in March. It must have hit Gram hard. Mom said she went and stayed with friends in Vermont for most of the summer. Just a vacation, as far as Mom believed at the time, but of course now we know it was more than that. Mom didn't go away herself. She had a summer job and she'd just gotten engaged to Dad."

"Mmm, that's right." Linnie folded up the letter. "It's hard to keep track."

"Oh, trust me, I have a million family dates at my fingertips now!"

"This next one's dated a week later." Linnie read silently for a moment. "It says she's cutting short her stay and coming home."

"Read it out."

"I will. Here we go. 'Please don't rush into anything until I get back, and please, please talk to Mr. Starke. I know you've explained exactly why Stewart's plan makes sense and I'm looking forward to discovering that he's just as wonderful as you say.'"

"So it's Stewart now?"

"If it's the same man."

"It must be."

"I guess so. I'll keep going. 'You're right to keep it a secret. As you've said, people have no right to, but they do talk when there's an age disparity, particularly if the woman is older, and when there's a fast courtship. Yes, some people do have nasty minds, and it isn't always the ones we suspect, dear Ivy, so please, please just keep up a little reserve and discretion and caution, please, until we can see each other. And please, tell Mr. Starke *all* of your plans and intentions before you act on them.'"

"Mr. Grausam, then a week later, Stewart," Shallis said. "But the tone sounds more urgent."

"Still, I think you're right. It has to be the same man. Gram's talking about him in the same way."

"He wants to marry Ivy, and Gram thinks he's out to con her."

"Which she might be right about if he's already borrowing money. I wonder how much."

"Please, please be careful. Please, please talk to Mr. Starke. I wonder if Ivy does."

"Question is, does she wait until Gram gets back?" Linnie had been through all the letters in her pile. She looked across at the ones Shallis held. "Does she marry him? Wouldn't we know about it?"

"Problem is," Shallis said, "this is all happening thirty-five

years ago, even though we're talking about it like it's this
week's episode of our favorite soap, and the next letter—unless they're out of date order, and on Ivy's prior track
record..." Shallis gestured at the boxes she'd already been
through. "I don't think they will be—" She took a breath.

"So the next letter's dated when?"

"July 1976."

"And is there any mention of Stewart Grausam?"

"I'm reading..."

The doorbell pealed again. "I'll get it," Linnie said.

"It'll be Mr. Lonsdale for our Envisaging the Possibilities tour."

Linnie headed for the door. "You really want the Grand Regency to buy this place?"

"I think it could be a win for the hotel as well as for Mom
and Dad...and I'm kind of reluctant to let the place go. If the
hotel owns it, I'll still get to visit."

As expected, Shallis's boss had arrived. And there was
no mention of any Stewart or Mr. Grausam in the rest of
Gram's letters. He'd apparently faded out of Ivy's life—or
he'd been pushed.

Linnie continued to go through the bundles of personal letters in the box, while Shallis conducted the tour for her boss.
She showed him the shared forty yards of rear fence that divided the garden of Fifty-six Chestnut from the grounds of
the hotel. The Grand Regency's pretty garden softened the
back view of its buildings from this angle. She asked Mr.
Lonsdale to imagine an exclusive restaurant, a character-
filled tearoom, or—her personal favorite—a boutique conference center, and he soon saw her point.

But he had questions.

Could the house's contents be included in the sale? He'd

noticed some rather fine pieces of china, for example. How long would the business of Mrs. McLenaghan's estate take to settle? Had Shallis perused the zoning regulations for this street? Liquor licensing laws? Noise and parking statutes?

With each question, he moved closer to the front door.

"Let me research that for you tomorrow, Mr. Lonsdale," she told him.

"You see, Shallis, I'm not just a pretty face. Not that I'm implying, of course, that you could be considered in that—"

"No, I understand, sir."

"So we'll regard this as a promising thought, but one that requires considerable further investigation."

She'd rarely heard him speak with such firm authority. "Thank you for taking the time to look over the place."

"Not at all. I like your initiative." He smiled, opened the door, took a step toward the porch, then stopped. "Now, I understand you're dealing with Jared Starke on all of this?"

"That's right. His grandfather is taking some time off, and Jared's thinking about whether he wants to take over the practice permanently."

"Can I give you some advice, Shallis? Fatherly advice."

Well, it was better than certain other kinds.

"Sure, Mr. Lonsdale, of course you can."

"Take the man with a grain of salt. My youngest brother was at school with him. I've heard a few stories from his college days, and I can't imagine Chicago has made him any more principled. Look carefully over everything before you sign it, and don't be taken in by his charm."

"I'm not usually taken in by anything that's not genuine, Mr. Lonsdale," Shallis answered, hoping it was true.

She'd spoken to Jared on the phone a couple of times this week, but that was all—Attorney Ken on one end of the line, and Career Girl Barbie on the other. Nothing that her boss or anyone else could have objected to. For her own part, she was very tempted to object to Mr. Lonsdale's interference, but managed to hold her tongue.

Didn't manage to keep in check a rising tide of stubbornness. She had to make up her own mind about him, not listen to anyone else.

Mr. Lonsdale gave her a pat on the shoulder. "I'm sure you'll keep your eyes open." Then he closed the door and left. He'd spent eleven minutes on the property.

"Is he an easy man to work for?" Linnie asked innocently.

"He might be, if I could get a better handle on him. He's smarter than he seems. You heard him just now."

"Warning you off Jared Starke, as if you didn't have better reasons than most people to know what he's like."

"I think I do know what he's like, yes…" Shallis said.

Now, there was a comment you could take two ways.

"…but I was talking about Mr. Lonsdale's questions about the house. Do you think he'll go for this place?"

"I think he might if you can give him the answers he's looking for. You'll have to talk to Jared."

This time, Shallis noted, Linnie said his name quite naturally, the way all the women in town who *weren't* sleeping with him would have said it. Her heart gave a little kick.

I must try to remember how that sounds.

Jared.

In a natural way.

Is that about right?

As if I'm not sleeping with him.

As if I'm not spending half my waking moments working out how I can get to see him again without being the one to step up to the plate and straight out ask.

On further reflection, after Linnie had gone home to Ryan, Shallis wondered what was so wrong with the straight out asking approach. She called Jared with Mr. Lonsdale's questions about the house, and suggested they meet for dinner.

Which the first runner-up in the Miss America pageant didn't usually have to do, because most of her dinner invitation transactions happened the other way around.

It felt…interesting. Different.

The heart pounding sensation was certainly new, in this context.

"Well, that would be very nice," Jared drawled in reply. "You're thinking…not tonight?"

"Oh, no, not— Actually, yes. You know my boss wants to get—"

"Tonight would be great." Not quite so drawly. Almost a lick of a nuance of a puppy-dog note in there, somewhere. Couldn't be that he was feeling as *non* laid back about this as she was, by any chance? "Can I pick you up? We can go over to Carrollton. You're still at the spooky house?"

"The Templeton house, yes. We are not calling it the spooky house, because I like the place. But make it at my apartment, can you? I need to change."

"That house is using you as a dust magnet again?"

"Not to mention smears of fifty-year-old typewriter ink on my fingers from going through a bunch of old letters."

"Make it not too early, then. Seven-thirty?"

"Seven would be fine, if you want it even earlier."

Any later, and we might not fit in…well, we might only fit it in twice.

As the female of the species, am I supposed to think about things like that, or are we doing a complete role reversal, here?

* * *

But then there was tomorrow morning, also, Jared calculated, if he could get Shallis to stay the night this time. Because if they had to drive to Carrollton, have a long, slow meal and drive back again, it was a little unrealistic to expect more than two—

Stop right there.

Why the obsession with quantity? Quality counted more. Shallis would certainly think so. Going to Carrollton was the right decision, even if it meant they only had time for one incredible session of—

Stop again.

Carrollton would work. The Grand Regency had the best restaurant in Hyattville, but Jared didn't think Shallis would want to eat there in the middle of a two week break which barely counted as vacation time, what with all that she and her mom were trying to get done at two houses. Carrollton had a five-star establishment which had deserved its top rating last Thursday night when Jared had taken clients there.

He made a reservation, and asked what time they closed. Just gathering data. Not hoping he and Shallis would get politely pushed out at ten, or anything, so they had nowhere to go but his place.

Or hers.

She was ready and waiting for him at seven, as promised, although she was a little slow answering her door. Yeah, he'd used that strategy a few times, too, he thought when the handle finally turned. When they were standing face to face, however, he couldn't think at all. He could barely even breathe.

With superb fluency, he did manage to get out the word, "Wow!"

She grinned and gave an apologetic shrug with her bare, satin-smooth shoulders. "Sometimes I like to revisit my old lifestyle."

Which he had to assume consisted of looking this drop-dead gorgeous every minute of every day.

Her dress was clingy, shimmery, skin baring, blue like a night sky. It hid her knees but not much else. In spiked heels, she was tall as a spring sapling, and her perfect nose was chin-height on him. He'd only have to lower his mouth a few short inches to bring it against hers.

Lord, he wanted to kiss her! He wanted to take her in his arms and get rid of this powerful need for her, after ten days of only dreaming about this, before it ate him alive. Her lips were dewy and soft, just a shade bolder than their natural color, and she'd darkened her eyes somehow. Darkened? Brightened? He didn't know what she'd done, except that they looked wide and deep and full of sultry secrets.

Her hair bounced around her face, swinging when she gave a little toss of her head as she turned to lock the door. He stood there like a piece of petrified tree, watching her do it, with his power of speech still gone AWOL and all the blood in his body converging below his belt.

She smelled like the best shower he'd ever had. It was probably the result of some two hundred dollar an ounce fragrance, but he couldn't think of it that way, didn't have the vocabulary, just knew the way it hit him as she stepped closer and smiled once more—fresh and clean and like a rush of sheer dizzy energy.

"Shall we go?" she said.

"No. Not yet." He sounded like a hungry bear waking up after winter, like Neanderthal man coming out of his cave and getting blinded by the sun.

Ug, me gotta kiss woman now.

Smooth, Jared, real smooth.

His hand was almost shaking as he touched her jaw and coaxed her close. Maybe she liked Neanderthal men. Her mouth had dropped open a tantalizing fraction. He caught a flash of pink as her tongue lapped against the inside of her lower lip. She pouted a little, waiting for him while he still moved in a daze, as if actually reaching her mouth was a tough task, like getting a drunk to walk a straight line.

Contact.

His eyes closed and the universe swam into a blur. He curled his fingers lightly around her neck, feeling her hair whisper and tickle against his knuckles, while her mouth whispered against his, stealing his soul and giving it right back again, glowing.

She said something. "Mmm," or something. Something encouraging and…well…generous, under the circumstances, because he couldn't remember ever feeling so at sea and so clumsy with his moves before.

She wound her arms around his neck and sighed her whole body against him. His blood converged faster. He ached and pulsed and throbbed already. She would have to feel it. Oh, yeah, she did. And she liked it. He groaned.

"How seriously does the restaurant take its reservation system?" she whispered.

"We can call. Tell them we'll be late."

"Before or after?"

"After."

"Good decision."

Still clinging to each other, they looked at the locked door.

"I was a little hasty on the home security," Shallis concluded.

"But you have your key." He kissed her neck while she searched for it in her bag. She laughed and kissed him back, whichever bit she could reach—some nose and some cheek. He tipped his face up to make it easier for her to find his mouth, and it was another ten minutes before they got the apartment door open.

Five seconds before he kicked it closed again behind them.

Fifteen seconds to reach her room.

Thirty to undress down to a strapless black bra and matching thong, and his pair of navy briefs that were almost bursting at the seams. At this point, for several minutes, progress stalled. But who cared about progress when the part you were stuck at was this perfect?

Her breasts swelled over the top of the bra. Her flat, tanned stomach shelved down to the tiny scoop of fabric that hid her heat. Her cheeks filled Jared's hands, and when he slid his fingers between them and down between her thighs, she gasped and twisted her head back, clinging to his hips as if she was on horseback and about to get thrown off.

He loved the responses he drew from her, played her like a musical instrument and felt himself vibrate all over in tune with the sounds she made. She bit into his shoulder, her lips soft and her teeth just staying on the pleasure side of pain. Working her way up his neck, she nipped his ear lobe and breathed hot air over the sensitive skin.

He crushed her hard against him, wanting to speak but not knowing how to express any of this in words. He said her name. Twice. A whisper and a groan. And then he entered her, without meaning to yet, only she was so swollen and steamy and ready he couldn't stay away. She had her legs wrapped around him, letting him in deeper, and then she tipped her body out and back, toppling them onto the bed.

They lost contact with each other and both of them almost sobbed with impatience to get it back again. Yes. Yes. Now. Again. Breath hissed between her teeth when she felt him fill her once more, and she lifted her hips from the bed, pushing harder, pushing him over the edge and following him seconds later.

"So we'll only be around ten minutes late," she whispered. "We've saved ourselves a phone call."

"That's why we went so fast?"

"You're suggesting another reason?"

Clever line. Come on, Jared. Think. Nope? Nothing?

He went with honesty instead. "I couldn't stop." His voice felt like gravel in a cement mixer. "I couldn't stay away or hold back or think or anything. I didn't want to. I didn't think you wanted to."

"I didn't."

"And even if you had…" He swallowed and shook his head. "Tell me why this is so good, Shallis. Tell me why it feels so different."

She lay silent in his arms for at least a minute, tracing patterns with her fingertips on his chest. "Can I get back to you on that?"

Another minute of silence.

"You think the answer is something I might not like?"

"I think I'm the one that might not like it. I wasn't looking for this, Jared. I wasn't looking for this part of it—" this naked part, he knew she meant "—to be this great, or this necessary, or this important. It makes it harder to…oh…work out a few things."

Yeah, and he had a few things to work out, also.

"Shall we just go to dinner?"

"That could be a good idea."

"Because if we lie here like this for much longer, we won't be able to save ourselves the phone call, after all."

She seemed a little shy getting dressed. He turned his back to step into his pants, then ruined the gesture by peeking. He discovered Shallis peeking at him. They laughed. Got to the restaurant twenty minutes late, without a phone call, to find their reservation hanging by a thread.

"And there was something interesting that Linnie and I found today, too," Shallis told Jared, after they'd talked about Alan Lonsdale's reaction to the house.

She didn't mention the way her boss had warned her about Jared himself. Now, why was that? Because she trusted Jared totally now, or because at some level she still didn't?

"I don't know if it's significant," she went on, "but after five boxes of, 'Thank you for your letter regarding the state of the road surface on County Route 39 between Angle Line Road and Route 41,' and such-like, it definitely caught our attention."

"Tell me."

Their entrées appeared, and they thanked their server, who didn't linger at the table.

"A couple of letters from Gram to Ivy, written back in the summer of 1970," Shallis said. "Well, there were about twelve letters from her all told, but two that got us curious, talking about a guy called Stewart, or Mr. Grausam."

"Unusual last name."

"Gram's handwriting is hard to make out sometimes, but I'm pretty sure Linnie and I read it right." Shallis spelled it out for him. "I'm not sure if we're saying it right, though."

Jared nodded, obviously trying to picture the spelling in his head. He said the name three different ways, but concluded, "It's not familiar to me. I think I would have remembered it, if I'd come across it in any important setting." He pushed a piece of duck in orange sauce onto his fork, and the aroma of the food mingled with wine and hot bread and her own French perfume in Shallis's nostrils. "Who was he?" Jared asked.

"He did some yardwork for the sisters, was the impression we got. Then he borrowed some money, but we don't know how much."

"Hmm."

"Then he wanted Ivy to marry him, and Gram sounded quite worried about it in the letters. She wrote that she was cutting short her stay in Vermont and coming home, at which point, of course, she and Ivy didn't need to write to each other any more, so we don't know what happened. Seems like Ivy can't have married the man, or we'd have surely known about it somehow."

"In 1970," Jared said. "The year my parents got married. The year before I was born."

"Yes, Linnie and I pinpointed it that way, too. It was the year Mom and Dad got engaged."

"So you think it might have something to do with your grandmother's secrecy?"

Shallis sighed. "In all honesty, I can't see why it would have. No, I think Linnie and I focused on it because it was the only little bit of juice in a very dry box of fruit, if you know what I mean."

"I'll keep an eye out for the name, all the same. Grausam. Want me to do some kind of search?"

"You're going to Google him on the Internet?"

"I'll do that, if you want. There are better ways."

"I really don't think it's important, so don't go to a lot of trouble."

"You have an instinct about it, though."

"Not even that. We were just curious. Along with that action movie and about twenty Elvis CDs, makes me wonder about Ivy. I can imagine her rocking along at night, to the sound of the King on a scratchy LP, with the lights turned low, thinking about this yard man who's courting her... She was in her forties then, and we gathered from Gram's letter that Stewart Grausam was some years younger—enough for it to be the source of gossip. I hope it ended okay for Ivy, not in floods of tears."

"And an empty bank account."

"Exactly. You know, that first time you came into the house with me after I'd gotten spooked, so I could prove to myself that nothing was there, I think you were wrong."

"Yeah?"

"I think there *is* something there. Not ghosts. Nothing supernatural."

"Then what?"

"I don't know. Maybe it's just the same thing that every long life leaves behind. An intricate sense of richness and detail, for anyone who's prepared to look carefully enough."

He drank some wine, then leaned a little closer. "You know what? We should all write a running account of our lives, so we don't keep our descendants guessing like this."

"A Web diary?"

"Maybe something a little more discreet than a Web diary."

"You see?" She leaned closer, too. Their table was small, situated in a quiet corner. The buzz of conversation from other diners was like a curtain, separating herself and Jared in their own space. "It's harder than it sounds to be truthful with the next generation. What do you put in this running account? 'Dinner with J. S. Got naked afterward.' Who do we want reading that, after we're gone?"

"Well, since we got naked before dinner, not after, our readership had better not be the sticklers for accuracy."

"I was editing out the before dinner part," she drawled, letting her gaze skim over Jared's face. His mouth was curled up at one corner, and his eyes were soft and liquid in the low light.

"So that means we're getting naked again later?"

"We'd better, if we've put it in the diary."

"So I can write the diary in advance, and then you have to complete every fantasy that's in it? *Awwright!* We're stopping at a stationery store on the way home. And we'd better not order dessert, because I have a lot of pages to fill tonight."

Shallis sat back and laughed.

She shouldn't enjoy this kind of conversation with Jared. It was—

No, okay, forget "shouldn't." She *did* enjoy it. It was fun. Skirting the edge of good taste at times, but with nothing one-sided about it. She wasn't fending off the suggestive one-liners from a man who held no attraction for her. She was enjoying the company of someone who could match her in so many areas, including trading smutty lines back and forth.

Jared was laughing, too, but when the laughter died out things suddenly got intense again. "Hey, I know you still have a lot of work to do with your mom on the contents of the houses, but next weekend…"

"Yes?"

"Want to…uh…" He stopped as if he didn't know the right way to finish.

"I want to do something, yes. See you," she said. "If that's what you mean."

And I don't want to play games about it, so that had better not be what you're doing, with this self-doubting-teen-in-a-grown-man's-body thing that's getting to me so bad. I gave myself some breathing space and it didn't work. I'm going full-on now.

"There's an estate sale I thought you might be interested in. Bigger than your grandmother's would be, but with some similarities in the contents. I'll send you the flyer. Your mother hasn't decided whether to go that route, yet. If you haven't been to something like that before, you might want to try it out and report back."

Oh. An estate sale.

"Oh, an estate sale?" She nodded brightly. "Yes, that might be useful. I can see if Mom's free."

"Much as I do like your mother, Shallis," he said, in a voice like a slow curl of smoke. "Please don't see if she's free. That wasn't what I meant."

"No?"

"No."

"Um, good. So what did you mean?"

"The sale's at two, but the house is open from ten, and it's on some very pretty acreage which is open, too, since the whole place is on the market. I thought we could take a picnic. Look at what's on offer, then sneak away and explore a little, come back at two for the sale."

"Is that going to be a popular move, as far as the owners are concerned?"

"The Starke law practice is handling the estate, and the family is pretty pleased with us so far."

"So as long as you put a clipboard and pen in the picnic basket…"

He laughed. "You're getting the idea."

"I was a little slow."

"Slow is good. I like slow, too."

And an hour later, back at her apartment, he proved it by taking their lovemaking very slow indeed.

Chapter Ten

Neither Shallis and Jared nor the people involved in running the estate sale at Clarewood had counted on rain the following Saturday. When Shallis had looked at the date on the flyer Jared had sent her yesterday, she'd realized it was his thirty-fourth birthday. Linnie had fussed over the occasion in each of the three years they'd dated during high school and college, and the date had lodged itself permanently in Shallis's head.

But the rain didn't care about sales or birthdays and came anyhow. It threatened all morning and commenced in bucket loads just as Jared pulled his car into a parking spot in the paved driveway. They ate their picnic in the vehicle, and the raindrops came sliding down the windscreen so thick and fast, they didn't even have time to take bets on which ones would hit the wipers first.

"It's lucky the auctioneer hadn't planned for the sale to

happen out of doors," Jared said. "I'm sorry about this. Do you want to bail out?"

"Actually, it's kind of nice." Shallis didn't want to tell him how nice, because that would sound too…um…*interested*. She didn't want to tell him about the impromptu birthday surprise she had planned for him, either.

He'd had the heater running while they drove, and the car was still warm. The windows steamed up, and the rain pattered and drummed like children's fingers in a kindergarten concert. It was cozy. And special, too, because how often did you sit in a foggy car in someone else's driveway on a hot date, eating thick sandwiches and drinking warm, sweet chocolate from a flask?

"Ready to go inside?" Jared asked when they'd finished eating. He sounded as if he wasn't. Like Shallis herself, he was in no hurry to break the mood.

"Not yet," she said. "Can you pop the trunk for me?"

"What, you want to warm up your rain jacket before you put it on?"

She had told him the rain jacket was in the extra bag she'd brought.

"That, and fizz up my bloodstream," she answered, grinning.

"Wh—?"

"You'll see."

She hadn't brought a rain jacket, she'd brought champagne and a cake. She'd even remembered candles, picnic champagne flutes and matches. Balancing the boxed cake on her lap, she opened the lid. "Ta-da!"

"Wow!" he said. Then in a slightly different tone, "Wow. It has a Boston Red Sox team logo on the frosting."

"It sure does." She beamed at him. "You can do that on cakes now, thanks to the miracle of modern technology."

"Um, Shallis, it may not be that tactful to tell you this, but my team is the Chicago White Sox. Socks, red, white, I know it's confusing."

"He thinks I don't know his team," she told the raindrops on the windshield. "He has no concept of my strategy, here. I've told you, Jared, you have to talk to my dad about the Shallis Duncan jinx factor. This was the only way I could celebrate your team without having them lose their next five games."

He frowned. "That many, huh?"

"Desperate times call for desperate deeds, or whatever. It didn't click that this was your birthday until yesterday, so I didn't have a lot of time to get clever." She fluttered her eyelashes at him. "Doncha wanna open the champagne?"

He laughed. "Hold out the glasses. And thanks. For thinking of this. And for not jinxing my team." Their eyes met for a moment, sparking and smoking and promising all sorts of things that had nothing to do with baseball, but then they let it go.

Later.

Jared eased the cork out of the bottle with his thumb, and foam swelled over the glass rim into the waiting flutes. They clinked the glasses together—or more like clunked, because they were picnic ware, made of plastic—and Shallis proposed a toast. "To the St. Louis Cardinals."

"And the Green Bay Packers."

"They're not even in the same sport, Jared."

He shrugged. "I'm spreading the risk."

"You're really catching onto this whole concept, now."

"I'm a fast learner."

"Got any other birthday celebrations planned?"

"Lunch with my mom tomorrow. Traditional Fourth of

July boating weekend in Florida with some guys. We always count it as a birthday thing for two of us, even though it's a month late for me and a week early for Luke. That's about it. This is going to be the most memorable of the three."

"Sitting in a damp car with champagne in plastic picnic glasses, eating the wrong baseball team's sugar logo with some cake attached?"

"Yeah, that's memorable. In the right company, it's unforgettable."

Their eyes met again. His dropped to her lips, promising a kiss he didn't intend to deliver just yet.

"Thanks, Jared," Shallis said, husky-voiced. "That's a nice compliment."

"You're welcome. The cake and champagne are nice compliments, too."

When they'd finished their cake and champagne, the rain still hadn't eased, so they made a dash for the house and spent an hour browsing the items in the sale. China and linen and books and tools. Silver and paintings and baseball cards and furniture.

"Going to bid on anything?" Jared asked.

"Actually there's a box of books that looked pretty interesting."

"I'd have thought you'd be done with old boxes of stuff, after the work you've been doing at your grandmother's and the Templeton sisters' lately."

"Those boxes were mainly letters and papers. Books are different. I saw a whole set of L. M. Montgomery first editions in there. Eight or nine, at least."

He gave an apologetic shrug. "L. M. who?"

"You don't know her? I guess not. She was my mom's favorite, as a child. The *Anne of Green Gables* series."

"Bid away, then. But don't let the champagne affect your judgment."

The sale began, with prices that zigzagged up and down, and lots in which odds and ends were grouped together in a way that sometimes made no sense to Shallis. Sometimes the prices made no sense, either. Who knew someone would pay so much for sets of old playing cards? Who knew the big, heavy sideboard in the dining room, numbered Lot 14, would get such a lackluster reception when its turn came up?

"This is interesting," she told Jared. "I'm not sure that Mom will want to go this route with Gram's things, though. A lot of these people aren't here to bid, they're just being nosy."

"She can work privately, through a selection of dealers, if she prefers."

"She might, I think. You gave me a couple of valuers' business cards. And she'll give a lot of things away to charity. She's not interested in squeezing out every last dollar."

"Here comes your box of books. Lot 27. Don't get carried away."

Well…she did. A specialist book dealer next to her said, "You overpaid. But you got some nice ones," then proceeded to bid up twice as high on the next box.

"Did you overpay, do you feel?" Jared asked. "Getting a dose of buyer's remorse?"

"No, I'm thrilled. This could get to be a habit. I love all these old books for young girls. *Little Women* and *What Katy Did* and *Hundreds of Things a Girl Can Make*."

"Ready to go?"

"Yes, I want to gloat over my stash in private."

"Your stash can visit my place for a while and the three of us can hang out."

"You're prepared to gloat with me?"

"Can think of worse ways to spend the rest of a rainy Saturday."

"Oh, but I never asked if you had your eye on anything. They're not even a third of the way through, here."

"Yeah, I have my eye on something, but she says she's ready to leave, and I'm okay with that. I'm even okay with watching her leaf through old books half the afternoon."

"She might prove distractable if you handle her right."

"Maybe I could read out some of the sexy bits."

"I hate to break it to you, Jared, but there are no sexy bits in *Anne of Green Gables*. Romantic bits, but no sexy bits."

"Romance is sexy."

"Guys are supposed to think it's the other way around. Sex is romantic."

"Some guys think both. Rare, incredible, highly bedworthy guys think both."

"And you're one of those?"

"I could be, in the right circumstances."

"Then I'd better provide them. How about we go to my place so I can bring the books inside?"

It was still raining when they reached Shallis's apartment. She ran ahead of Jared to unlock the door, while he carried the box of books. Slid through the gap beneath the door, she found a manila envelope scrawled with her mother's handwriting.

Jared put the books down in the middle of her square of living-room carpet and she told him, "I'd better take a look at this, in case it's important."

"You think I'm in that much of a hurry?"

"Oh, I mean, no, but—"

"You're absolutely right. I'm in that much of a hurry."

"Ah."

"But I have a little self-control. Open your envelope."

Shallis read her mother's message on the front, then decided out loud, "No, I won't look inside. Mom says she's found the letters from Ivy that match the ones from Gram about the yard man and the marriage proposal. Fills in a couple of gaps in the story, apparently, but it's not earth-shattering."

"Well, if you're looking for earth-shattering..."

Shallis was.

And Jared delivered.

The rain eased, then cleared away and they went for a half-run, half-power-walk that had their different exercise paces meeting in the middle. Late sun came out and made the wet grass steam. The bright flowers of azaleas and other late spring bloomers were soggy with rain. Foliage glistened, and everything smelled earthy and fresh.

Back at Shallis's apartment, it was five-thirty—the logical time at which to tell him she had plans for the evening, so she could give herself some more space. Problem was, she didn't want to. She didn't want to let go of this yet.

Jared didn't, either. "If you don't have anything on—friends or family—want to grab some pizza and eat at my place?" He leaned one knee against the arm of her couch and did some warm-down stretches, his breathing barely challenged by the slower than usual pace.

"You don't have anything on, yourself?"

"Yes, but mentally I've already canceled."

"Don't, if it's important."

"No, it's not." He didn't explain further, and she kicked herself for being too curious on the subject.

"Pizza at your place would be great, then." She knew that

his grandfather had gone back up to his mountain hideaway after just two nights spent in town for golfing with his friend, two weeks ago now. They'd have the place to themselves.

"We can pick up a movie, as well."

"No offers of taped British cooking shows and historical dramas, tonight?"

"I'm sorry, I know the evening won't be much of a thrill without those, but we have to ration our pleasures in this uncertain world."

"Right. Ration our pleasures. So I should expect to be tucked up alone in my own bed by ten?"

"Uh…no. Please. I don't care where you sleep or when, but tuck me up with you, okay?"

"Okay."

"And…you know…if you get lonely in the shower…"

"Ooh, terrible problem, loneliness in the shower. I struggle with it all the time."

"That's too bad. We can fix it right now, if you want."

"I want."

They didn't reach for their towels until the water ran cold.

When they got to his place, with two DVDs and hopefully only about ten minutes ahead of the pizza delivery, he told her, "I'd better call Shaun and cancel our pool game for tonight."

"Oh, that was your plan?"

"Semi-regular event. Very casual. He has a new and very colicky baby, so he's cancelled a couple of times lately. He's the only high school friend I still see. We cut each other a lot of slack."

"Know too much about each other?"

"Know just the right amount."

"Including the way you leveraged your position on the high school football team?"

"Including that. I know a couple of underhanded tactics he's used with his girlfriends in the past, also, but he's settled down since he got married. I tell him every time I see him that Christie's a better wife than he deserves."

"I bet he appreciates that."

"He's constantly and humbly grateful for the insight."

"And what does he tell you about the football thing?"

"That I would have gotten the quarterback spot anyhow, so why did I have to cheat? Next time you're in my office, let me show you my Sore Loser trophy."

He explained its history and Shallis laughed, felt something settle into place inside her—something peaceful and confident and nice.

This is right. I don't know where it's going, but for now it's right.

Their pizza arrived and they opened two beers and put on a DVD, and everything stayed right...even better than right...the whole evening.

Four hours later, Shallis shot awake for no apparent reason in the uneven darkness of Jared's bedroom and thought about something that she should have thought about much earlier in the week. Five days earlier, to be exact, because one thing she could be sure of since her doctor had put her on a contraceptive pill back in L.A. six months ago, her cycle was regular.

Except that this month it wasn't.

She took the kind that had twenty-one active pills followed by seven days of sugar pills. She'd finished the active ones last Friday and then, trusting to her memory and her diary, had thrown the sugar ones in the trash. She should have taken the first active one in the new packet this morning, but she hadn't thought of it because she'd been thinking about going to the estate sale with Jared.

And all last week, thinking about Jared, appreciating the fact that he was giving her time and letting her take this slowly, wishing he wasn't so damned patient and would start to take it lightning fast, she hadn't thought about the period that always started two days after she finished the active pills…

Deep breath.

Except that this month it hadn't.

Jared lay beside her, warm and heavy, breathing steadily, fast asleep, not wearing a stitch of clothing. Some light seeped around the edges of the drapes that covered the big window. Moonlight or a street lamp, Shallis couldn't tell. It made the shadows in the room look strange.

Why had she awoken so suddenly?

Couldn't be that her subconscious was trying to tell her something.

It was really annoying, because she knew it wouldn't be easy to drift back again, even with Jared setting such a great example of innocent and appetite-sated slumber beside her. She snuggled a little closer to him—close enough to feel the way his body fitted against the spoon-shaped curve of hers. Not wearing a stitch of clothing, either, she put her arm around him and felt it lift and fall gently with the rhythm of his breathing.

He didn't stir, so she had plenty of wide-awake opportunity to think about the little blip she'd belatedly cottoned onto.

I couldn't be pregnant.

I just couldn't.

I have been taking those little blue pills religiously every single day.

What had the doctor in Los Angeles said? That she might go the occasional month with only light bleeding. He hadn't mentioned no bleeding at all, but still...

I couldn't be pregnant.

I really couldn't.

Linnie and Ryan have been trying for more than three years, and I haven't been trying at all.

She remembered the complaint she'd made to Linnie last Friday when they'd found the packet of letters from Gram amongst Ivy Templeton's things—that she'd been looking through dull boxes of business letters and bank statements all day, and then Linnie went and hit the jackpot with something personal and interesting at her very first try.

Yeah, things like that happened in life. Some people worked and agonized and got nowhere, while others didn't even have to think about it and hit the jackpot at their very first try.

Only not this time.

Because she couldn't be pregnant.

For a start, she was having no symptoms. Point number two, she'd only just gotten going on her first sexual relationship since...well, in a long time, given the standard of men she'd met in L.A.

She tracked back through the past couple of weeks and counted. Eighteen days. She and Jared had first done the wild thing exactly eighteen days ago, but then they'd had a gap of ten days. Okay, so maybe eighteen days ago was theoretically the right timing if she hadn't been on the pill.

But I was. I am. I'm a modern, intelligent, responsible woman and I take contraception seriously, even when I leap into bed with my tragically nonpregnant sister's ex-boyfriend and heartbreaker, just like shallow beauty queens and ruthless corporate attorneys are supposed to do.

Outside, a car swished by and made new shapes of light and shadow angle through the room. A dog barked. Jared laughed in his sleep—Jared, who couldn't possibly have made her pregnant.

Shallis lay awake for another hour, convincing herself that it really wasn't possible, and when she got home the next morning, scandalously close to lunchtime, she did the not very intelligent, responsible or medically advisable thing and took both Saturday's and Sunday's little blue pills at the same time.

Jared had suggested a movie tomorrow night, but she'd turned him down with the suggestion that they call each other later in the week. What was that saying about locking the stable door after the horse had bolted?

There were also these things called pregnancy testing kits, expressly designed to put a woman's mind at rest, one way or the other, but she didn't pick one up because...

I just couldn't be.

None of it made sense. Not the suspicion, not fobbing Jared off, not taking two pills at once, or superstitiously refusing to consider a test. Linnie and Ryan had gone on their Caribbean vacation two days ago, and they'd be back Wednesday.

By then, she'd be over this ridiculous scare. She'd laugh at herself. And then she would pick up the phone and call Jared and say yes to the movie idea after all, because she wasn't going to be pregnant, and she was going to see Jared again.

Chapter Eleven

"So you read those letters?" Mom asked Shallis for the third time in as many days. They were on their way to the Douglas County Airport to pick up Linnie and Ryan after their vacation.

"Yes, last night." The other two times she'd had to answer no. Her mind had been…uh…on other things.

It was Tuesday.

Also known as Day Three of the pregnancy scare. Even when she had skimmed through the letters, Shallis had found it hard to concentrate on Ivy's neat, round handwriting. And she still hadn't seen Jared or picked up a pregnancy test, because…because…

"What did you think?" Mom said.

About what?

Oh, right. The letters.

"Pretty mushy and gushy," Shallis answered. "I'm not surprised that Gram was concerned."

"She took on too much concern for everyone else's problems, though, your grandmother." Mom's voice had an edge that concerned Shallis a lot. "I've found all sorts of thank-you cards from people she went the extra mile for. Names I recognize and names I don't, but even when I do recognize them it's not because Gram herself told me she contributed to someone's college tuition, or visited someone else in the hospital day after day for weeks."

"Don't sound so bitter about it, Mom. A lot of people feel that a good deed counts for less if they broadcast it around."

"We're not talking broadcasting, we're talking telling her own daughter."

"She was never a gossip."

"Then she carried discretion too far!"

Shallis asked gently, "Mom, do you really mind that much about hospital visits she didn't mention?"

"No. I don't. But I mind about Flip and Ivy and Rose. A lot. And that's spilling into everything else." With one hand on the wheel, she snatched a tissue from the box on the console between the car's two front seats and began dabbing at her eyes and nose and muttering under her breath about her makeup.

"Do you want to pull over?" Shallis suggested.

"I'm fine."

She wasn't fine. She was displacing her grief over Gram's death into this whole mystery over the Templetons and causing herself even more grief in the process, but Shallis couldn't tell her that, or coax her out of it. Maybe the displacement was necessary.

"Did you check that Linnie and Ryan's flight is on time?" she asked, wanting to change the subject.

"It was when it took off from Miami."

"Have you spoken to them? Gotten a postcard?"

"No, and I'm glad. They needed this time so much, Shallie, and I hope they didn't think about home once."

Linnie and Ryan certainly looked relaxed when they appeared out of the arrival gate. Shallis's expert eye took in the details. A salon hair treatment for Linnie, just as Shallis had wanted. Highlights, conditioning and a trim. Nicely done. A facial, too, if she wasn't mistaken. There was a certain glow.

And Ryan's walk had lost the stiff-hipped look that came from spending too much time on a horse. He had the fresh memory of sand between his toes instead, and he was holding Linnie's hand.

They all waved at each other, grinned and hugged.

"We didn't want to come home," Linnie said wrapping her arms warm and tight around Shallis and Mom in turn. "Only now that we've landed... How is everything, Mom? Where's Dad?"

"Hosing the barn floor so we can lick our dinner off it tonight, from what I could tell when I last saw him. I tried to tell him your standards weren't that high, Ryan, but he didn't believe me."

"Because his standards *are* that high, aren't they, sweetheart?" Linnie hugged her husband's arm, leaned in and kissed his cheek.

Ryan slid his hand down her back and gave her bottom a squeeze which he obviously didn't think Shallis could see.

Wrong. She saw it, and she loved it.

Her heart flooded with relief and she almost cried.

"We made a decision, Mom," Linnie said. "I'm going to take a year off teaching. To unwind a little, support Ryan more, get the bed and breakfast cabins up and running and do the math on how much it contributes to our income. If it's paying its way, I'll go back to teaching and we'll take on some paid help."

"You might be pr—" Mom began. She stopped when Shallis glared at her.

Pregnant by then and not ready to go back to your school? *Don't say it, Mom!*

"—able to take on paid help sooner than that if it's going real well," Mom said instead.

"Good save," Shallis murmured as Linnie and Ryan walked ahead of them to the baggage carousel.

"Thanks for heading me off at the pass, Shallie. I want to bite my tongue out, sometimes. Caring this much can make a person real tactless sometimes, and Linnie and I are both trying so hard to be close right now!"

"I know. But they look good, don't you think? She might not have gotten pregnant, but their marriage looks in better shape."

The phone jangled Jared out of sleep at a time of night when his body's sluggish state told him no one should be calling. It was right beside his bed and he lunged for it, expecting a prank call or a wrong number or someone with slurred speech in search of friends to continue a Friday night party.

Instead, he heard his mother. "Jared?"

"What's wrong?" Because just the shaky sound of his name told him that something was.

"I'm calling from the county hospital. It's your grandfather."

His body chilled as if he'd jumped into an ice-encrusted pond. "He's okay? Tell me he's okay."

"He's had a heart attack. He managed to call 911 on his cell from the cabin, I don't know how."

"How bad?"

"They don't know yet. They're still getting him stable. They called me twenty minutes ago, and I was so—I should have called you from home. I'm sorry."

"It's okay. I'll be there in ten minutes."

When Jared reached the hospital, Abe was still lying in a curtained-off bed in the E.R. with his daughter-in-law seated on a chair beside him. He had monitors and leads snaking out of him like railroads snaking out of a big city, but he looked better than Jared had feared, and there was no tense knot of medical personnel working frantically over him. He had a little color in his face, his eyes were open, and he managed a smile.

The smile didn't last long. It drained away as soon as he tried to talk, and after a couple of words, he just shook his head.

"Don't try," Jared told him. "There's nothing you have to say."

"There is. Important."

"That important? Can't it wait until morning?"

"What if I don't make it until—?"

"Just shush, Abe," Mom scolded him. "We would have six doctors and nurses still hovering over you if they thought you were in any danger of not making it until morning."

With a stubborn look on his face, Grandpa Abe closed his eyes and lay still and silent, as if taking some time to gather his strength. He was clearly on a mission, and he wasn't going to listen to reason from anyone.

"Any idea what he's on about?" Jared murmured to his mother.

They both moved away from the bed and Mom kept her voice low, also.

"Oh, I can guess, I think," she said. She sounded uncomfortable.

"Then you tell me, since he can't. If he's left the gas switched on up at the cabin, or whatever, I can head up there and deal with it." In his heart he knew it wasn't something like that. He had a strange tingly feeling in his spine, and his legs felt as hollow as dried-out gourds.

Mom shook her head. "This is something he and I have been fighting about for years. And I knew this would happen. He told me the other day—three weeks ago, I guess, the last time we all had lunch—that I could do what I liked once he was gone, but I knew when it came to the crunch that's the last thing he'd want. He'll want to be here, oversee the whole thing, make sure it's done his way."

"What's done his way?"

"You know, Jared, the good and wise King Solomons of this world like to be in control just as much as the evil despots do, if that makes sense."

Jared sighed. "Not really, Mom."

They both heard Grandpa attempting to speak, and it was terrible to hear how feeble he sounded. "What're you saying to him, Judy? I need to be part of this. I have to."

"See what I mean?" she muttered.

"Okay, spill, Mom, you're scaring me."

"What you said at lunch the other day about secrets—" she began.

Grandpa cut in, struggling to drag himself up higher on his pillows. "Come *over* here, darn it, Judy! Don't you dare, after all this time—" He stopped, panting for breath.

"All right, old man." Jared's mother stepped back to the bed and cupped her hand against her father-in-law's cheek. "Stop me if you don't approve how I'm doing it, okay?" she drawled.

"I will!"

"Oh, I know you will!" She touched his cheek again, in a physical demonstration of the kind of love that definitely wasn't blind. She knew all her father-in-law's faults, but cared about him anyhow.

Then she turned to Jared. "Son, there isn't a pretty way to say this."

"Judy—"

"Let me do it my way, Abe. Jared, your grandfather has spent the past fifteen years convincing me not to say it at all, but now he's changed his mind because he thinks he's on death's doorstep and he wants to put in his version of the story, and so there's nothing to hold me back anymore."

"Okay." Jared nodded cautiously, his legs still oddly unwilling to move, or even bend so that he could sit.

"You see…" She trailed off, took a deep breath, tried again. "You see, your dad wasn't your biological father." She waited for a heartbeat or two, but Jared's throat had closed over and he couldn't speak.

Or even react.

It was like an out-of-body experience. A part of him listened. A part of him felt numb. A part of him analyzed those last four words with a lawyer's sense of language and realized, okay, she's not saying I'm adopted, she's saying something else, something worse. And a really strange part of him wanted to burst out laughing at how sheerly and utterly weird and impossible this felt.

We *know* secrets in this family, yes, all sorts of secrets, but we don't *have* them. We keep *other* people's secrets. That's the way it works for the Starkes, after four generations in the law. We guard people's secrets with professional discretion and care. But we don't have secrets of our own. Not secrets like this.

Mom apparently didn't need to chip at him with a mason's chisel to understand that he'd turned to stone. She kept going—steady voice, careful words. Behind Grandpa's head, some piece of equipment started a low, irritating beep which all three of them ignored. "I gave birth to you, yes, but I didn't get pregnant by Ray, I had a stupid, starry-eyed fling with a…well, in hindsight a scummy guy…while your dad was away in law school."

"Tell him that I said—" Grandpa began.

"Of course I'll tell him what happened next. Your father—or Ray, I should say. No, to hell with it, Jared, I'm going to keep calling him your father because he *was* your father in every way that counted—he was pretty angry and upset. We'd been going out for a while. He hadn't proposed officially, but he'd thought it was understood between us. And it was, or it would have been, if I hadn't been so naive and silly and lacking in trust. I wanted a ring, and Ray hadn't given me one. Anyhow, he talked to your grandfather and I don't know what you said, Abe, because neither you nor Ray were somehow *ever* able to report enough detail on the talk you had…"

"Bottom line that counts," he said.

"Yes, but women like a little detail to back it up, you know!"

"Told my son to marry her anyway, Jared."

"Stop it, Abe, I'm the one who's saying this," Mom said, but Grandpa was on a roll now.

"Told him your mother was young and she'd made a mistake and she wasn't the only woman in town to have been conned by Grausam."

"By—" Jared croaked out.

"Yes, yes, you know the name, now, thanks to little Miss America, there, reading through all those letters of her grandmother's, like they were a bestselling novel." Grandpa paused and struggled for breath, but he looked stronger now, energized by his need to speak. "Same man who convinced Ivy Templeton he wanted to marry her, even though she was well in her forties and he was thirty-three and they'd only known each other a few weeks. Same man who conned forty thousand dollars out of poor Ivy for some nonexistent operation for his nonexistent mother and then skipped town and disappeared."

"Forty thousand."

"Ivy was old enough to know better. Your mom was just twenty-one, and if my son had done the right thing and proposed to her before he went off to law school, it never would have happened.

"'I know you love her, Ray,' I told him. 'So if you can raise the baby as your own, if you can give it every scrap of love and attention and pride you'd have given your biological child, then marry her. If you can't do that, if there's going to be a speck of resentment or withheld feeling, if you think you'll ever once hold the past over Judy's head or punish her for it, or even worse punish the child, then cut loose now. This may be the biggest decision of your life, son, so get it right, and then follow through.' Didn't soften it, just said it. Like I'm doing now, because there's no time left for me."

"Abe, don't say that!" Jared's mother scolded him.

"And Ray thought about it, and he made his decision. And the two of you were happy for twenty years, Judy, isn't that right? Until he started commuting to Nashville and you both grew apart."

Mom was half-laughing, half-crying by this time. "Almost thirty-five years, Abe, and I've just gotten more detail from you about what you said to Ray, here on what you think is your deathbed, than you've ever managed to give me before!"

"Maybe I am on my deathbed, and that's why!"

"A man on his deathbed can't manage a speech that long."

"Stop it, you two," Jared said. Still croaky. Still with a heck of a lot of unanswered questions. He managed to get out one of them. "Why didn't you have more kids of your own, Mom? Belonging to both of you, I mean."

Again, it was his grandfather who answered. "Because Ray couldn't, as it turned out. Tried for a long time. Hoped for a miracle. But it didn't happen."

"I think when he finally accepted it wasn't going to, that was when we first started to have problems," Mom said. "Without that, we might have been okay until the end."

"And does this happen to have anything to do with why Caroline McLenaghan never told her daughter that she'd been Flip Templeton's lover and that she owned his sisters' house?" Jared asked.

Grandpa Abe got fretful again, and less direct. "Oh, that's complicated."

"Did Mrs. McLenaghan know about our family's personal angle? Did she know that Stewart Grausam was my father?"

Grandpa hesitated before he spoke, but finally admitted, "Yes, she did."

"And she didn't see that that was why you didn't want her to tell her own daughter about Flip and Ivy and Rose? I'm assuming it was you who pushed her in that direction, and I'm assuming Grausam is the reason why…" Jared let the comment trail off, baiting his hook for his grandfather's answer.

"I told you, it's complicated," Grandpa repeated. "I'm certainly the one who urged secrecy on her, and I guess, yes, I did have my own reasons, beyond the fact that it was a protection for the sisters themselves if no one knew who really owned their house or paid their expenses."

"What reasons, Grandpa? Get a little clearer on those, could you?"

"Protecting you and Judy and Ray. Cascade effect gets going. One thing comes out, and people ask questions, and that brings down the whole kit 'n caboodle on everyone's heads. Couldn't see the point. Could see all of the risks and none of the advantages. In my position, you start to conclude that honesty is overrated. Didn't want you to know who fathered you, Jared, because how could it do you any good?"

"You mean because he was pond-scum."

Neither his mother nor his grandfather denied the statement.

Nobody spoke at all for what had to be two or three minutes.

A nurse appeared, checked the monitors and the IV, got rid of that annoying beep, took Grandpa Abe's blood pressure and pulse, made a couple of notes on a chart, then looked at the three of them suspiciously.

"Someone's been upsetting someone." Must have been some give away detail in the quality of their silence, Jared decided. She looked like a pretty experienced nurse. "Mr. Starke?" she asked, bending toward her patient. "Need some peace and quiet?"

"Family stuff," he growled. "Don't send 'em away. I'm fine."

"You seem to be," the nurse agreed. "Medication's going in, doing what we wanted it to. Heart rhythm's making a pretty pattern. Doctor's going to be real pleased, when he's back with you in a couple of minutes."

"You're telling me I'm not going to be dead before morning?"

"Just you try that kind of a trick and see what happens!"

"You're serious? I'm really not going to be dead?" He still

sounded scared, and almost penitent, like a little boy who's sure he's going to get punished and can't believe it when he hears that he's not.

Jared understood that this must have been a huge wake-up call for his grandfather, to have made him so desperate to unlock a secret he'd convinced his son and daughter-in-law to hold for so long.

The nurse put her hands on her ample hips and fixed Grandpa with a look that was almost a glare. "Do you want to be, dearie?"

"Hell, no!"

"Good, because you'd be up for a disappointment."

She left, and Grandpa slumped back in the bed. "I'm a silly old fool!" he said. And then he laughed. After a moment, he shot a sharp glance at Jared. "You going to be okay with this, son? It shouldn't change anything. It can't and won't, after thirty-five years. It doesn't!"

"No, I guess it doesn't," Jared agreed, because he wasn't going to argue to the point with an eighty-two year old man in an E.R. bed.

But in his heart he wasn't so sure.

Maybe it changed everything.

Chapter Twelve

Pregnancy scare Day 9—although most people would probably think of it as the second Monday in June.

Shallis woke up when the alarm on her clock-radio buzzed at seven, feeling sluggish and tired and bad-tempered and edgy, none of which she could afford. Five days from now, the Grand Regency would host its biggest wedding of the season—the kind where Shallis bent over backward to accommodate the couple's every whim.

The thirty-year-old bride was wealthy. She divided her time between glittering social scenes in Nashville and New York, she had lots of gorgeous friends of marriageable age and if she loved the Victorian-era luxury and charm of her wedding reception venue she would talk about it far and wide, and the Grand Regency would get more big, lucrative weddings in the future.

"As if I'd want more brides like this one in my lifetime,"

Shallis muttered to herself in the shower, soaping her body and refusing to believe in the way it had recently changed. Her breasts were so tender and swollen, they felt like a clinical description of the mumps.

She'd already dealt with at least a dozen panicky changes to the Lancaster-D'Emilio wedding reception menu, decor, entertainment, table layout and cake, and since the bride wasn't working with a wedding planner because she believed in "personal attention to detail" it all happened in the most hysterical, least professional way possible, which meant that Shallis had to—

Coffee.

She needed coffee, brimming to the top of the biggest mug in her kitchen, before she even got dressed. Wrapped in a robe, she filled her two-cup plunger with rich dark grounds, added boiling water, sniffed in some urgent molecules of caffeine from the rising steam...and almost threw up.

Eww! When she wanted it so bad, why did it not smell good?

I'm tense. I need...

Chips. Nice, salty, crunchy original flavor kettle-cooked potato chips to settle this weird feeling in her stomach.

It's the stress over the Lancaster-D'Emilio wedding, that's all. I'm not even going to think about the other possibility.

She found an eight-ounce packet of chips in back of her pantry cupboard, ate most of them, drank a quarter of the coffee and chased it down with water because...maybe the grounds were stale. Maybe that was why they didn't taste right. The packet had sat open in her pantry for too long. She often waited for her breakfast coffee until she got in to work.

At work there was a message already waiting for her from Courtney Lancaster. Courtney wanted to change the menu again, as well as one tiny, tiny insignificant detail about the cake.

Half an hour later, thanks to years of military-style training in charm, Shallis came away from the head chef's chaotic office just off the hotel kitchen without having lost any fingers to any of his large, steely-sharp knives and with an agreement that, yes, three out of the four proposed menu changes were possible this late in the process but, no, changing the cake frosting from white royal icing to chocolate petals on a five-tier masterpiece that was scheduled to be photographed out of doors at around four in the afternoon in Tennessee's June heat for a lavish spread in *Wedding Belle* magazine was just not going to work.

Fighting a headache, she broke the news to Courtney, who insisted that there had to be a special kind of no-melt chocolate available. Back in the kitchen, the head chef assured Shallis that there wasn't, if you actually wanted it to taste anything like real chocolate. He suggested moving the cake photography indoors, including the special canopy of climbing roses that Courtney had designed for the cake-cutting ceremony herself and was paying a fortune to her florist to create.

Courtney didn't want to move the cake photos or the cake-cutting canopy indoors, nor did she want to risk upsetting the people from *Wedding Belle*. She announced her intention of researching dry ice, instead.

Shallis attempted to drink another cup of coffee, brewed at the hotel's five-star restaurant coffee station.

More *eww*.

Fighting nausea as well as the headache, she gave a detailed tour of the hotel's wedding facilities for a proposed six-course dinner reception in October to a couple who acted as if they were highly likely to break up before the end of the week, and an equally detailed rundown of the conference facilities to a woman who promised an attendance of "somewhere between fifty and four hundred" and didn't see why she needed to narrow down that range until two weeks in advance of the event.

When lunchtime arrived, Shallis didn't even try for more coffee, just headed straight for the nearest sandwich shop and had plain turkey breast on whole wheat. Then she drove all the way to Carrollton so that she wouldn't be recognized by any drugstore staff and bought a pregnancy test which sat like a smoking gun in her purse all afternoon.

Just before leaving for the day, she won an apologetic, effusive victory in the royal icing versus chocolate petals standoff. "I'm *so* sorry I gave you such a hard time today, Shallis!" This made her remember why she mostly loved her job—poor stressed out Courtney, she had acute bridal jitters and she was a perfectionist and the two didn't sit well together, but she was going to love her special day—and then Mom called.

"Two things, honey."

"Yes, Mom?"

"I was out at Linnie and Ryan's today, and you know how regular her cycle is, and I've been keeping count—"

"Which you shouldn't do, Mom, seriously! How does that help anyone?"

"I can't help it, honey. I'm so racked over it, and my mind just works that way and I know hers does, too. That way, for once, she and I are alike. And it's twenty-eight days, and you know how sensitive those tests are now, and—"

"You're trying to tell me she's *pregnant?*"

And some weird sister-related transference thing is going on and I'm the one having the symptoms?

Shallis almost let out a whoop of happiness and relief.

"Well, no."

"*No?* All that build up and *no?*"

"Not definitely. Not that I know."

"Well, thanks for the burst balloon!"

"But Shallie, the thing is, she hadn't been crying. And she was walking around practically on tip-toe, as if she hardly dared to breathe, and when she went to the bathroom she had a completely different look on her face when she came out to how she looked when she went in—a hopeful look, instead of terrified—so I'm thinking she has her fingers crossed about it, she has reason to hope, and I'm wondering if I should suggest that she puts herself out of suspense and takes a—"

"No. Absolutely *totally* no, Mom."

Shallis looked at her black leather purse sitting on the desk. Yeah, was that a wisp of smoke rising from it? She wouldn't have been surprised to hear the *whoosh* of spontaneous combustion and witness an eruption of crackling flames.

"Do *not* suggest that she takes a test," she told her mother. "Don't you realize the games she's probably playing with herself about it? Taking a test is a huge thing. Buying a test is a huge thing. It has superstitions attached to it like shiny Christmas balls on a tree. She's not even going to think of buying a test for days, because she's sure that as soon as she does, she won't be pregnant."

Oh.

So that's the real reason *I* bought the test, to make me *not* pregnant.

The upside-down logic made total sense.

"She might not ever do a test," Shallis predicted. "And she's probably wishing right now that tests had never been invented."

The way I am.

Mom sighed down the phone. "Okay."

"Just like that?"

"Oh, I knew all of that. I did. I just needed to have someone else tell me, and I knew your father would tell me in three words, subject closed, and I needed the detail. Men just don't do detail like women, do they? So thanks, honey."

Shallis sighed, also. "You're welcome, Mom. But I might start charging you for the service. You said there were two things?"

"Oh, that's right." Mom's tone changed. "Abraham Starke had a heart attack on Friday night."

Shallis's stomach flipped. Ug. The flip felt as bad as coffee smelled, and the news was not something she felt equipped to hear, right now. "Omilord!" was all she could say, and she was glad she was still sitting down. "Oh, no!" Her mind flew at once to Jared—flight time about two seconds, since he wasn't far from her thoughts already.

"I had a phone call from his office this morning. From the receptionist, but then I called Jared back and got more detail. Abe is doing well, and his doctors are optimistic, but he's still in the hospital. They're planning a bypass operation sometime this week. Jared sounded pretty cut up about it. He has a good soul, in some ways. He's always been very loyal to his parents and his grandfather."

But he hasn't called.

And I haven't called him.

And is my purse glowing red hot, or is it just a trick of the light?

"Yes, he does have a good soul," Shallis said out loud.

"I wouldn't have expected it, but I think he's changed these past six years."

"Don't sound so surprised, Mom. People do change. They can, I believe, if they try."

"Mmm, maybe." But Mom didn't want to talk about how much Jared Starke might have changed. "I thought your father and I would visit Abe in the hospital tonight. We may not get to see him, because cardiac patients have restrictions on visitors, but we can leave flowers. You'll want us to add your name to the card, won't you?"

"Yes, please. I'll go see him myself later in the week."

"And will you try and get out to the farm to see Linnie, too? Because I want to hear your impression on whether she might be—"

"No, Mom. I'm not going to look for impressions. I'm not going to risk Linnie guessing that we're watching her every move and every expression on her face. We'll know soon enough, one way or the other. Let's leave her alone."

A wave of deep nausea hit Shallis as soon as she got off the phone.

I can't be pregnant, because if Linnie isn't…

I have to take that test, because if I am, then telling the baby's father is going to be the easiest of a whole raft of tough conversations, and I'm going to need time to prepare.

Is my purse actually rattling *now?*

Ten minutes later the purse wasn't rattling, because the test wasn't in it anymore. The test was sitting in the cream porcelain sink of the freshly cleaned administrative staff bathroom at the Grand Regency Hotel. And it was positive. Deep purple in all the wrong places.

Back in her office, with the door tight shut and a chair propped under the handle—certain people such as Mr. Lonsdale didn't always knock—Shallis called the Ask-a-Nurse service listed in the phone directory. She had to key in the number three times to get it right. She then told the female voice at the other end of the line exactly why it couldn't be possible that she was pregnant.

She desperately wanted to tell the nurse, also, why she absolutely couldn't afford to be pregnant, why she didn't dare to be pregnant, and why she would suffer so much thinking about Linnie if she was pregnant and Linnie wasn't, but managed not to get quite so personal. She also managed not to mention her feelings about the baby's father, because she didn't know what they were.

The nurse drew her attention to some of the fine print in the instructions for those little blue pills and the penny dropped.

That stomach upset. That vague and annoying but totally insignificant stomach upset she'd had the weekend before encountering Jared in his grandfather's office for the first time four weeks ago. When you had a stomach upset, you could lose your hormonal protection for the rest of that month. She hadn't even thought about it.

"And that's all it can take?"

"That's all it can take," the nurse agreed, then suggested prenatal counselling and an appointment with an obstetrician.

Shallis knew she didn't need the prenatal counselling. The only thing worse than being pregnant when her sister was the one who so desperately wanted to be, would be if she terminated the pregnancy or gave the baby up.

Linnie would never forgive her.

She'd never forgive herself.

She did need the appointment with the obstetrician. She was going ahead with this.

At the moment, it was "this," it wasn't a baby, because that was too enormous and life-changing to think about. In the abstract, yes, she'd always assumed she'd have children someday, but she'd never thought it would happen like this. Beauty queens were organized when it came to their bodies. And they were in control.

Take it in small steps, Shallis, she told herself.

Baby steps.

I can't tell Linnie or Mom, yet...

Instead, she would start easy, and tell Jared, work up to the really tough ones later.

Yeah. Right. Pressing the electric bell at the Starke house on Chestnut Street at a quarter till six, she revised her use of the word "easy." Nothing about this could possibly fit that label.

Jared looked terrible when he opened the door to her just when she was on the point of concluding that he wasn't at home, and her first thought was his grandfather. Could Mr. Starke have taken a turn for the worse? She asked Jared about it at once and he shook his head.

"No, he's doing fine...great. Are you coming in?"

"Um, if you're not busy."

"Let me just—" He didn't finish the sentence, just disappeared inside and went along past the stairs to the little room off the back hallway that he was using as a home office. Shallis closed the front door behind her and followed him, in time to see his computer screen darken at the touch of a key.

Coming out of the room again, he kissed her and squeezed her arm. The squeeze was too tight and the kiss was as short and pecklike and absent in spirit as if they'd been married a hundred years and bored with each other for most of them. In a reflex gesture, Shallis touched her fingers to her mouth and he noticed and kissed her again.

Much better this time. He lingered a little, parted his lips, touched her hair, whispered an apology. But his heart still wasn't in it.

Meanwhile, Shallis's heart was in her mouth.

I hate this. I don't know what it is, but I hate it because I know it's not going to be good.

"Want to grab a beer and sit out back?" he said.

"Um, sure. Maybe a few pretzels…?" Because that anti-nausea salt craving was back again. She hadn't eaten enough today, and a stomach that was both empty and churning felt… *Eww!*

"Pretzels and beer. Perfect." His tone seemed flat.

He looked as if he hadn't shaved in three days, and if he'd been to the office today he wasn't dressed like an attorney now. He wore a gray sweatshirt so ancient that he'd at some point, probably around five years ago, cut the sleeves off at bicep height to turn the top into a T-shirt. This was teamed with sweatpants that would have matched the top except that he'd recently used them to paint the outdoor furniture in.

Shallis knew it was the outdoor furniture because when she sat down in one of the Adirondack chairs on the deck in the balmy June air, she could see it was the same forest-green color as the messy splodges on the fabric. And she knew it was recent work because both the furniture and the splodges looked bright and fresh.

Strange what a person's mind chose to focus on at a time like this.

Jared brought the pretzels out still in the packet, and his own beer in the can, but he'd managed one concession to etiquette and poured Shallis's beer into a big glass, which was somewhat of a waste since she only intended on drinking a few token sips. Maybe that might be a good way to introduce the subject?

You may wonder why I'm not drinking much tonight, Jared, wanna guess?

No.

She took a handful of pretzels and felt her whole body burning with nerves. "Is he in good spirits, though, your grandfather?" she asked.

"Getting bored. Better than the phase when he was seeing the Grim Reaper in the doorway."

"Like my ghosts at Number 56."

"No," he answered heavily. "Not like that."

Okay, so we're not doing humor tonight.

"I guess you've been sitting with him, not getting much sleep."

Small silence.

Shallis replayed her last words inside her head. How pathetic, working so hard to find Jared's excuses for him.

It was a gorgeous afternoon, heading into evening with a slow softening of the light. The spring green glowed on the trees, and a neighbor's cat streaked across the grass like an antelope on an African plain, glad to be alive. In theory, Shallis was glad to be alive, also, but if she could have changed places with the cat at that moment, she would probably have done it.

"I'm sorry, Shallis." Jared looked across at her, eyes narrow and tired, blind to the beauty of the day. "Something's happened. I've got a few things to think about. This is nothing to do with you." He stopped, as if listening to what he'd just said. "I don't know if it has anything to do with you," he corrected himself. "At the moment, it's just about me…"

Good time to tell you I'm pregnant, then, obviously.

"…but I guess that could change."

"Would you care to apply a little legalese to that statement, Jared? I'm not finding it confusing enough, yet."

He laughed—one gruff, weary bark of sound.

Bi-i-ig silence, this time.

Shallis focused on the pretzels because now her stomach was churning like an industrial washing machine. Nature seemed to be protecting her unborn child against harmful substances, because the beer tasted worse than her breakfast coffee. She put it down on the deck beside her chair and doubted that Jared would even notice.

Jared knew that Shallis had to have noticed how much of a mess he was, even before his cryptic apology.

Had to have noticed. She seemed a little stiff and vague and off-line in response, and he didn't like seeing her this way, didn't like doing this to her. But he couldn't find it in him to pretend, to drag the usual smooth, adept facade back into place.

In any case, he knew he had to tell her about what he'd learned from his mother and grandfather on Friday night. He owed her that much, because he suspected it might be all he had left to give her. They'd done pretty well with honesty so far, the two of them. Shame to spoil their track record now.

"You wanted me to tell you if I came across the name Stewart Grausam in any other context," he said, breaking the silence at a point where it was so uncomfortable that the air seemed to shriek.

Shallis sat up straighter, leaned forward, wrapped her hands around her trouser-clad knee, squeezed a different expression onto her tense, beautiful face. "Oh, and you obviously have. And obviously it's important."

She had her hair twisted on top of her head today, in what might have been a casual, thirty-second maneuver or might be that fake untidy look that took hours to achieve. She wore a clingy, short-sleeved knit top that matched the trousers.

Both were colored a subtle green that was probably called Eau de Something. Jared didn't know, didn't care, just liked how the little touches of gold jewelry looked against the soft shade, and liked even more what it did to the color of her eyes.

Today, that sort of liking didn't feel good, it just felt like an ambient ache centered somewhere in his chest—the kind of pain that Grandpa Abe would feel after his bypass when the medication began to wear off.

"Don't keep me in suspense, Jared. That's the last thing I need. *Is* it important? I'm guessing it has to be."

"Uh, yeah. Important to me. Stewart Grausam was my father."

He told her the story.

He couldn't tell her quite what it was doing to him, or why, probably because he didn't understand himself yet just why this had hit him so hard, why it had changed so much. So he didn't hit the clean center of the honesty target, and it all came out more cynical and hard-edged than he meant it to, as if it didn't much matter to him who his father was. He dimly recognized that this was wrong and unfair, so he compensated by moving quickly to how it concerned Shallis and her family.

"So there's been a hidden agenda on my grandfather's part from the beginning," he told her. "And I have to apologize for that on his behalf. He was the one to urge secrecy on your grandmother all these years, regarding her past with Flip Templeton and her ownership of the house. He still insists that the Templeton sisters needed the secrecy as a protection against other men like—"

He stopped. *My father.* He couldn't say it. His father was Dad…Ray Starke…the man his mother had married.

"—Grausam." He took a controlled breath. "But he admits

that he had our family's interests in mind, also. I don't need to explain that, do I?"

"No, I— It makes sense."

Jared watched her watching him, seeing her wariness and her concern.

Yeah, you don't know how I'm taking this, do you, Shallis? You don't want to say the wrong thing. You're wondering how much blood and genes count. Don't worry, I'm wondering the same thing.

"Are you going to try tracing him, Jared? Does anyone know if he's still alive?"

Jared hedged for a moment on that one. "To be honest, I think my grandfather was hoping he wouldn't be. He didn't want me to look for him."

"And your mother?"

"Understands why I had to."

"Had to. So you do have to? And you've started."

Better than that. Or worse…

"I've found him. With an unusual name like that, and knowing his approximate age, it wasn't hard. Now I just have to decide what I want to do with the information."

"Is he still in the area?"

"Chicago. Ironically enough."

She didn't need him to explain the irony. He'd left Hyattville thinking that he was moving on from his family's clearly defined traditions, when instead he was conforming to an even truer pattern that he'd known nothing about. She understood that. He could tell by the watchful expression and the little nod. "So you might arrange a meeting, if he's willing, and fly up there?"

"If I can fix it for a weekend. With Grandpa in the hospital, I can't abandon the practice."

"What would you be hoping for?"

He laughed at that one. "Do me a favor and you tell me. That may be the only reason I haven't yet picked up the phone. I'm not sure what I'd be hoping for. I'm not sure of anything. I have to be honest about that, Shallis." To make sure she didn't miss the significance to her in what he was saying, he repeated it. "Right now, in my life, I'm not sure about anything at all."

Her face changed, and she nodded.

Okay.

Message received and understood.

He stood up, not so much ready for her to leave as finding it unbearable to keep her here, when he didn't have anything to offer or even anything left to say. She followed his lead, looking as numb and bewildered as he felt. Moving toward the French door that opened from the screened-in porch onto the deck, they met up and he couldn't stop himself from reaching out and putting a hand on her arm.

Mistake.

The contact of skin on skin froze them both in place. His fingers slid across the soft swell of her muscle and nudged into the crook of her elbow, where she felt as fine and silky and warm as a rich fabric draped in the sun. They arrived in a kind of monkey grip, each clutching the other by that one safe piece of arm—a tree branch in a raging current, or something.

Shallis's mouth was pressed tight shut, damming back what looked like a million things she wanted to say but wasn't going to, and he told her on a croaky rush of breath, "I appreciate *so much* that you're not delivering a speech about this. No advice, no wisdom, no accusations. Really, Shallis, I can't tell you! I just don't need it or want it right now, when I have no clue what this news does to my future, and the fact that you understand that and you're not doing it… Man! To say I appreciate it, it's not strong enough."

Still gripping his arm, she lifted her free hand to his face, stroked it from his forehead down to his jaw. "I'd better not kiss you," she said. "I think that would be—"

"Yeah. Okay. Yeah, it would."

A kiss would be wrong. Too much. Inappropriate to the current state of their relationship, under the circumstances.

Thinking this, he wanted to do it anyhow, and the desire surged through him like wildfire. Wouldn't the smell of her and the taste of her put the universe back in balance? Wouldn't it solve everything?

Damn it, let's get a little less ambitious, here! Wouldn't it just *feel* good, and allow him to pretend for a while?

Her mouth stayed closed and motionless, its shape so perfect, its color so soft and pink. His center of gravity dropped low into his groin, which felt as heavy as base metal.

Kiss her, Jared.

Just once.

Goodbye, maybe.

Goodbye, more than likely.

Did he really belong in Hyattville now, taking over Abraham Starke's law practice? He didn't think so. He belonged in Chicago, scamming his way to a comfortable old age like Stewart Grausam, armed with a law degree so that he knew how to keep everything just the right side of legal.

Don't think about that. Don't think about anything. Just do it. Kiss her. She's waiting for it, isn't she? That's what the frown and the big, troubled eyes and the still, expectant mouth are all about. That's the reason for the little lap of her tongue-tip at the seam of her lips. That's the reason for the sharp in-breath.

Isn't it?

No.

It wasn't.

"Small complication in all this, Jared," she said. "It's only fair to tell you. I'm pregnant."

Jared had never been sucker punched before. He'd had no idea that *anything* could flatten a man's lungs so fast.

Chapter Thirteen

Somehow, Shallis got herself out of Jared's house, into her car and home to her apartment.

Without crying.

Without yelling.

Without hitting him.

Understanding that the yawning chasm between them had just gotten twice as wide in the space of the past half hour. Not blaming him for it. Not blaming herself, either. No idea in heaven or on earth what to do.

Raise a baby on her own.

Break her sister's heart.

Lie to her child about who its father was.

She had no choice about the first two, but the third she could control. She wouldn't lie and she wouldn't keep secrets, the way her family and Jared's had done. Her child would be told, and so would anyone else who had the right to an answer.

Although not quite yet.

It seemed pretty clear that Jared wouldn't actually be around to make his role as a father obvious to the whole world at first glance. She'd never seen such an appalled reaction to any piece of news. He'd looked like the underdog boxer in the last round of a fight, when the impact had first hit home.

Then when she'd explained a little—pointless detail about the stomach upset, that first Tuesday night on Chestnut Street, the testing kit and the call to Ask-a-Nurse—he'd just closed off, gotten the same hard, guarded expression on his face that Stewart Grausam had no doubt worn a few times in his life, also.

She's pregnant? I'm not going to give her any leverage by agreeing that it must be mine. Just get me outta here!

He'd told her, "I'm sorry, this is the worst time. I'm sorry, I know you're not in control of that. I'm just… Sorry. I need— I don't know what I need. Time. Space. I'm sorry."

Yeah, well, she was sorry, too.

And as much of a mess as he was.

She tried to ground herself, stay rational, for the baby's sake and her own.

Of course it had hit Jared hard. Two major slugs of news in the fatherhood department in the space of a few days. She hadn't expected a miracle, even before he'd told her about Grausam. Hadn't cherished any illusions about some oh-darling-you've-made-me-the-happiest-man-alive type response.

There was no basis in their relationship so far for anything like that. Neither of them had mentioned love or a future. But she had at least expected to be able to talk about it.

The legal implications.

His financial involvement.

Whether he had any interest in being present at the birth.

Whether their open-ended, not-too-deep, sexy little early-mid-life-crisis-style fling might sizzle along for a few more weeks before limping to a halt under the weight of morning sickness and blood tests and an expanding waistline, or whether it was over as of this moment.

But they hadn't gotten to any of that. He hadn't even asked the due date, which the Ask-a-Nurse lady had cautiously agreed, based on what Shallis had told her, should be around Valentine's Day.

She felt exhausted, utterly wrung out and limp, every muscle as weak as wet tissue and her stomach like an empty cave.

Okay. There's something I can do. I have to eat. And eat right. That's important.

She found a can of cream of celery soup, some salad greens and some bread for toast, which wasn't brilliant—a little lacking in the protein department. But it was a start. There were vitamins present there someplace, a few minerals in the bread and calcium in the cream.

Next, she took a bath—not too hot—because it couldn't be good for the baby to have a mom who was this stressed, so she needed to relax. Lying in the bath, she wondered what Linnie was doing at this moment, and how she was feeling. Was Mom still obsessing over the fact that it was a Monday four weeks after the last significant Monday in Linnie's life, and Linnie hadn't cried? Did Ryan know what was or wasn't going on?

And as for Jared, for all she knew, he could still be standing thunderstruck on his grandfather's back deck.

* * *

"It doesn't change anything about who you are and who you can be!" Grandpa Abe said. He sat high in his hospital bed, his body moving with restless impatience. His bypass surgery was scheduled for tomorrow and he wasn't in a mood to take care with his words or to conserve his energy.

"Take it easy, Grandpa," Jared told him, half expecting the alarms on the monitors to start their electronic dinging at any moment.

If the monitors had been attached to his own body, they'd already be going off. His blood pressure felt stratospheric, his pulse had to be erratic and his breathing resembled the shallow pantings of a woman in labor—which, by the way, he'd only ever seen on TV.

How did you deal with losing a father and gaining an unborn child in the space of a few days? Who did you talk to? What did you say? Was history repeating itself? Grausam had left Jared's mother on her own. He'd disappeared the day she'd told him she was pregnant. Was Jared himself now planning to do the same thing to Shallis? Where did any of this fit into his winner's mentality?

What the hell counted as a win in this situation? What did he want?

"Take it easy?" Grandpa Abe said. "No, I won't! I don't get this, Jared. I have no patience with it. Ray drummed the right messages into you your whole life. You make your own destiny. You start with a clean slate. You use the material you're given."

"This is what he was talking about, all those times? The fact that the Starke heritage wasn't really mine, and someday I'd find it out?"

"The Starke heritage is yours! In what sense is it not yours?

You're a good lawyer with a bright mind. You know how to work hard. Yes, this is what he was talking about, but you're not hearing the right message. This is exactly what he didn't want. You're questioning things that don't need to be questioned. Don't go through with this trip to Chicago. Don't make contact. What purpose can it possibly serve?"

Jared skipped the purpose question, because he didn't have an answer to that yet. "I have made contact," he said quietly. "I called Grausam today. Told him I'd fly up on the weekend. He sounded…rather affable about it, actually."

"Affable? When do you use a word like *affable,* Jared?"

"Okay, perky, then."

His grandfather swore, then fell into a stubborn silence, his mind turning over so fast that Jared expected to start hearing engine sounds. It had to be at least five minutes before he opened his mouth to speak again, and since Jared wanted the old man to rest, he didn't attempt to keep the conversation going during the interval.

"Don't make it the weekend," Grandpa finally said.

"I thought you didn't want me to go at all."

"Oh, and you were going to take a blind bit of notice? No, since you're going, get it over with."

"But the practice—"

"Close the practice for the week. Do it properly. What kind of a rapport can you build with the man in a day and a half? Keep Andrea in the office handling any calls. I'll phone Gerard Banks at home now, and he'll be happy to take the urgent business."

"There are a couple of real estate closings."

"Which he could do in his sleep. Nothing serious though, is there? No court dates. No tight deadlines on filing paperwork? If you're going to go to Chicago, leave yourself open to staying as long as the situation requires, long enough to make an informed judgment about whether you're going to have any kind of future dealings with this man."

"With my father," Jared corrected deliberately.

"Ray was your father, Jared." His face darkened to red. "In every way that counted. Don't insult me or his memory by calling him anything else."

"We won't talk about this any more tonight," Jared said. "You're going to get me thrown out of here, Grandpa. The nurses don't want you getting—"

There was some movement and sound in the doorway of the private room, and Jared cut off his words and turned just as Sunny Duncan's cooing greeting came. "Abe! We stopped at the desk, there, and they said the surgery's happening tomorrow?"

She approached the bed, carrying an elaborate flower arrangement, which Jared knew that Grandpa wouldn't appreciate, no matter how well he pretended. He liked flowers, but only when they still had their roots in the soil—one of the many things he was stubborn about.

Bob Duncan reached out and shook Grandpa's hand. "You old fraud," he said.

"Shh, don't let on, Bob." The angry red was draining from his face, thank the lord. From Jared's perspective, the Duncans' arrival was well-timed. "I'm letting them think I need this bypass, but you and I both know I'm strong as an ox. Sunny, what a beautiful arrangement! The best of the bunch." He waved at the windowsill where several others were already grouped. "I won't miss the last days of spring at all, at this rate."

Yes, Grandpa Abe could pretend well, when he wanted. The Duncans would never guess that they'd come in on the tail end of a very tense conversation. They'd never know that

Jared had learned just an hour ago that he'd fathered their first grandchild-to-be. They had no idea that he and Shallis had ever been involved....

While Jared himself had no idea if they still were.

Three Hyattville-born generations in the room, two different families, three generations of secrets and three generations of unspoken feelings. He wondered what hidden emotions might be simmering beneath the perfect surface that Shallis's mother presented to the world. Was it his imagination, or was there something a little distracted in her manner tonight?

"You got here right when we needed you to, Bob," Grandpa said. "Worst thing about being in the hospital, you run out of conversation so fast. Poor Jared and I had nothing left to say to each other, did we?"

"Yeah, Grandpa, we'd pretty much covered the whole gamut," he agreed in the same cheerful tone.

"Are you busy, Shallis? Is there a function at the hotel tonight?"

"I'm busy, and there's a function, but I don't have to be there for all of it."

"So can you drop in at Linnie's, kind of casual, and see how she's doing?"

"Didn't we have this conversation yesterday, Mom?"

"Yes, and I listened to you, which is why I'm not going out there myself."

"I'm not going out there, either."

Mom wailed a protest.

"Not today, Mom. I'll go Thursday—"

Another wail.

"Okay." She sighed. "Tomorrow. And I'll take her some of

the flowers left over from tonight. *If* I haven't been swallowed whole by the Lancaster-D'Emilio wedding."

"That's this Saturday? That's why you're tense?"

"Yes, it's this Saturday."

No, it's not why I'm tense. I'm not telling you why I'm tense until I've thought it through enough to have some concrete answers, and until we've found out more about how Linnie's feeling this month.

I can't tell her I'm pregnant, if she's just had her monthly bourbon-and-Coke episode. I just can't.

But on Wednesday evening when Shallis showed up at the farm, the jury was still out on how Linnie was feeling. On the surface, she seemed bright and smiling and busy. *Too* bright, smiling and busy? She took Shallis on a tour of the two cabins, which had hosted their first two groups of guests on the weekend.

"They said all the right things, loved the food, loved that the antique mall was so close, loved the trail ride Ryan took them on, said they'd tell their friends, and be back here themselves," Linnie reported as she and Shallis walked back to the main house. "And both cabins have couples on the weekend and families staying all next week. Those flowers you brought are gorgeous, but they're too big and formal for the cabins. I'll break them down into smaller bunches. Do you want to help? We can do it now, while we talk. Grab some coffee, too."

"Sure… But no coffee, thanks," Shallis said.

If Linnie was pregnant, she wasn't having symptoms yet. Or not the same symptoms as Shallis, anyhow.

And if she'd been drinking her bourbon-and-Coke this week, then she'd put the liquor bottle away.

They brought the flowers into the laundry room that

opened off Linnie's little kitchen, and she covered the top of the washing machine in a sheet of plastic and a wooden cutting board. They recut stems, snipped off tired blooms, filled vases with clean water, added a florist's freshener and grouped the flowers and greenery into pretty, woodsy arrangements that would suit the country-style cabins.

"So, Linnie, was it about the same amount of work you expected? Were the guests polite and not too demanding?"

"It was fine."

"Because we don't want you losing the ground you gained in the Caribbean."

There's an opening for you if you want it, Linnie. I'm your sister, you can tell me.

Is she going to bite my head off if I tell her she's looking tired? She's not looking tired. She has color in her cheeks, but every time she thinks I'm not looking at her she starts biting her nails and frowning, and I think her eyes are too bright....

"You're the one who's looking tired, Shallis," Linnie said, as if she'd read her little sister's thought track like a printout on a heart monitor.

Shallis gave a neat, fake shrug. "Oh, it's that big wedding we have on Saturday. I'm losing sleep over it."

I'm losing sleep, because I feel like I'm lying to you, Sis.

Ryan's boots thumped on the back porch. "Where are you, Lin?" he called. *You okay?*

"Laundry room," she called back. "With Shallis. *Doing fine.*"

He appeared in the doorway, darkening it with his bulk. He smelled pleasantly of horse. *"Yeah?"* he asked. His eyes flicked to Shallis, and he pasted on a neat smile. "Hi."

"Hi, Ryan."

"Yep. Fine," Linnie answered her husband, quick and bright, as if she hoped the little marital exchange, a whole

seven words, starting with "You okay?" and ending with "Fine," would go unnoticed by Shallis.

Shallis wasn't fooled.

But she wasn't part of the marital unit, either.

What would that be like, she wondered—to be able to communicate so much, with so few words, because your lives were so closely entwined and you understood each other so well?

I want it, she knew. I want a chance at having that. And if I don't get it, I don't want it to be because I failed the first forgiveness test. If Jared shows up at some point and wants to talk, I'm at least going to listen.

Meanwhile, however, how did she interpret Linnie's answer to Ryan? Was it, "Fine, I'm over the disappointment for this month, and I don't want you worrying," or "Fine, and my period still hasn't started, and I don't want you worrying."

One or the other, but which?

"Which, Shallis?" her mother wanted to know, later that night. "You must have *some* intuition about it!"

She'd called thirty seconds after Shallis walked in the door, and she admitted to a responsibility for three of the four messages on Shallis's answer machine.

"Mom, I don't dare to have any intuition, because if I'm wrong…"

"So you do? You think she's pregnant?"

"We all want her to be, so much. How can I separate out the wishful thinking? Don't do this to me!"

"I'll go out there tomorrow."

"You don't think us alternating days like this is going to make her just that little bit suspicious? Mom, I'm starting to think you need a hobby."

"I want to babysit my grandkids. That's the only hobby I want."

Babysit, or take care of full-time while I'm at work?

"Put Dad on the phone, can you please?" Shallis said out loud.

"He wants to babysit, too!"

"Just put him on."

"Hi, Demon-child." Dad had always refused to call her Princess and Beautiful and Sweetheart. Enough other people did that. He'd gone the opposite route.

"Don't let her go out to the farm on Thursday, Dad."

"Well, I promised Ryan I'd help him with—"

"Cancel. Or send Mom for a facial and sneak out there on your own. She is not to be trusted with Linnie right now."

He sighed. "Yeah, are any of us? Don't worry, I'll keep her away. Maybe Friday…"

"Friday. Pick me up from the hotel after work and I'll come with you."

Grandpa's bypass surgery had gone well.

Jared settled into his seat on the flight from Nashville to Chicago on Wednesday evening, knowing that almost thirty-six hours after the operation, the old man had hit all the right benchmarks on his recovery and was safely resting in the Douglas County Hospital cardiac ward with his daughter-in-law keeping watch.

Jared was free to make this journey north to meet his biological father. Meaningless sperm donor? Or the man who'd made him who he was?

He tried to empty his head of expectations and fears, but it wasn't easy. When he looked at himself in the mirror in the airplane bathroom, he no longer saw his own face in the same way. He could trace the genetic heritage he'd gotten from his mother—the wheat-and-amber coloring, the shape of his mouth and nose. Everything else, he wondered about.

His jawline and chin, his sturdy build, the slant of his brows. None of those things came from the Starkes or from his mom, as far as he could see. So did they belong to Grausam?

And what about his manipulation of the football tryout all those years ago? The lawyer in the rival practice whom he'd slept with so she would spill a few secrets? The way he'd massaged certain information about certain companies to give himself an edge?

Did those actions belong to his biological father just as definitively as did his physique?

If they did, he didn't know how to take it. Had he just given himself a very convenient genetic excuse for past behavior that he regretted? Was he condemning his future to a repetition of patterns at least two generations old?

He could almost hear his father's voice in his head—the father he'd grown up with. *"You start with a clean slate. You use the material you're given. You make your own destiny, in this world."*

Were you right about all of that, Dad, or does it just sound good?

When the flight landed, he picked up his rental car and drove straight to the downtown hotel he'd chosen, glad that he'd taken the last flight of the day so he didn't have too much time to fill in here. He ordered room service and did a full thumb workout with the TV remote, getting sleepy during late-night talk shows at around midnight. He was meeting Grausam here at the hotel's street-level restaurant for breakfast at eight.

The man was late—the requisite twelve or so minutes that

balanced on a knife-edge between flagrant rudeness and a strategy for getting on top of the power balance. A few years ago, this would have given the two of them something in common. These days, Jared considered punctuality to be a better way of showing his strength.

He was halfway through his first coffee when he saw Grausam coming toward him. He stood and held out his hand, but the man didn't take it, clapping him on the arm and shoulder instead, while giving a laugh and a sniff and a manly sob.

"Jared! I knew it. The moment I saw you. Son! This is too much, a discovery like this. When you called, I—" He stopped and shook his head, as if struggling for control.

For no good reason, Jared's skin crawled. He knew he was looking for reasons to dislike Grausam, so of course he could find them. But all the same, weren't the words and the emotion way too pat and smooth? They didn't fit with the flick of his father's cool green eyes toward the expensive watch he wore, and then down to confirm the same impression with Jared's shoes.

Good, said the eyes. Expensive hotel, status symbol watch, Italian shoes, filial obligation. How much can I get from him?

"Yes, it's been a big week for both of us," Jared said. "Sit down and take a look at the menu. This is on me, of course."

Grausam didn't argue.

They ordered, and then they talked. It was the kind of conversation you had on a first date with someone you hardly knew, full of standard questions and spin-doctored replies.

Grausam had been thirty-three to Jared's mother's twenty-one when he'd made her pregnant. Now he must be sixty-seven or sixty-eight, although at first glance he didn't look it. He might even have had some work done around his eyes. They looked a little too round and wide. And his hair was a

disaster, dyed too dark and combed over too far from a parting line at the back, to hide the receding hairline. It looked
blatantly unnatural, and it jarred.

Grausam was still working, he said, but wasn't very spe-
cific about what he did. "You know how it is, a bit of this, a
bit of that. Venture capital. Brokerage."

"You were working as a yard man when you knew my
mother, weren't you?" Jared said.

His father laughed in a comfortable way. "Oh, I moved on
from that a long time ago. That was just to get a start."

"A forty-thousand-dollar start?"

Across the table, Grausam froze for a fraction of a second.
"Oh, you know about that?" And then he winked. "Not to be
crude, son, but trust me, I earned it. You know what I mean?
Anyhow, fools and their money, and all that."

"Yes, I know exactly what you mean," Jared said, and in a
strange way he felt as if a weight had lifted from his shoulders.

*I don't owe this man anything more than the round of golf
I promised him this afternoon.*

The Lancaster-D'Emilio bridal party checked in to the
Grand Regency Hotel at three o'clock on Thursday afternoon. By four o'clock, the bride-to-be was in floods of tears
in Shallis's office—or to be more precise, on Shallis's shoulder. This was not a new experience for her, but Courtney
Lancaster had put her heart and soul into every detail of this
wedding, and the sobbing-and-threatening-to-call-it-off phase
was no exception.

Shallis really had not intended to go out to Linnie and
Ryan's farm today, but after it had taken her an hour and a
half of high-energy supportiveness, mutual soul spilling and

a promise to be there for Courtney every minute of the whole event, in order to get the hotel's biggest wedding of the summer back on track, she just had to have some country air.

Or was this only an excuse?

She hadn't seen Jared since Monday evening at his place, when they'd exchanged their parenthood-themed emotional bombshells. She knew he was in Chicago, and she knew his grandfather's bypass operation had gone well, but she'd only heard these pieces of information secondhand. He hadn't called, and she hadn't expected him to. Naturally, this did not stop her legs from starting to shake every time she heard the phone.

She'd been so-o-o tempted to tell Courtney Lancaster. "You think you have problems? Here's a quick rundown of how my life is going so far this week. Now, do I win?"

Instead, she'd ended up talking about Miss America, and about Linnie's wedding six years ago—Jared's interruption, Linnie's doubts, the way she'd panicked that she wasn't cut out for the starring role as bride. "It's totally normal, Courtney, I promise you."

Courtney had gotten very indignant when she'd heard about the scene with Jared at the altar. "Some men just don't know when to quit!"

This was truer than Courtney knew. Some women didn't know when a man *had* quit, either. Had Jared quit Hyattville? Quit Shallis? Acquitted himself of any responsibility as a parent, the way his father had before him?

She was racked over it, frozen in limbo, no idea what she wanted to ask of him, no idea how to start planning her future, and she didn't know who she could talk to. Friends? She hadn't had enough time to make new connections here since her return from L.A. Two of her oldest friends were no longer in town, and a third had given birth to her second child about six weeks ago, while child number one was the most active eighteen-month-old Shallis had ever seen. Julie was loyal and fun, but both her parents were staying with her in order to help out and—

No, it wouldn't work.

There was no one Shallis could safely spill her heart to, if she couldn't spill it to Jared himself.

Going out to see Linnie was a mistake. She was busy in the kitchen, cooking and making shopping and To Do lists ready for the next batch of guests who were due tomorrow. They had chosen a package that included both breakfast and dinner, three days in a row, which meant extra work.

"You can sit and watch, or you can help," Linnie told her, "But I can't stop till I'm done, here. Don't worry, I'm getting to bed early tonight, so you can report back to Mom that I'm not overdoing it."

"Do you want me to report to her?"

Translation—is there anything special you want me to report to her?

"Isn't that why you're here?"

"Um, no, Linnie, I just felt like seeing you."

In fact, I told Mom we should stay away. I'm breaking my own rule. If she finds out, she'll jump right in the car and muscle in on this.

"Oh." Linnie stretched a smile onto her face. "Well, that's nice. Pour yourself something cool to drink and watch me cook."

"I could cut onions, or something."

"Sure. Tell me about how that big wedding's coming for Saturday."

So they talked about Courtney, talked about horses,

chopped herbs and vegetables, talked about herbs and vegetables. Words that Shallis knew she couldn't say crammed into the back of her throat so thick and tight they threatened to make her gag. Her jaw felt as if it was wired shut…which somehow made her eyes sting.

This felt exactly like grief—the same heavy, draining weight inside her that she'd experienced after Gram's death. That grief had been tempered by the knowledge that Gram herself would have been happy to go, after such a long and full life…fuller than any of them had known. There was nothing to temper the power of what she felt now.

I'm having a baby with a man I might never see again. A man whose questionable track record we've just discovered stretches back a whole extra generation. And I think I'm in love with him, only I don't quite dare to be. And if you're not pregnant, Linnie, then whether I'm in love or not is the least of my troubles… although how that can be when it hurts so much, I don't know.

Linnie asked another question about the Lancaster-D'Emilio wedding, but it was so obvious she wasn't really interested in the answer. For her, as for Shallis, their conversation was just the tip of the iceberg, with all the real weight of what was going on in their lives hidden deep in their thoughts.

As soon as she got home, Shallis called Mom and told her, "Don't go out there tomorrow, Mom. Something's going on. I feel like we'll jinx it if we go."

"You mean you went today?"

"I'd had a tough day at work. But I shouldn't have gone."

"And now you're buying into this jinx idea of your father's."

"I bought into Dad's jinx idea fifteen years ago. I'm just

applying it in a different area. Let's both wait until she calls us, or tells us something."

They went round and round about it a couple more times, but then Mom caved and changed the subject.

"I took the inventory of Gram's things over to Jared's office today, but he's still in Chicago. I heard he's considering a couple of partnership offers. Do you know if he's gone for an interview, Shallis? Andrea is so discreet! She wouldn't give a hint."

"Maybe she doesn't know."

"Could be. But with the wake-up call over Abe's heart bypass, I can't see what's going to become of the practice if Jared doesn't stay on. Abe will have to sell it to a stranger, and fast, before all his clients have gone somewhere else."

"That kind of thing happens all the time. The idea of going into the family business seems old-fashioned to a lot of people."

"Yes, I know, honey, but I was starting to think Jared might have more of those values than we'd thought."

Shallis changed the subject and ended the call as quickly as she could.

Chapter Fourteen

Jared had a clock running in his head even before he woke up in his Chicago hotel room on Saturday morning. Alarm set for seven-fifteen. Five minute shower. Grab coffee and Danish in the lobby and eat in his room. Check out by eight. Get to the airport at nine, for a ten o'clock flight. Touch down in Nashville at one-twenty.

The whole program ran as smoothly as had his various meetings and meals with colleagues and friends over the past couple of days, and he sank back into his roomy premier class seat on the aircraft fifteen minutes before takeoff.

He'd talked and he'd thought and he'd listened to professional propositions and personal advice. He'd lain awake for a good two or three hours each night, staring into the broken darkness of his hotel room while he thought some more. Or rather, while he tried to correlate the driving, unbrookable emotions inside him with some kind of rational analysis.

In the end, he'd given up on the rational analysis, and now he was going with his gut.

If this airplane would ever get itself off the ground.

He looked at his watch. Five after ten, and they hadn't pushed back from the gate. The thumping, chaotic activity of carry-on bags getting stowed in overhead lockers and flight attendants giving safety demonstrations had ceased some minutes ago. The cabin felt stuffy and hot. He heard the pilot's voice, beginning with the ominously cheerful words, "Well, folks, sorry, but…" and his heart sank.

Apparently a red warning light in the cockpit had begun to signal that the heating system was malfunctioning in the cargo section used for pet transportation, and they had a cat on board this flight. Could be just the red warning light that was malfunctioning, the pilot said, but they had to make sure. Couldn't risk arriving in Nashville with a chilled or roasted feline.

In the past, Jared had always liked cats. Today, he wondered why the hell they thought they could spend their weekends jetting across the country in airplanes, and why their owners wanted them to.

He wasn't any happier twenty minutes later, when the mechanics decided the problem ran deeper than red warning lights, jet-set cats and cargo heating, and the passengers were told to disembark the aircraft.

How long would this take?

At least a couple of hours, Jared was told. He checked available flights and managed to find one that left Chicago at eleven forty-five, delivered him to Memphis and then provided a connecting flight that touched down in Nashville at three ten.

By the time his cab pulled into the driveway of Grandpa

Abe's house on Chestnut Street, it was after four o'clock. He called the hospital as soon as he walked in the door, using the direct line to the phone beside his grandfather's bed in the cardiac unit.

His mother answered and gave an upbeat summary, confirmed when he heard Grandpa's voice, clear and strong in the background. "Ask him when he's coming in. I want a full report. And I mean a *full* report. No, don't tell me in Jared's own good time, Judy, it isn't good for a cardiac patient to be stressed like this."

Jared heard his mother sigh. "He's been milking the cardiac patient thing like a dairy cow since he came out of the anesthesia. So what do I tell him, Jared?"

"Tell him I haven't got a final draft of the full report, yet. Couple of sections still need work. Key pieces of data need to be plugged in. Shareholders in Starke Unlimited deserve a complete picture. Is it a merger? Is it a takeover? Is it a divestment of major capital assets? Bedside board meeting scheduled for tomorrow morning, and he should make sure he's there."

Another sigh, and some tongue clicking. "You're worse than he is. I can't tell him that."

"Then hand over the phone, and I'll tell him. I'm picking up his lead and running with it. And I have a critical interview lined up for this afternoon, so I can't make this a long call."

He heard his mother say, away from the phone, "He says he's coming in tomorrow morning and you have to wait. Do you want to talk to him?" Then he heard more growling in the background, said a quick goodbye even though he didn't know if anyone still had their ear to the phone, and cut the connection.

He dialed Shallis, and got her machine. Drove to her apartment in case she'd heard his message—his cryptic, emotional message—and just hadn't wanted to pick up. But unless she was hiding under her bed because she knew it was him, she wasn't at home.

She could be anywhere, and his brain wasn't making the right connections. Impatience had built inside him like a fire in a hardwood log, and with all those white hot coals and crackling flames, he couldn't think.

He cruised past Fifty-six Chestnut, but there was no sign of life. Remembered Caroline McLenaghan's address from the ever-thickening McLenaghan-Duncan-Templeton files in the office and cruised past there, also. Sat at the curb and called up Linnie and Ryan's farm on his cell, left another message, didn't even think about his murky past with Linnie until after he'd put down the phone.

Finally he remembered something about a big wedding at the Grand Regency, today, and realized that was where Shallis would be. Yeah, and it fit somehow. They'd shared some confrontational moments at a Grand Regency wedding once before. He'd thrown the dice that day and lost—or that would have been the public perception, anyhow. Today he would throw it again, but the stakes were far higher.

The stakes were everything.

He would lose everything if Shallis didn't give him the answer he wanted, because he'd already turned his back on Chicago, turned down the partnership offers, told a couple of people what he thought of their morals and their principles—yeah, that fourth beer had possibly loosened his tongue a little too much last night, although if he should regret what he'd said, well, folks, sorry, but he didn't.

So if Shallis couldn't forgive all the real, tangible things she had reason to be angry about, or if she just didn't feel the way he did…

This has never happened to me before, he realized.

Pushing for the big, splashy win had always been easy, because he'd never put anything important at risk. He'd always had a strong fallback position.

Today, for the first time, he didn't have any fallback position at all. If Shallis didn't feel the way he did, then he would lose everything that mattered.

He was as jumpy as the cat must have been in the airplane cargo hold. His hands were damp on the wheel as he drove, his head was stuck in an ever-tightening vise, and his stomach was heavy and hollow.

The epic dimensions of today's Grand Regency wedding didn't help. It was a far bigger and more elaborate event than Linnie and Ryan's had been, since theirs had been arranged in weeks instead of months.

The cocktail hour was already in full swing and the parking valets had abandoned their posts at the apex of the sweeping driveway out front. The guest vehicles overflowed the hotel parking lot. Jared had to go so far down the street to find a space that he might as well have walked from home, around the long block bordered by Chestnut Street, North Street and Main. Better yet, only it was too late now, he could have cut through the rear yard of the Templeton house and jumped the fence.

Walking back toward the hotel entrance, car keys in his pocket, he saw a flurry of activity in the Grand Regency's gorgeous rose garden. Wedding photos? It looked more like a movie shoot. Bride in a huge dress. Cameras with lenses like cruise missiles. Juniors fussing with metallic reflectors and tubs of flowers.

And there were so many bridesmaids in a rainbow of pastel gowns that he ran out of fingers counting them off. Finally, he saw one woman whose dress didn't fit with the rest of the group, because it wasn't a full-skirted girly pastel, it was pale on top and dark on the bottom, it fit the figure beneath it the way wood fit around the lead of a pencil, and it was neat and professional and not splashy enough to steal attention from the bride…except that of course it did, for Jared anyhow, because this was Shallis.

She hadn't seen him yet. He wasn't ready for her to see him yet. He just wanted to watch her, like a voyeur, in case this was the last time he ever got to see her without the kind of hostile look on her face that he'd seen on the faces of the two women whose child custody disputes the Starke law practice was currently handling.

Stewart Grausam had done the Starke family a favor, in some ways, by disappearing so completely from Jared's mother's life. She had never needed to wear that look. Jared's gut lurched at the prospect that Shallis might wear it one day, because of him. If they couldn't resolve this the way he wanted… If he didn't need to run away from fatherhood because he'd gotten a great big push…

What in the heck was going on with these photos?

"Shallis, do you think we can get the cake out here now? We'll set it against the roses? You're sure it will it handle the sun?"

"Shallis, I'm sorry, but if there's any way that climbing vine could get pruned back a little for these shots? Is there a gardener you can page?"

"Shallis, my dress! Ohmigosh, he's trodden on my dress!"

If this was a movie shoot, then Shallis appeared to be the first assistant director, the go-to gal for the problems everybody else created by the bucketload. Jared had found it easier striding down the church aisle at Linnie and Ryan's wedding six years ago to interrupt their ceremony than he found it to interrupt Shallis's smiling attempts to keep everyone happy today.

Finally, glancing away from the gardener's efforts with his pruning shears, she saw him. Her face froze.

"Shallis, is the mark gone now? Does it show that it's damp?"

She turned back to where she was needed. She hadn't smiled or waved or spoken. Did that tell him everything he needed to know?

"I have a little battery cooling fan here, Courtney," she was saying. "That'll dry it off faster. Matt, you have to take those vine clippings with you, every scrap, and you'll have to sweep off the paving. Bridesmaids, watch your dresses!"

No, he decided. He wasn't going to leave on the strength of one frozen look. He had to talk to her, or at least find out if she would talk to him, and settle on a time when they could do it without all this activity.

He stepped beneath the arch of greenery that led into the rose garden, and went toward her like a space voyager journeying toward the center of the universe. Everything else shifted in chaos, while Shallis was the only fixed point in his vision.

Still some yards from the vortex of activity, he stopped beside a rosebush covered in a profusion of dark pink blooms and waited while Shallis solved another problem. At last, cameras began clicking and she turned in his direction as if she'd somehow known exactly where he'd chosen to wait. Their eyes met.

Oh, Lord. Oh, damn.

Okay, yes, their eyes met, their gazes locked—happens all

the time, eye contact between two human beings—but this was such a pitifully inadequate description of the connection, the cliff-edge awareness and uncertainty, the rush, the vibration, the breathlessness, the wanting.

Emotion and need and fear slammed at him like a professional hit. His heart was hammering and he felt ill. If she turned away again... If her beautiful face wore the wrong look... If she wouldn't even give him a chance...

No, okay, so far that wasn't happening. The jury was still out on what she thought and what she would say, but she was coming toward him, at least, with her eyes huge, and her expression still ironed into its careful professional shape.

"You're back," she said.

And she was speaking to him, even if it was only two cool, prickly words.

"Shallis, there's so much I want to say. I don't know where to start. We can't talk here. What's going on?"

"*Wedding Belle* magazine is doing a story on Courtney and Daniel's wedding, with a full photo spread. It's huge publicity for the hotel. And of course the two of them have their own photographer, and video operator, on top of that." She gave a tiny flick with her hands, and a tiny shake of her head. "You don't need this detail."

No, he didn't. All he wanted was to pitch himself against her body and hold her, kiss her, drown himself in her, but he knew he couldn't. Not yet. Not until they'd talked. "Will you be done here, soon?"

She smiled briefly and shrugged, wary about showing very much. Whether that was for personal or professional reasons, he didn't know. "Around midnight, maybe?" she answered.

"Oh good, getting off early," he drawled. "Do you earn a coffee break at some point?"

Her face went tight again. "Tell me why you're here. Twenty-five words or less, Jared. So I know if it's worth risking my job for one conversation." She looked wary, her attitude ready to go either way, but the awareness and pull clearly as powerful in her body as it was in his.

Before he could answer her, another voice cut in. "Shallis, someone's here for you."

"Right. Of course. I'm coming." The professional smile was back in place, along with the perky professional willingness to be on call for completely unreasonable requests every tick of the clock.

This wasn't professional, though. Jared realized the fact before Shallis did, because she was looking in the wrong direction, smiling her now glaze-eyed smile at the bridal party.

This was family.

This was Linnie.

Close to tears.

With Ryan right behind her, looking worried about his wife.

"Shallis…" Linnie fell into Shallis's arms just a half-second after she first realized her sister and Ryan were here. Linnie's voice sounded strange, and it pulled Shallis's already shattered focus in yet another direction.

Oh, no. Oh, no.

The *Wedding Belle* photographer was shooting the cake. The *Wedding Belle* makeup artist was touching up Courtney's face. Jared stood back, possibly composing his twenty-five-words-or-less answer to their entire future. He was dressed casually in baggy gray canvas shorts and a paler gray polo shirt, and he looked strong and gorgeous and very stressed.

From the moment she'd first caught sight of him, Shallis had wanted to go up to him and smooth out his forehead with her fingers, kiss him and hold him and tell him everything was going to be okay. She'd also wanted to yell at him and tell him he was a jerk and she didn't want him in her life.

Logical, Shallis.

Consistent.

She'd yearned for it all to be simple. Way more simple than it could possibly be. She'd really wanted something from him that could be said, right here and now, in twenty-five words or less.

If he's slippery about it, not straight with me, she thought, if he has some token solution to this, I don't know what I'll do. The disappointment…the disillusionment…will shred my heart to pieces. There's only one way I can forgive him for the way he reacted when I first told him, and that's if he reacts the right way now.

In her heart, she didn't know if it was possible. Did she trust him that much? Did she trust herself to be strong enough to let him go if he had some shallow, slippery, open-ended proposition about their future?

And Shallis couldn't think about any of that right now because Linnie was crying in her arms, great heaving, emotional, gut-wrenching sobs which made Shallis hate the whole universe, with her own body at the epicenter of it, the place where the earthquake started from.

Linnie's not pregnant and I am.

How are any of us going to bear this?

How many relationships are going to get destroyed?

Even if Jared's twenty-five words do, by a miracle, manage to include "love" and "baby" and "father" and "involved" somewhere near each other and in the order I want, how can we deal with having a baby together when Linnie and Ryan want to be having one so much and aren't?

She wished that she'd stayed in L.A., or that Jared had never left Chicago, so that she couldn't have gotten herself into this situation. For about three seconds she burned with a regret so intense that it was like an electric shock charging through her.

Why had they ever met up again? Why had they let it get so important, so fast, without nearly enough of an attempt to think it through? Why hadn't she allowed herself more of the space that Dad had always managed to find for her, when important things were at stake?

Then, just as suddenly, something in her rebelled and she knew that she could never wish any of this to be different, because she loved Jared—she'd known it for certain the moment she'd seen him standing by the rose bush a thousand heartbeats ago, but weeks before that, had she really been in any doubt?—and that part of the story was so right, felt so right in her heart, that she couldn't wish it away, whether that was useful or sensible or workable or not.

She still didn't know how they'd get through this, but even so, she couldn't wish it away.

"I'm sorry, I can't talk yet," Linnie sobbed.

"Don't then, Lin." Shallis's own voice came out ragged and jerky. "It's okay…it's okay."

It's not. It's tragic. It's wrong. Why am I saying it's okay? If I was Linnie I'd—

"I'm sorry, I don't know why I'm suddenly reacting like this." Linnie sobbed harder. "Ryan?" She appealed to her husband for help, and he stepped awkwardly forward and—

Grinned.

Grinned?

Yes, from ear to ear. As dazzling as the camera flashes popping at frequent intervals on the shaded terrace as wedding guests took their own candid pictures. As wide as the moon. As happy as ten pigs in mud.

"Guess it must be the hormones," he said.

The *what?*

Now Linnie was grinning, too, through her tears. "Oh, Shallis, we're going to have a baby! And I'm so h-h-happy, my heart is bursting!"

Jared took a step back and muttered something, but after that, for at least a minute, no one said anything coherent at all. Linnie and Ryan and Shallis just laughed and cried and hugged.

"Do Mom and Dad know?" Shallis finally asked.

"Not yet. We called by their place just now, but they weren't home and I just couldn't wait to tell someone. I knew you'd be here because of the photo shoot and the article." She gestured at Courtney Lancaster's cake and the people fussing around it. "Oh, Shallis, we bought the test this afternoon. I told Ryan I was going to wait until Monday, but I've been such a mess, I just couldn't."

"We both have," Ryan said. "Couldn't take it another minute."

"We drove to the nearest pharmacy, drove right home again. Two minutes till we got a result, oh, the longest two minutes of my life. I've been holding my breath all week, walking on tip-toe, not daring to think it was possible. I've been terrified you or Mom would notice and start asking questions."

"Oh, we noticed…"

"You *did?* And you didn't say anything."

"Linnie, we didn't dare, either." Shallis wiped her shaking

hand across her wet eyes, then found a clean tissue in her pocket and handed it to her sister. "We just didn't dare in case we were wrong. At one point I thought I was going to have to handcuff Mom in her basement to stop her from going out to your place and blurting something."

"She's going to blurt out a few things when she hears. She's going to take all the credit for making us go on that vacation."

"You must have been pregnant before the vacation, Lin. I mean, um, don't you think?"

As soon as she'd said it, Shallis wondered if Linnie would get suspicious about what a close watch she'd been keeping on the calendar this month—her sister's dates, and hers. She'd already worked out that her sister's baby had to be due about nine days after her own, and she'd done that particular calculation when she was only wondering and praying about Linnie's possible pregnancy, not during the past few minutes when she'd begun to celebrate the reality. She'd been way too emotional to be capable of any form of math since Ryan had started grinning.

But Linnie missed the implication and only blushed. "Well…but the vacation still gets the credit. We were looking forward to it so much that we, um, got a good head start on certain aspects of it the day we paid for the tickets."

Ryan laughed and his neck went red. He tipped his baseball cap forward a little, because a mature and capable married man shouldn't be caught blushing like that. Standing behind his wife, he wrapped his arms around her then bent and buried his face in the curve of her shoulder, while Shallis's gut lurched.

This was how life should be. This was how two people should act and feel when they'd just learned they were going to be parents. They shouldn't feel stunned and terrified. They shouldn't have parted from each other without the slightest clue about what they should have said. And they shouldn't be standing within a few yards of each other five days later and still have no idea if they had a future together.

Jared unwound his big, capable body from its tight position in the background and took a couple of paces forward, clapped Ryan on the shoulder and pumped his hand.

"That's great news. Congratulations," he said, and Shallis watched Ryan let go of a hard little knot of dislike for Jared that he'd held inside him for six years, because when he and Linnie were having a baby at last, the whole world was a good and forgiving place. He didn't need to dislike Jared Starke any more.

"And we called my OB/GYN—her emergency number but she said, yes, this definitely counts as an emergency, and she was so thrilled," Linnie continued, leaning into Ryan's body. "And I told her what a dark line showed up on the test and she said that was great, meant my hormone levels were nice and high, and just the past couple of days I've been feeling…"

Yeah, Shallis knew all about how Linnie had been feeling. Queasy. Tired. Sore-breasted. Emotional.

And in her own case, squeezing her muscles like iron bands, sometimes, also, to keep from cracking and totally losing it. Her focus blurred and she couldn't go on listening to Linnie's bubbling, teary-eyed, emotional description of every single damned symptom and every single damned moment since Monday afternoon when her period had failed to happen.

Queasy, tired, sore-breasted, emotional and *bitchy,* Shallis added in her head.

I am so happy for you, Linnie. I am. *So* happy.

But the pregnancy thing is happening to me, too, and I can't celebrate—not yet, maybe not *ever,* the way you and Ryan are—and, oh, I'm getting an inkling of how you must have felt, these past few years, whenever you saw pregnant women in your doctor's office, or moms pushing strollers in the street. This crippling, horrible, irrational jealousy, because the world is working out right for other people, and it isn't for me.

I'm pregnant, too.

And I want to tell you, but I know I can't. Not now. Not today. Not when Jared and I haven't talked—although he's listening to every word of this. Not when you're so happy. This has to be your moment, Linnie, your day. Yours and Ryan's. Look at you, you're like the champagne fountain Courtney and Daniel are having for their reception tonight. You're overflowing. And I am so happy for you, and such a mess inside.

"Excuse me, Shallis, we're done with the cake and the bride and groom, and we're ready to shoot the table settings now," said one of the magazine people.

Just shoot me, too, while you're at it, could you, please? With a nice tranquillizer dart? You know, the kind they use on tigers?

"I'll be there in two seconds," she answered, painting on her smile, playing the right tape of her voice. She turned back to her sister. "Linnie, Mom and Dad are probably in the clubhouse after their golf game. Go tell them. Go celebrate. I am so h-happy for you."

There. She'd managed to say it, and to make it sound as if she meant it, because she did. Strange that even though she did mean it, it was still so hard to say.

I am so happy for you, but so scared and uncertain for me.

I want to freeze-frame the whole world except for Jared and me, because if I don't find out soon how he feels and what he wants and doesn't want, what he can give and what he can't, and how much my heart can forgive, I think I'm going to forget how to breathe.

"The golf club?" Linnie said. "Ryan, shall we?"

He grinned again. "Horses can wait a little longer, I guess, while some of us have a beer to celebrate. I'm sorry you can't come with us, Shallis." He looked at the bridal party, the photographers and Jared, saw something significant in Jared's face, frowned again and shook his hand. "Thanks for the help you've given my wife's family over her grandmother's estate," he said, courteous and formal.

"No problem, Ryan," Jared answered.

He zeroed in on the art director from the magazine, and almost dragged her across to the bride and groom for a conference. Linnie and Ryan wandered out to the street hand in hand and along to their pickup, parked almost out of sight.

"Look, guys," Jared said, "Ms. Duncan, here, is very good at her job. We can all see that. But is there a chance you can do without her for the next, oh, twenty minutes? Maybe longer? Because I've just flown in from Chicago and she and I need to talk. Right now. Before one of us explodes."

Courtney looked terrified that some of the shrapnel might land on her dress, and said, "Gosh, of course!" The magazine art director only had three more questions and requests. Shallis answered one of them and delegated the other two. The bridesmaids made various offers of help which would have slowed things down by an hour, so Shallis politely fobbed them off.

Jared took her hand and would have dragged her away,

only she went willingly so he didn't need to. He didn't go very far. The hotel was way too busy today to offer any privacy, but behind a screen of climbing roses and painted wooden lattice in the far corner of the garden stood the old board fence that made the boundary between the hotel grounds and Fifty-six Chestnut Street, and he was in no mood to be put off by the lack of a gate.

He wrestled a huge half-barrel of summer flowers against the fence, trampled the flowers as he jumped onto them, then used one hand as an anchor and did a pole vault without a pole, to land between two bushes on the far side. Through the gaps and warps in the paling, Shallis could see that the grass in the yard looked green and lush and inviting. It was overdue to be mowed.

Jared dragged Ivy Templeton's ancient garden seat against the fence right opposite the barrel, pulled off his shirt to leave himself bare-chested, and draped it over the top of the splintery palings. "So you don't ruin another outfit at this place."

"This place is pretty special. I've forgiven it for the other outfit."

"Can you do it? Can you make it across? I am *not* going to compete with *Wedding Belle* magazine, three hundred guests and a bridal party the size of a small Pacific nation."

"Quit complaining," Shallis told him breathlessly, as she arrived in front of him, her chest level with the top of his head. She pulled down the tight skirt she'd had to hike up to give her legs room to move. She tried to banish the intimate sensation of folding her hands over the warm fabric of his shirt on the top of the fence, because she still didn't know if she was allowed to let herself feel that way. "I'm over."

He put his hands around her waist, but didn't lift her down. Didn't reply, either. Didn't say a word, let alone twenty-five.

Just went still and slow and soft, pressed his face against her lower stomach, slid his hands down over her bottom and wrapped his arms tighter, then turned his head a little, to nestle his cheek against her.

Shallis stroked her fingers through his hair, not daring to speak, waiting for him, wanting to melt on the spot but wondering if she had to stay stronger than that. Oh, she wanted him so much, loved him so much. It seemed so simple, standing here like this in the quiet of the old yard. She didn't want the complexity of family history and family secrets and family law. Was it possible?

Finally Jared lifted his head. "This is our baby in here?"

It wasn't really a question, but Shallis answered it anyway, her voice husky, with the answer she hoped was true in heart and soul as well as in clinical fact. "Yes, it's our baby."

"I can't believe it. It's so incredible. It's overwhelming, but it's great, and I reacted so badly when you first told me, Shallis, I'm not sure why you're still here. I'm…*ecstatic*…that you're still here, but tell me why."

Moment of truth. Tell him I'm only here to tell him what a jerk he is? Or tell him what's in my heart?

She took a shuddery breath then firmed her voice. "Hey, before I say something totally pathetic and naked about why I'm still here, can you please give me the twenty-five words or less? I don't want the soul-searching and the explanations, I just want the bottom line, and I want it straight."

He tilted his head and looked up at her, lifted her from the garden bench and swung her down to the ground. Her body slid against his bare, warm chest, and the melting happened all on its own before she'd made any coherent decision as to whether she was going to let it.

"I haven't counted the words," he said.

"Well, you've just wasted five of 'em." She looked deep into his eyes, but didn't let herself smile. Didn't dare. Behind them, his shirt still hung on the fence.

"You're serious about this, aren't you?" he said.

Well, she seriously wanted to be, was seriously pretending to be.

"Six more," she said. "I don't want long, legalese-type hedging, Jared. I want the fourteen words you've got left."

"Okay."

"Thirteen."

She watched him struggling manfully not to waste any more. He took a deep, careful breath, his chest squashing against her breasts through the silk of her top. "I'm not going back to Chicago. I love you. I want our baby. Marry me."

"You overshot by two words."

"So we can't get married, now?" But he was grinning as he said it. He knew he had her right where he wanted her. And he'd made it way more simple than she'd dared to hope. Not that she'd let him know this yet...

"Try again." She cupped his face and stroked his strong jaw. "I think you can edit it down." She brushed the ball of her thumb across his lower lip. "And reverse the sentence order, I think that could work better."

"Marry me." He kissed her, one sweet, slow press against her mouth. A kiss wasn't a word, so it was okay. "I want our baby." Another kiss, longer and slower. "I love you." Deeper, making her lips part and quiver. "I'm staying in Hyattville."

She counted the words on her fingers, as he gave his winner's grin. Yeah, he knew he'd nailed it this time.

"Perfect," she whispered. "That was perfect."

"You're telling me that's all you need? Wait, I asked you to marry me, are you saying yes?"

"Of course I'm saying yes."

"And you don't first want, oh, the grovelling apology about running out on you all the way to Chicago, about not finding a way to tell you Monday night that I'd somehow be there for you so you wouldn't be going through it alone, about not calling you for five days, about not even damn well *knowing* that I loved you until, probably, Thursday…?" He paused for breath.

"Of course I want the grovelling apology. But I wanted to know how much time I had for it, first. Now I know. I have the rest of my life."

"Oh, you do? Your whole life, for one apology?"

"Didn't you read the fine print?"

"I got stuck on the twenty-five words or less."

"You're marrying a former beauty queen, Jared, and you're a lawyer. You need to read the fine print. Everyone knows what high maintenance we are, and what sticklers for perfection."

"So we can't sit down on this garden bench, I guess. It's not perfect at all. It's dusty, and it would mark your skirt."

"You're learning fast. You'll just have to stand and hold me while you kiss me. And remember, pregnant former beauty queens are made of spun glass."

"So I have to hold you like this? Hardly touching?"

She laughed. "No. I'll stop pretending, now. I'm not made of glass, and I'm not going to make you apologize for the rest of your life."

"Well, that's good to know."

"You didn't take me seriously for a second."

"Nope. One of the things I love about you, actually. I have a ball not taking you seriously."

Which was a line that Shallis herself didn't take seriously, because he followed it with a very serious kiss. Closed eyes, soft murmurs, tightly wrapped arms, the works. Sighing against his shoulder, Shallis saw a movement near one of the second floor bedroom windows of the old Victorian house.

If she had been the imaginative type, she might have thought it was an elderly woman watching them from the room with a smile on her face, happy that unfortunate secrets had unravelled at last, and were being knitted up into something new and wonderful and right.

But of course she wasn't the imaginative type. It was just the cherry tree moving, against the outside of the glass.

Jared pulled away a little, and looked at her. "What are you thinking about? I'm planning to kiss you again, and you look as if you're miles away."

"Just thinking about this house, its past and its future."

"Shall we buy it from your mom? The hotel doesn't have to have it. Grandpa's talking about coming back to the practice part-time once he's fully fit again, and the office space we have is really too small, even if he only puts in a few hours a week. We could set up Starke and Starke here on the first floor, live on the upper floors. We can put a gate here in the back fence and you can walk to work. Imagine it, if we fixed up the garden there'd be plenty of room for our kids to play."

"Our kids with an S," she noted.

"I think we'll need the S at some point, don't you?"

"Now that you mention it, yes, I'd like the S."

"Can't you just see it?"

"Oh, yes! Yes, I can!"

And she could, as clear as this June day. Fresh paint and polished floors, a blue and gold sign hanging out front, reading Starke And Starke, Attorneys At Law, junior Duncan-Starkes running in the yard, where there would be a swing set and a sandbox, freshly mown lawn and borders of shrubs and flowers.

Maybe she was the imaginative type, after all…

Although right now, with Jared holding her and smiling into her eyes, sharing her vision of the future, it really didn't seem as if much imagination was required.

Epilogue

Shallis and Jared decided to wait a week before taking a deep breath in unison and breaking several pieces of pretty impressive, left field news to their families—that they were in love, getting married, and having a baby.

"And it's not because we're terrified about their reaction," Jared said. "Not at all."

"Not at all," Shallis agreed.

"Seriously."

"Seriously."

Seriously, that was part of it—possibly quite a large part of it—but there was also something so magic and special in having a week all to themselves, using every second that they could squeeze out of their schedules to be together. At the end of it, they felt as if their relationship had deepened and grown by months not days, and they felt ready to go public.

Well, kind of ready.

There was still the question of exactly how to say it, and when, and to whom.

"Mom and Dad are having a barbecue at their place for Sunday lunch," Shallis told Jared. "How about I tell them I'm bringing a friend?"

"How about we set up an appointment in my office? Grandpa might be fit enough to come in—he's doing well at home since his discharge—and my mom can be there, too."

"Or we invite everybody over to your place, then your grandfather doesn't have to go anywhere."

In the end, the decision was taken out of their hands. Linnie just happened to cruise past them while they were out walking together down Shallis's street, and the hand-in-hand thing was a bit of a giveaway. Not to mention Shallis's head on Jared's shoulder, and the moment where they stopped walking so he could kiss her, hold her in his arms and slide that warm, possessive hand of his against her belly.

By the time Linnie had screeched her car to a halt, jumped out of it, crossed the road and planted herself on the sidewalk right in front of them, she'd had plenty of time to put one and one together, come up with two, and even get an inkling that maybe this time one and one added up to three.

"Shallis?" she almost shrieked. "Jared? You two?"

They tried to say something, but Linnie didn't give them time, and anyhow something seemed to have gone wrong with both their voices.

"Jared, why do you have your hand on Shallis's stomach like that? Ryan does that to me all the time, since we found out—since we— So does that mean—? Omigosh! Shallie, I can't breathe and that can't be good for the baby, so please tell me what in heck is going on, as if I didn't already *know!* Omigosh!" She made some incoherent sounds.

"Did you, uh, have any idea about it, Linnie?" Shallis ventured to say.

"Not the slightest clue! Till this minute! *How* could I have had a clue, when you have obviously been deliberately—! Unhh!"

"So, um, is it okay?"

"That you've been keeping this *secret?* That you and *Jared*—?" Linnie's cheeks were bright pink and her eyes were wide and glittery. Was she angry? This was her own sister, but Shallis couldn't tell.

Jared clearly thought that Linnie was. With his arms still close around Shallis, he cleared his throat, lifted his jaw met Linnie's intense expression full on.

"I love her, Linnie," he said. "Nothing in my life has ever made so much sense or felt so right. Shallis getting pregnant, probably the first night we slept together, wasn't in the plan, but sometimes it's the things you don't plan for that really matter, that put everything in the right place, don't you think? We're getting married as soon as we can, just a little ceremony and a quick honeymoon somewhere. If this, I don't know, hurts you or—"

"Are you *kidding* me?" Linnie shrieked again. "I have everything I want, there's no way I'd be hurt about something like this. It's water under the bridge, what you're talking about. But you kept it *secret?* From *me?* For I don't know *how* long? I am *outraged* about that!" She grinned suddenly. Her outrage evaporated, and she started to cry. "Well, let me tell you, Shallis Duncan, baby sister, *I* am the one who is going to get to tell Mom and Dad about this, not you, because otherwise there is no justice in this world!"

Later, going back over the whole scene, Jared said to Shallis, "And the best part was, she never realized how happy we were that she wanted to tell everyone for us."

"Yeah, because if you think that Linnie can pack some decibels in her shrieking, you should hear Mom."

A few weeks after this, in a sister-to-sister talk, Linnie admitted that she might have found the whole thing a lot harder if she hadn't been pregnant herself, and Shallis admitted how scared she'd been about that, too. "But we would have gotten through it, I think," Linnie said. "With some work."

Still...

Relationships between sisters could get complicated, and you had to be careful when you wanted the bond to stay strong and close. Shallis couldn't shake an intuition that maybe their bond wouldn't be completely safe until after their babies were born, and intuition was a dangerous thing in a pregnant woman...

Through her entire pregnancy, Jared's darling, hormonally intoxicated wife insisted to him that her baby just had, had, *had* to come late. Around a week to ten days late, thank you, while Linnie's baby could, pretty please, come a week or two early so that Linnie could get to be a mom just that little bit sooner than Shallis, since she and Ryan had been trying for so long.

Jared did not get this at all.

"Shallis, your sister does not look to me like a woman who's running a race," he told her more than once, both before and after their late summer wedding. "She wants the baby to come when it's ready to come, and she wants it to be healthy. That's all."

"You think so?"

"And Ryan feels the same."

And when they got as far as the early hours of February

17, in the maternity unit at the Douglas County Hospital, when Shallis had been in labor for thirty-six hours and still wasn't ready to deliver, Jared really, really did not get it.

Sweetheart, darling, love, just push that baby out, never mind that Linnie's still at home with no twinges at all, as of our last phone call to your mom about a thousand hours ago, because watching you working so hard and looking so tired is practically killing me. You cannot *hold* this baby in!

"Jared…?" Shallis moaned at that moment.

"Still right here, sweetheart."

"You know, I was so good at all of this in childbirth class. Now I'm failing the—" Another contraction hit, hard and unrelenting, and she couldn't finish.

"—the exam," he finished for her, loving that she could still attempt some humor at a time like this. "No, you're not failing it."

"Uh…"

"What's up?"

"Uh…" Shallis repeated, with a panicky look in her eye that Jared caught right in his gut a quarter second later, like a virulent disease.

"Should I press the buzzer?"

"No!"

"You mean I shouldn't wait for that? I should go right now and get the—?"

"Yes!"

Hating to leave her, Jared rushed out into the corridor and along to the nurses' station, where he encountered an unexpected flurry of the same panic he was already feeling himself. "Where's my wife's doctor and nurse?" he yelled.

"I'm sorry," someone answered. "We have someone threatening to deliver in the parking lot, and she's—"

"Is she with Dr. Kerr?"

"No, she's—"

"So can we please have Dr. Kerr?"

He caught sight of the older obstetrician and almost fell on the man's neck. "Hey, do we have something happening now?" the doctor said casually, and didn't seem to realize how close he'd just come to getting strangled on the spot.

"She's ready. It's coming."

But it took another hour or more. Oh, when it happened, though…

She was a girl. She slipped free, and Dr. Kerr told Shallis the news about the baby's sex at once, only he could hardly be heard over the baby's strong, healthy cries. Shallis burst into tears. "A girl? We have a girl?"

Jared cried, too. It just overtook him like a speeding car, one minute he was grinning, laughing, kissing his beautiful wife, the next he had a rock in his throat and these strange shuddering heaves shaking his shoulders.

What an incredible thing! Every second of it!

She had a damp fuzz of black hair stuck to her head, and a red face and splayed hands and a wide mouth and a perfect little body, complete down to a set of tiny, translucent fingernails more precious to his sight than diamonds. They'd already decided to call her Abigail Caroline. A. C. Starke. Could look good on a brass plate one day…

I'm a dad.

This is my daughter.

This is an experience neither of my two fathers ever knew, seeing this new being formed from both of us, knowing my own flesh and blood from the very moment she takes her first breath.

Watching Shallis take the baby in her arms, listening to her voice filled with a new note of tender love he'd never heard in it before, Jared felt awed, yet determined to rise to the challenge and win the best that fatherhood could offer, for his wife, his daughter and himself.

He wanted to tell the whole world what had happened, but had just enough perspective to know that certain people would be a lot more interested than others. This probably wouldn't make the evening news, but Mom and Grandpa, Linnie and Ryan, Sunny and Bob would be waiting to hear… and he knew from first hand experience that Linnie could get a little miffed when she wasn't kept up to speed on family news.

"Shall we make some calls?" he said to Shallis, kissing her damp forehead, feeling the heat in her smile as she looked up at him. "There's a phone right here by the bed."

But, damn it, no one was home. A miracle had just happened, and no one was waiting by the phone to hear about it. Checking his watch, he discovered it was eight in the morning. Which explained why it had suddenly gotten light outside, and might explain why answer-machines were picking up instead of people.

"I'm going to check to see if they're already here," he told Shallis. Dr. Kerr and two nurses were still checking mom and baby, and making all the right noises. Weight eight pounds five ounces. Length twenty inches. Mother and baby in perfect health.

Jared kissed his darling wife, touched his precious baby's cheek, felt dizzy as he stepped into the corridor. Felt dizzier when he saw Ryan coming toward him, grinning the way he'd grinned that day eight months ago when Linnie had announced her pregnancy news on a stranger's wedding day.

"Did you hear?" they both said to each other at the same moment. "We have a—"

"—girl," said Jared.

"—boy," said Ryan.

"Huh?" said both their faces. They explained to each other in snatches, joined by Sunny and Bob, Judy and Grandpa, and Ryan's mom Belle, who'd driven up from Florida yesterday.

"Almost born in the parking lot…"

"Thought it would never end…"

"Little guy, just six pounds."

"Bit of a bruiser, eight pounds five."

"Perfect…"

"Beautiful…"

"We're calling him Sam."

"Abigail."

"Born right at six-thirty…"

"Born at seven forty-five… Hey!" Jared clapped Ryan on the shoulder. "This is what Shallis wanted the whole pregnancy. For Linnie to have her baby first. Congratulations!"

Ryan grinned again. "Yeah, I guess we got in under the wire on that one."

"In a week, who'll care?" Bob Duncan said. "They'll have the same birthday. Big saving on parties, down the line. That's all it'll mean."

"Oh, Bob, you have no sense of occasion!" Sunny complained to her husband, but she was smiling wider than he was.

"So you weren't rooting for Linnie, hoping she'd go first, Bob?" Jared asked.

"Nope. I was rooting for my darling devil-child Shallis. That way, I *knew* Linnie would go first," Bob answered, and then he winked at his two sons-in-law, admitting them both to a secret and very exclusive club that only the right kind of father could join.

* * * * *

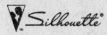

SPECIAL EDITION™

At last!

From *New York Times* bestselling author

DEBBIE MACOMBER

comes

NAVY HUSBAND

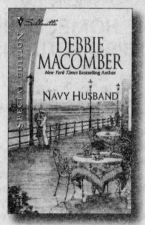

**This is the final book in her beloved Navy series—
a book readers have requested for years.**

The Navy series began in Special Edition in 1988
and now ends there with *Navy Husband*,
as Debbie makes a guest appearance.

Navy Husband *is available from
Silhouette Special Edition in July 2005.*

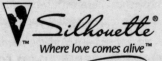